Praise for *Long Trail Home*

Hold on to your heart—Vickie McDonough is about to steal it away with an irresistible love story so unique and fresh, it will leave you breathless. It may be a "long trail home," but the pages have never flown so fast! This is prairie romance at its very best—I loved it!

> —JULIE LESSMAN, award-winning author of the Daughters of Boston and Winds of Change series

McDonough fans rejoice! Vickie's given you another winner, this time bringing post–Civil War Texas to life in a memorable story of loss and love, of regret and redemption. You won't want to miss this poignant tale of two wounded souls searching for the true meaning of home.

> —AMANDA CABOT, author of *Tomorrow's Garden*

Sweetness, sass, and suspense . . . readers will laugh at the banter between characters who fast become their friends, cry at the heartache they endure, root for them against incredible odds, and sigh at the tender romance. What more could you ask for in a book?

> —MARYLU TYNDALL, bestselling author of the Surrender to Destiny series

Vickie McDonough has created a riveting tale of loss, survival, and new beginnings set in the early days of Texas. Her charming characters will touch your heart, and the intriguing subplots will keep you guessing. The heroine's long-guarded secret and hero's tragic homecoming are heartbreaking. You'll root for this couple until the very end—and turn the last page with a smile.

> —M
> be

Long Trail Home is a wonderful novel filled with interesting characters. The action plays out across a panorama of authentic historical Texas. I had a hard time putting it down. The whole Texas Trails series is a must-read in my book.

—LENA NELSON DOOLEY, author of *Maggie's Journey,* book one in the McKenna's Daughters series

Set in the heart of Texas, *Long Trail Home* continues the saga of the Morgan family. More than a simple tale of love and faith, Vickie McDonough weaves a story of change and growth that comes from facing adversity with courage. The final tapestry is one you will remember long after the end of the book.

—MARTHA ROGERS, author of the Winds Across the Prairie and Seasons of the Heart series

I love the characters, especially Annie and Riley. Ms. McDonough knows how to put you into the characters' minds and make it feel like you are right there with them through their pains, their joys. *Long Trail Home* is a wonderful read.

—MARGARET DALEY, award-winning author of *From This Day Forward*

A tale of truth cloaked in a necessary lie, where misfortune and two wounded souls collide and their paths merge. *Long Trail Home* captures your heart and attention the moment abandoned Annie discovers a way to stay alive.

—DIANA LESIRE BRANDMEYER, author of *A Bride's Dilemma In Friendship, Tennessee*

Author Vickie McDonough has again delivered a story that demonstrates the power of love and determination.

—DIANN MILLS, author of *Attracted to Fire*

TEXAS
TRAILS

←— ★ —→

LONG TRAIL HOME

VICKIE McDONOUGH

A
MORGAN FAMILY
SERIES

MOODY PUBLISHERS
CHICAGO

© 2011 by
VICKIE MCDONOUGH

Edited by Pam Pugh
Interior design: Ragont Design
Cover design: Gearbox
Cover images: 123rd.com, photos.com, Veer and iStockphoto.com

· Library of Congress Cataloging-in-Publication Data

McDonough, Vickie.
    The long trail home / Vickie McDonough.
        p. cm. — (Texas trails: a Morgan family series)
    ISBN 978-0-8024-0585-2 (alk. paper)
    1. Texas—History—1846-1950—Fiction. I. Title.

PS3613.C3896L66 2011
813'.6—dc23

2011029008

We hope you enjoy this book from River North Fiction by Moody Publishers. Our goal is to provide high-quality, thought-provoking books and products that connect truth to your real needs and challenges. For more information on other books and products written and produced from a biblical perspective, go to www.moodypublishers.com or write to:

River North Fiction
Imprint of Moody Publishers
820 N. LaSalle Boulevard
Chicago, IL 60610

1 3 5 7 9 10 8 6 4 2

Printed in the United States of America

This book is dedicated to Chip MacGregor, my agent. The original idea for this series was his, and I thank him for inviting me to take part in it and for promoting and selling the series to Moody Publishers.

Thank you to all the helpful ladies at the Waco Tourist Information Center. Your maps and brochures were a wealth of help.

Thank you to the friendly staff at Baylor's Texas Collection and University Archives. I wish I could have stayed a full week and researched all the wonderful historical documents preserved there.

And a special thank-you to Holly Browning, Curator, at the Historic Waco Foundation, for answering my many questions and taking time out of her busy schedule to give us a private tour of the fascinating East Terrace House.

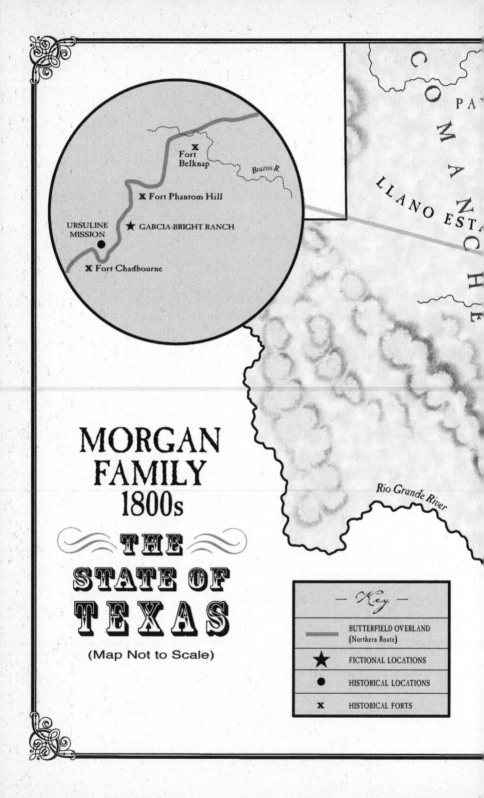

MORGAN
FAMILY
1800s

THE
STATE OF
TEXAS

(Map Not to Scale)

Fort
Belknap

Brazos R.

Fort Phantom Hill

URSULINE
MISSION

GARCIA-BRIGHT RANCH

Fort Chadbourne

COMA
PA
LLANO EST
N
C
H
E

Rio Grande River

— Key —

BUTTERFIELD OVERLAND
(Northern Route)

★ FICTIONAL LOCATIONS

● HISTORICAL LOCATIONS

✕ HISTORICAL FORTS

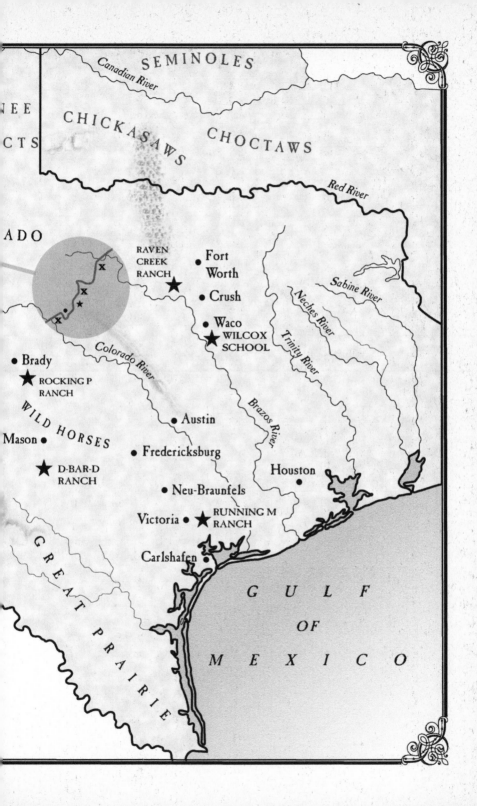

WACO, TEXAS, 1858

*T*hat one right there—he's your mark."

Annie Sheffield slipped past her daddy and peeked around the corner of the building. A handsome youth with wheat-colored hair stood in the dirt road in front of the mercantile, a shiny pocket watch dangling from his fingers on a silver chain. Annie squinted when a shaft of light reflected off the watch, and she blinked several times, refocusing on her prey. A much younger boy with the same color hair reached for the watch, but the other boy lifted the treasure higher to safety.

The older boy's look was stern but gentle. "No, Timothy. Remember this watch was Grandpa's. It's very old, and we must be careful with it."

The younger boy's face scrunched up but he nodded. Then the comely youth bent down and allowed Timothy to hold the shiny watch for a moment before he closed it and put it back in a small bag, a proud smile on his handsome face.

Ducking back into the alley, Annie leaned against the wall in the early evening shadows. She glanced at her daddy. "Do I have to?"

"You wanna eat, don'tcha? We need that watch."

"But that boy looks so proud of it."

Her father narrowed his gray eyes. "I'd be proud if'n it was *mine*."

Annie sighed. If her father possessed the watch, he'd just go hock it or gamble it away.

"Go on with ya." He flicked his thin index finger in the air, pointing toward the street. He tugged down on the ugly orange, green, and brown plaid vest that he always wore. "Scat!"

Annie peered around the building again, taking a moment to judge how fast she'd have to run and where she could hide once she'd taken the watch. She'd come to hate being a pickpocket. Ever since she heard that street preacher several months back in Galveston hollering to a small crowd of spectators that stealing was breaking one of God's special laws, it had nagged her worse than a swarm of mosquitoes. But she was hungry, and they had no money.

She studied the boy's long legs. Could she outrun him? And what about his little friend?

Her daddy was an expert pickpocket. He could snitch a wallet and disappear into a crowd like a crow in a flock, but when it came to running away from a target, well, that's where she came in.

The tall cowboy was probably only a few years older than her thirteen years. He motioned to the younger boy, and they hopped up on the boardwalk and strolled toward her, completely unaware they were being spied on. He held one hand on the younger boy's shoulder, as if wanting to keep him close. Now that they both faced her, she could see their resemblance.

They had to be brothers. The big boy glanced at his watch bag, tucked it in his vest pocket, and gave it a loving pat.

Annie jumped back. "He's coming," she whispered over her shoulder.

Her father scowled. "I want that watch. Go!"

He gave her a shove. She stumbled forward and turned.

The youth's blue eyes widened. "Hey, look—"

They collided—hard. Annie was knocked backwards, arms pumping, and her cap flew off. The youth grabbed her shoulders, and in a quick, smooth move that had taken Annie her whole life to master, she slipped his watch from his pocket and into hers. She ducked her head and stepped back. "Sorry, mister."

Her apology was more for stealing his treasure than crashing into him. She spun around and ran, hating the baggy trousers her father made her wear so she'd look like a boy. Hating the life she was forced to live. Hating that the handsome youth would hate her. She ran past a bank and a dress shop, then ducked down another alley. Behind the building she turned right instead of going left and back toward her daddy. Right now she didn't want to see him.

"Hey! Come back here, you thief!"

Annie's heart lurched, and she switched from trot to gallop. She could no longer see the watch's owner, but she knew it was him hollering. Bumping into that young man had flustered her. She hadn't expected him to be so solid for a youth not even full grown yet. Men grew taller and tougher here in Texas than in the other cities of the South where she'd mostly grown up—a different city every few weeks. A thief wasn't welcome in town for long.

Loud footsteps pounded behind her. She ducked under a wagon that sat behind the smithy, rolled, and dove into the open doorway. She crawled into the shadows of the building and curled up behind a barrel that had oats scattered on the ground around it. She took several gasps of air and listened for footsteps. The watch pressed hard against her hipbone, causing her guilt to mount. A horse in a nearby stall snorted and pawed the ground. Annie's heartbeat thundered in her ears as she listened for her pursuer's footsteps. Would he thrash her if he found her?

She peeked around the barrel. The tall boy stood in the doorway, looking around. She shrank back into the shadows like a rat—like the vermin she was.

After a moment, he spun around and quick steps took him away. Annie leaned against the wall, hating herself all over. Why couldn't she have been born into a nice family who lived in a big house? She'd even be happy with a small house, if she could have regular meals, wash up every week or so, and wear a dress like other girls.

But no, she had to be born the daughter of a master pickpocket.

The blacksmith—redheaded, with huge shoulders and chest—plodded over to a shelf directly across from her, pulled something off it, then returned to the front of the building. He pounded his hammer, making a rhythmic *ching*.

What would he do if he found her hiding in his building? Would he pummel her like he did that horseshoe? He'd have to catch her first, and surely a man that muscled couldn't run very fast. And if she was anything at all, she was fast.

Annie yawned and glanced at the door. Was it safe to leave yet?

Nah. She'd better wait until dark. Her stomach gurgled, reminding her that she hadn't eaten since early this morning, when her pa stole a loaf of bread right off someone's table. The family had been out in the barn, doing chores, and he'd walked right in as if he owned the place. He'd laughed when he told her that the only person who saw him was a baby in her cradle—and she wasn't tattling.

The sweet scent of fresh straw and leather blended with the odor of horses and manure. Annie leaned back against the wall, wincing when it creaked, then closed her eyes. She was so tired of her life. Of moving from place to place. If only her daddy could get a real job and they could live in a real house. . . .

Riley chased the boy, running until his side ached, but the little thief had disappeared. He bent and rested his hands on his knees, breathing hard as he watched the street for any sign of the pickpocket. Few people were on the streets of Waco this late. Most businesses had closed before suppertime, except the saloons. The lively tune of a piano did nothing to soothe his anger. How could he have not noticed that thief had slid his grandpa's watch right out of his pocket?

Movement drew his attention to a couple strolling arm-in-arm on the far side of Main Street. Maybe he should ask if they had seen the pint-sized robber, but then they only seemed to be looking at each other. Riley glanced toward the boarding-house where his family's wagon was parked. They'd stay there tonight, then travel to their new ranch, a few miles outside of town, along a river called the South Bosque.

Riley heaved a sigh and shoved his hands into his pockets. He studied the small town that sat all cozied up to the Brazos River. He hadn't wanted to come here in the first place—and neither had his mother. Their old farm had been perfectly fine, but his father said there were new opportunities in Waco and inexpensive land, too. Riley scowled and blew a heavy breath out his nose. He hadn't wanted to leave his friends, especially Adrian Massey, a pretty neighbor girl he planned on courting once he was a few years older. He hoped that she would follow through and write to him as she promised.

His mother's tears hadn't swayed his father, though they made Riley's heart ache. She wanted to go back to Victoria where her family and the rest of the Morgans lived. But not Pa. He loved his siblings, but he had a need to be independent, to play a part in developing Texas—and now they were even farther away.

At least his pa had pacified his ma by taking her for a visit back with her family and then on to the ranch where the Morgans had been raised, so they could see his aunt and attend her wedding. Talking with his aunt Billie about her time as a captive with the Comanche had been the most interesting part of the trip—that, and seeing the beautiful Morgan horses his uncle Jud raised. At least he could look forward to the delivery of the dozen broodmares and the young stallion his pa bought.

Staring down the street, he watched his pa take a small box off the wagon and hand it to Timothy. Riley winced, as the realization hit that he'd run off and left his little brother. Pa slowly turned in a circle, looking all around. Riley ducked into the alley. He couldn't head back without searching for that thief again. The boy had to be here somewhere, because the town wasn't all that big.

He ran his fingers through his hair, dreading seeing his father's disappointment. Riley had overheard his pa's initial objection to giving him the watch when Uncle Jud had suggested it—said that he wasn't responsible enough to have something so valuable to the family. Riley kicked a rock and sent it rolling. Why didn't his pa have more faith in him? Gritting his teeth, he had to admit he'd been right—at least in this instance. He raked his fingers through his hair and gazed down the alley, realizing that somewhere along the way he'd lost his hat too.

Half an hour later, as the sun ducked behind the horizon and cast a pink glow on the clouds, Riley headed back to the boardinghouse. Maybe if he were lucky, Timothy hadn't tattled about him losing the watch. But as much as he loved his younger brother, he knew the truth. Pa would be waiting, and he would insist on hearing the whole story. And once again, his pa would be disappointed.

———— ★ ————

A horse's whinny startled Annie and she jerked awake. During the night, she'd huddled up in a ball to stay warm and must have pulled hay over her from the empty stall on her left. She yawned and stretched, her empty belly growling its complaint. Bright shafts of sunlight drifted through the cracks on the eastern wall, and dust motes as thick as snow floated in the air. The front door creaked open. She jumped, then ducked back behind the barrel and peered over it. Chilly air seeped through the cracks in the walls, making her wish for her blanket. She wrapped her arms tight across her chest.

Her daddy would be so mad that she'd disappeared all night.

At least this town—Waco, he had called it—was small enough she shouldn't have trouble finding him. The blacksmith plodded through the building and opened the back door, letting in a blast of cold air. Annie waited a few minutes while he fed the five horses, then grabbed a bucket and headed out the back door. She tiptoed to the opening and peered outside. The large man walked toward the river then bent down, lowering the pail into the water. Annie spun around and raced to the front door, peeked out, then dashed down the street and into the first alley she came to. Would her daddy be upset with her for being gone so long? Would he wallop her? Keeping as close to the buildings as possible, she hurried back to the spot she'd last seen him.

Three long days later, Annie nibbled on the moldy bread crust she'd dug out of someone's trash heap and gazed out over the small town from the tree she had climbed. Her pa had up and left her—as he'd threatened on so many occasions when she hadn't returned to their meeting spot with enough stolen goods.

She watched people coming and going, doing their Saturday shopping. Mamas held the hands of their youngsters and stood chatting with other women or walking between shops. Men compared horses, checking their hooves and sometimes their teeth. And the girls all wore dresses—some prettier than others—but dresses all the same. Her eyes stung. One man swung his daughter up in his arms, and even from so far away, Annie could see her smile. She rubbed her burning eyes. Her daddy wasn't much of a family, but he was better than none at all—most of the time, anyway.

She swung on a nearby branch and dropped to the ground. With so many folks around, she should blend in. Hurrying past the livery and several other buildings, she stopped only to dip her hand in the horse trough for a quick drink, then continued to the far end of Waco. The house she aimed for sat a short ways out of town. She'd been there the past two days, drawn by the delicious aroma of baking bread and the children's happy squeals.

Squatting down next to a sparse shrub, she peered through the wooden fence at the house she'd dreamed about—the one she longed to live in. Two stories, white with a dark roof, half a dozen rocking chairs on the porch, and even a few flowers out front, in spite of the chill that still lingered at night.

The children, all younger than she was, were an oddity, though. They walked around, holding their hands out in front of them, feeling their way along knotted ropes that lined the path. She decided they must be blind, just like some of the beggars she'd seen in New Orleans.

But these children wore nice clothes without ragged hems and torn sleeves, and their cheeks were rosy, and smiles lit the faces of most of them. Annie shook her head. What kind of person was she to be jealous of the blind?

The youngsters felt their way to the far side of the house, and Annie stooped down and ran around back. The odor of something delicious wafted out the back door. Someone inside banged cooking pots.

Annie hunkered down behind a rain barrel. A barn sat a short ways behind the house. Maybe she could sleep there tonight.

The back door opened, and a pretty woman who reminded Annie of her mama glided down the steps in a bright blue dress. Her yellow hair was piled up on the back of her head. Annie tugged at her short, plain brown hair. It had never been long enough to put up like that—not after her pa hacked it away with his knife. Besides, she wouldn't know how to fix it anyway.

Fragrant odors drifted toward Annie. Her stomach moaned a long complaint.

The woman clapped her hands. "Children, time for lunch."

As one, the youngsters turned toward her voice, carefully feeling their way toward her. Would anyone notice if she sneaked inside with them?

She glanced down at her dirty hands and fingernails. Her pants stunk, and her head itched. Maybe those kids couldn't see her, but they sure would be able to smell her.

The idea she'd been chewing on for two days sounded better and better. Those children had everything she wanted—they were clean, had decent clothes, ate regular meals, and lived in the house she wanted.

Come morning, she'd be sitting on the front porch. And if she had to pretend to be a blind orphan in order to be taken in—so be it.

CHAPTER ONE

LATE JUNE IN AUSTIN, TEXAS, 1865

*R*iley Morgan slid off the back of the freight wagon along with three other soldiers and waved his hand at the driver. "Thanks for the ride, Mr. Anderson."

The old farmer nodded his head. "Glad to help some of our brave soldiers get back home. Wish I hadn't been too old to fight." He clucked out the side of his mouth at his sad-looking mules as they plodded down the road.

Riley was thankful the old man hadn't been in the war, knowing he wouldn't likely have survived the hardships. Every soldier he knew was not much more than skin and bones, including him. He tugged on his baggy pants. He needed to find a new rope to keep his trousers up since the one he was using had nearly frayed through. In fact, he desperately needed a shave and a bath, but he had no clean clothes to change into.

Commerce Street spread out before him, and at the top of

the hill at the far end of the street sat the tall courthouse. This was only the second time he'd been to Austin, the first being on his way out of Texas as a green soldier, riding to Houston to join up with the 8th Texas Cavalry—Terry's Texas Rangers—unaware of the horrors to come.

"Sure was nice to have that ride from Houston. My feet still ache after walking all those miles to the Alabama coast." Harley Wayne scratched his beard, studying the town of Austin.

"Just think how your feet woulda hurt if we'd had to walk all the way from North Carolina. Lucky for us we got to hop that ship to Galveston," Allen Harper said. The oldest man in the group removed his hat and swiped his sweaty forehead with his sleeve as his gaze traveled the town. "Woowee! Have a look at that."

Riley followed Allen's pointing finger to where a trio of pretty gals walked out of a store. His heart stumbled at the lovely sight. Pretty women strolling down the street, as if they hadn't a care in the world, wasn't something he'd seen in a long while. The dark-haired one reminded him of Miranda and caused him to sigh. If he could get another ride on in to Waco, he would be seeing his fiancée in the next few days. Excitement swirled through his gut, and he longed to hop on the first horse he came to and race home, but he wouldn't steal a man's horse, not even if he had to walk the rest of the way home.

At least he was done with that miserable war and was back in Texas—and almost home. He leaned on a hitching post, trying to comprehend that the war was really over. No more officers barking orders at him. No more shooting at his countrymen. He'd miss his fellow soldiers and the friendships he'd built, but not the fighting.

Allen walked halfway across the wide street and stood with his hands on his lean waist. "Let's find something to eat. My belly's rubbin' a blister on my backbone."

J.T., the youngest of the group, stepped forward. "Ma'll feed you-all."

All three men, Riley included, stared at the boy. He'd joined their regiment over a year ago and had been so mercilessly teased at first because of his big ears and bumbling ways that the boy had pretty much quit talking. Hearing him speak now was a rare thing.

"Your ma lives in Austin?" Harley asked.

J.T. nodded. "Runs a café not far from here."

Riley felt his stomach letting out a cheer; Allen licked his lips.

"Where is it?" Harley walked down the street hoping to spot the eatery. He spun back around, rubbing his hands together. "I'm starved, boy. What's her place called?"

"Charlotte's Café, and it's two blocks down Commerce and a block north on Pecan Street." He pointed down the street they were on.

Three blocks to home cooking—and, they hoped, some real coffee. Riley's mouth watered, and he followed the men from his regiment. A home-cooked meal would be worth the delay in getting home. Walking home could take a number of days—maybe even weeks, and with the few coins in his pocket, he couldn't afford to ignore the offer of a free meal.

Surveying the town, he walked down the wide street lined with various businesses. He was thankful Austin was intact, unlike so many other southern towns he'd passed through. Women talked in small clusters, and a group of children chased one another around the only wagon on the street. That's what seemed odd about the place—a lone wagon, only a few horses, and almost no men.

Would Waco look as barren? He'd heard that over two thousand men from McLennan County had gone off to join the war effort. How many of those had returned? At least his pa had remained home to take care of his ma. Riley flinched, wishing he could erase the past four years from his mind and could go back to those quiet days of ranching—days he used to despise.

J.T. turned the corner, and the other men followed, Harley limping from a slow-to-heal battle wound he'd gotten months ago. They'd be done wolfing down all the food in the café if he didn't quit his lollygagging.

"Hey, Morgan!"

Riley skidded to a halt and spun around, looking down Pecan Street. Who could have called his name? He knew nobody in Austin except the men he'd fought beside, and in the condition he was in, it was highly unlikely anyone he'd known before the war would recognize him. His gaze scanned the street, but no one was walking his direction. He found a number of the town's men standing in a cluster around a small herd of horses. Disappointment pressed down his shoulders. Must have been some other man with the same last name. He headed back to the café, but something in his gut pulled him back around. He narrowed his gaze and focused on the horses.

His steps propelled him away from the food and toward the animals. There was something familiar in their sleek lines and proud carriage. They weren't the gaunt, exhausted animals he'd been used to seeing the past year or two. No, they were Morgan horses—just like the ones his father raised. His heart clenched. Was it possible his pa had come all the way to Austin to sell some? So many horses had been lost during the war that they were a scarce commodity and would bring a good price, even if they were scrubs, which these definitely weren't.

He saw a man slap another tall man on the shoulder, and both men grinned and shook hands. The man closest to the horses was the same height as his pa. Riley's heart pounded, and he picked up his pace, all but running. The tall man saw him hurrying his way and his hand lowered to his gun, but as Riley drew closer, disappointment slowed his steps. The man was not his father, though he had a similar stature. He glanced at the sleek horses again—yearlings and two-year-olds, if he had to guess. Beautiful animals, just like his pa's. His throat seized up, and he turned back toward the café.

"Hey, you there."

Footsteps sounded behind him. Riley didn't turn, not wanting to explain why he'd been gawking at the man, but to keep walking when someone had addressed him would be rude. His ma had taught him better. He pivoted and waited.

A healthy, well-muscled man probably in his midforties stopped in front of him. His blond hair had tinges of gray at the temples, and intelligent blue eyes studied him. "Don't I know you?"

Riley shook his head. "Sorry, I thought you were someone else." He nudged his chin toward the horses. "Nice animals you got there."

The man scrunched his mouth up on one side and shook his head. "I thought there for a moment you were my brother, but you're much younger than him."

A grief Riley hadn't felt in a long while washed through him. "Nope. Sorry. I only had one brother, and he's dead now."

The man's brows lifted then quickly lowered. "Sorry for your loss. Was it the war?"

Riley shook his head. "Rattlesnake."

"Tough luck. Had a young nephew that died of a snakebite a long while back. Sad thing." The man looked back over his shoulder at his horses. "You're not in the market for a good mount, are you?"

"Morgan horses, right?"

The stranger's head snapped back, and he smiled. "I see you know your horseflesh."

Riley grinned back. "I ought to. My pa raised Morgans. I've tended them all my life."

The man's weathered brows drew together. "There's not too many of us in these parts that raise Morgans. A distant uncle of mine started the breed way back east. What d'you say your name was?"

Riley blinked, trying to comprehend what the man had said. His family, too, was distantly related to Justin Morgan. "It's Morgan. Riley—uh . . . Raleigh Morgan."

The man's mouth dropped open and his eyes widened. "Not Calder's boy?"

"Yes. One and the same."

A loud cheer poured forth from the man's lips, startling the horses. "It's me, your uncle Jud." The man, his pa's brother, clapped him on the back, and seized Riley's hand and shook it hard.

No wonder the man had reminded him of his pa. Riley felt tears stinging his eyes. He was unable to recall the last time he'd seen the man, but that mattered not. Riley was back home in Texas, and he'd found his family.

———— ★ ————

Riley loped toward home on the horse his uncle had given him, excitement charging through his whole body. The town of Waco took form in the distance, the buildings growing larger the closer he got. As he rode down Main Street, he slowed his horse to a walk and studied the town nearest to his parents' land. There'd been times he didn't think he'd see it again, not that it was all that much of a town. Waco hadn't grown a smidgen in the four years he'd been gone, but that was understandable since the war had sucked funds from everyone's pockets. Other than the majority of the buildings needing minor repairs, it looked much the same.

Several folks turned and stared, but no one lifted a hand in greeting. Had he changed so much that people no longer knew him? He recognized Mr. Petree, the mercantile's owner, and his wife, the town gossip, who stood just outside the store's doorway. He couldn't catch a whiff of her, being as far away as he was, but he remembered how she always reeked of some flowery scent. She stared at Riley then leaned toward her husband, her hand held over her mouth as if trying to keep Riley from reading her lips.

He ducked his head and focused on the road ahead. He nudged the horse his uncle had given him into a trot as he headed out of town and passed the Wilcox School for Blind Children. A woman who looked a few years younger than he was swept the porch, her right hip swinging up each swipe she made. She cocked her head as if hearing Gypsy's hoofbeats, lifted a hand in greeting, and smiled. He wasn't sure if she could actually see him or just heard him. Still, he nodded and touched the tip of his hat. She continued her work, again sweeping the spot she'd just done. She was a pretty thing with her waist-length light brown hair tied at her nape and hanging down her spine, swinging back and forth like a pendulum. The blue ribbon holding all that hair captive matched her dress. Was she a teacher? A student who'd grown up while he'd been gone?

She crossed the porch and stumbled over a rocker that stuck out farther than the others. Her broom clattered to the floor. Her arms flailed—and Riley slowed Gypsy, ready to help—but she latched onto the porch railing and righted herself. He shook his head. Too bad such a comely gal was blind.

But that was neither here nor there since another beautiful woman filled his mind. Miranda Cooper. He was as anxious to see his fiancée as he was his folks. The six months since he'd received Miranda's last letter had been tense, anxious ones. He tried to explain to her how he'd gotten caught up in the initial excitement of the war, but she'd continued to be upset with him for not returning the first chance he got. She didn't understand why he stayed. He never found the words to explain the camaraderie he felt with the other men in his regiment. He was a soldier—a man—and not just his father's unruly son.

At the fork in the road, he stopped Gypsy. He longed to go see Miranda first—to hold her soft body close and kiss her inviting lips, but after the way he'd left and the pain he'd caused his parents, he owed it to them to return home first.

Home. He swallowed the lump threatening to choke off his breath. He'd dreamed so many times of coming back to the ranch during those awful years of war, and now he was almost there. What if his parents didn't like the man he'd become? War changed men. How much had it changed him?

Gypsy tugged at the bit tightening the reins, as if sensing an end to their journey. Riley glanced down at his hands. They hadn't shaken this much since that first skirmish at Tomkinsville. He'd learned fast that shaky hands could get a man killed and had worked hard to master control of his emotions and his body, no matter what he faced. But he seemed to have left that control on the battlefield. Gripping the reins tight in his fist, he nudged his horse forward across the final miles toward home. He allowed himself to smile at the thought of the *whoop* his ma would let out when she saw him again. Excitement overcame his jitteriness.

Finally, he reined Gypsy to a halt atop the hill overlooking his family's land. *Home.*

A grin tugged at his lips. How many times had he wondered if he'd see this piece of rugged ranchland again? The familiar green-brown hills were welcoming. The few trees he'd climbed as a boy had grown taller, just as he had. But where were the cattle? His father's broodmares?

Riley stiffened. Something wasn't right. A tightness clenched his chest. Why was there no garden, heaping with summer's bounty? Nothing flapping on his mother's clothesline? Not even a barking dog?

He yanked out his field glass and squinted shut one eye. Not a soul was out and about as should be on a sunny morning. Narrow sticks jutted from the front of the house like pegs one hung clothes on, except those weren't pegs. Nothing remained of the barn but charred dirt where it had once stood tall and proud. His gut twisted. Where were his parents?

He shoved the telescope into his haversack. "Heyah!" He thumped his knees against Gypsy's side and the animal lunged forward.

At the bottom of the hill, Riley slid off before his horse had completely stopped.

Indian arrows. Comanche arrows. The front of the cabin had seven, and two more lay just inside the broken door. A number of bullet holes freckled the house's chinking. He swallowed hard. What had become of his folks?

His mind wrestled to understand. Many of the Indians living in Texas had been rounded up like cattle and forced onto reservations back in the late '50s or sent across the Red River to live in Indian Territory, but there were renegade bands that evaded capture, ones who still attacked whites and sometimes kidnapped children, like his aunt Billie. One of those bands of Comanche must have attacked his home.

Though the battle had obviously taken place months ago, Riley deftly pulled out the Griswold and Gunnison pistol he'd taken off a dead soldier after the battle at Shiloh and pointed it toward the house. The pistol's brass plating gleamed in the sunlight.

Taking a steeling breath, he stepped inside the cabin his father had built shortly after they arrived in Waco. He barely recognized the place. His father's skillfully made furniture was broken or cast aside. The English china his mother had been so proud of, passed down from her grandmother, crunched under his boots. Leaves and dirt littered the floor, something his ma would never have allowed.

Riley gritted his teeth at the destruction around him. Pain stabbed his chest. This hadn't been war, it had been a slaughter. A band of highly skilled warriors attacking a peace-loving couple. For once he was thankful Timothy hadn't been here to witness the scene. If his brother were still alive, he would have fought with everything in him to save their parents and home, and the Comanche would have tortured him all the more for it. But what had become of his father? His mother?

He quickly checked the two bedrooms, amazed to find the room that had been his and Timothy's relatively untouched. The shutters were open on the lone window, allowing a stream of sunlight to illuminate the center of the room. A colorful quilt sewn by his ma covered the bed, which still sank in the middle, as if he'd slept there just last night. A familiar shirt and pants, now far too short, hung on a peg. A Comanche hatchet was stuck in the wood beside the clothing, its feathers lifting on the light breeze. Homesickness battled with rage. He wanted to shoot the brave it belonged to, but the Comanche was long gone.

Riley shoved his pistol in the holster and spun around, needing to get outside—away from the horrible images attacking his mind. Maybe his parents had made it out safely.

Maybe he was lying to himself.

Something under the dining table caught his eye, and he halted. Dark brown spattering stained a faded blue-checkered cloth. His mother's tablecloth. Finding it hard to breath, he slowly bent down and nudged it with his pistol. Bloodstains.

He tugged on the cloth, and something clinked underneath it. He tossed the tattered fabric aside and blinked his eyes, staring hard to comprehend what he saw. A single teacup from his ma's china still remained intact. How had something so delicate survived the carnage?

Reverently, he picked it up, turning it around, amazed to not find a single crack or chip. Grime coated the ivory cup. He rubbed it with his thumb, revealing the colorful floral pattern that his ma had loved so much. He ripped off a section of the tablecloth—a section without blood—and wrapped up the cup. He went outside, tugging his hat down to shade his eyes from the glare of the sun. Why should it be shining so brightly on such a dreadful day?

Riley carefully placed the cup in his saddlebag, then glanced at the hill where the family cemetery rested. He didn't want to go up there, but he had to know. Leading Gypsy, he walked past the house, forcing himself not to look at his father's rusty tools and the wood still stacked neatly behind the cabin. A few weeds grew along the charred spot where the barn had been, proving the attack hadn't happened recently. Why hadn't Miranda written and told him? Why hadn't anyone from town?

As he crested the hill, the scene before him blurred as tears filled his eyes. Instead of only three graves—one for Timothy and two for the baby girls who had not lived—there were two more.

The graves of Calder and Emily Morgan.

His parents were dead.

CHAPTER TWO

hildish squeals and laughter echoed off the walls. Annie stood out of the way in the corner of the dining room, watching the four youngest students from the Wilcox School for Blind Children search for the spoon she'd hidden within easy reach. The three girls and one boy, ranging in age from four to seven, felt their way around the long table, the hutch, and the bench seat that rested under the bay window of the house.

"I'm gonna find it first," Rusty bellowed. The redheaded boy with a smattering of freckles across his nose and cheeks never let blindness slow him down, and because of that, he always sported scrapes and bruises.

"Nuh-uh. I always find the spoon before you do." Lissa, a charming six-year-old, didn't let Rusty's constant bragging discourage her. Annie brushed her hand over the girl's light-brown hair, almost the same color as her own, and received a wide smile and a hug. Lissa leaned back and felt around Annie's apron, finding the big front pockets. "Shucks, nothing there."

Annie smiled.

Rusty patted the seats of each chair, drawing closer to the spoon. Annie was tempted to tiptoe over and move it so one of the girls could find it, but so what if Rusty found it first again?

Love for the children filled her heart and overflowed. They gave her life purpose. Without them, what would she have to look forward to each morning?

Miss Laura stepped into the room and smiled. "Ah, Seek and Find. Such a fun game. But Mrs. Alton almost has dinner ready. You children must wash up now and help set the table, and after we eat, I have something special planned."

Chubby, dark-haired Camilla turned her black, unseeing gaze toward Laura. "It is a sweet, *si?*"

"Perhaps. I *will* tell you it's something special for Miss Annie's birthday."

Camilla clapped her hands. *"Bueno."*

Annie crossed her arms. How could she have forgotten today was her birthday? She'd never celebrated as a child, except the time her daddy snitched a light blue hair ribbon for her from a store. This birthday was a big one—her twentieth. She shook her head. It was hard to believe she'd lived at the Wilcox School for almost seven years now—nearly one third of her life—the best third.

Becky, with her short blonde braids and crossed eyes, rounded the table, heading toward Rusty. The girl was quiet and shy, but competition brought out her tenacious side. She loved to win, but she never gloated about it.

Rusty reached toward the final chair, but Becky patted the seat first. Obviously hurrying in order to beat him, she caught her foot on the chair leg and she stumbled. Her hand smacked down as she fought to balance herself, hitting the edge of the spoon, and flipping it up. The metal *thunked* against the underside of the table and clattered to the floor. In an instant, the three nearest children dropped to their knees, their hands smacking the wooden slats as they searched for the treasure. Chairs squeaked as they were shoved out of the way and the children scrambled under the table. Lissa stood on the opposite side of the room, a scowl on her face. She knew she was too far away to reach the spoon before one of the others found it. Annie crossed the room, gently touched the girl's shoulder, and the child spun toward her.

Laura had cautioned her many times about caring too much, because it was so hard when the children had to return to their parents or move to a school for older children. The goal of the school was to educate the students, to teach them to care for themselves and do basic chores, so they could return to their families and live a fairly normal, productive life.

But what was normal? Annie had always argued that point. She'd never lived in a house before coming here. Oh, she and her daddy had spent the night in plenty of barns, abandoned shacks, and even a few abandoned sod houses, but never one of their own. She shivered at the thought of the smelly grass house. Dirt, worms, and worse critters had dropped from the ceiling onto her head and shoulders too many times to count. No, give her a solid floor, four wooden walls, and a permanent roof, and she was happy. Two or three meals a day didn't hurt either.

"Got it." Camilla backed out from under the table and stood, holding up her prize.

"Ah . . ." Rusty scooted across the floor, then sat in the middle of the room, his arms crossed over his knees. His lower lip stuck out, but Annie knew he wouldn't stay upset for long. He couldn't, and besides, it was time for dinner—and that always made him happy.

Later that night, after the children were tucked in bed, Annie stood at her window staring out at the half moon and recalled the enjoyable evening. Mrs. Alton had cooked a special dinner in honor of her birthday—a delicious turkey that a generous neighbor had donated, potatoes, and fresh corn on the cob, dripping with butter. There was a time of singing, a special treat of gingerbread, and then Annie opened her gifts— a new dress Miss Laura had given her and the precious trinkets the children had made. This had been one of the best evenings of her life.

She crossed the room that she and Laura shared and sat on her bed. She picked up her brush and ran it through her hair. One hundred strokes each night, just as Laura had taught her.

"I wonder what that smile's for, as if I didn't know." Laura leaned against the doorframe, looking more wrung out than she normally did at bedtime.

"Are you feeling all right?" Annie couldn't help her concern. She had grown to love the kind woman as much as if Laura were her real mother.

In four steps, Laura crossed the room. She flopped onto her bed, pulled the pins from her bun, and forked her fingers through her blonde tresses. Annie much preferred her own hair hanging down and tied at the nape, but Laura liked hers up and out of the way. The severe hairstyle made her friend look older than her thirty-four years.

"Thank you for the party and that beautiful blue dress. I love it, but you shouldn't have gone to such expense on my part."

"Think nothing of it. I enjoyed plotting with Miss Wishard and choosing the fabric I thought you'd like best. I just wish I could give you a better wage for all you do here, so you could purchase more things for yourself. I fear I'm taking advantage of your kindheartedness." Laura set the pins on the small table that stood between the beds and shook out her long hair. She scrubbed her scalp with her fingertips. "It always feels so nice to set my hair free from its binding every evening."

Annie lifted her eyebrows, giving her friend a teasing smirk.

Raising her hand, palm facing out, Laura gave her a mock glare. "Don't start on me, young lady."

Giggling, Annie laid her brush down. "I'm no longer a young lady. I'm twenty, and a full-fledged spinster now."

Instead of laughing as Annie had expected, Laura rose and stared out the window. The light breeze fluttered the ivory curtains and her friend's long hair.

"What is it?" All manner of thoughts assailed Annie, and her hand clutched a fold in her nightgown. Was her friend sick? Was the school in trouble? Had one of the children done something naughty?

Laura turned, leaning back against the windowsill. She pressed her lips together, then caught Annie's eye, but for a moment she didn't say anything. Finally, she sighed. "I think it's time you consider finding a man to marry."

An icy numbness held Annie stiff. A shaft of fear unlike any she had known, not since her mother had died when she was six, gripped her chest. "Y—you want me to leave?"

←——— ★ ———→

Darkness enveloped the camp as the last of the purple hue on the horizon faded to a deep navy. Night meant rest for most, if one could sleep, and a relief from the endless marches and battles. But night also meant opportunity—opportunity for the enemy to sneak in close and attack. Opportunity for homesick and fed-up soldiers to give up and slip away. He had to stay awake. Had to keep the enemy away and his fellow soldiers close. Don't go to sleep, Morgan.

His stomach growled, reminding him he was still alive. One of the lucky ones. He sniffed a sarcastic laugh. The lucky ones were the men free from pain and hunger. The ones who no longer felt anything.

He hung his head. His ma would be ashamed of him. But wasn't death preferable to this endless suffering? How much longer would Americans battle one another? The war was lost. The South had lost.

And yet the fighting continued.

Should he leave, like Roscoe and Smitty had? Just slip into the shadows and head home? He stared into the darkness, feeling its lure. Texas was so far away; if he ran, who'd ever find him there?

He glanced back over his shoulders to see dozens of campfires flickering like the evil eyes of a cruel monster that demanded a man give his all—his life. And for what? So one man could own another? To reunite a country whose people held such opposing viewpoints that cousin was willing to kill cousin over it?

As he stared at the fire, the soldiers faded away, and the blaze took the shape of a woman. Skirts flaming, she stepped from the bonfire, a smoky apparition. Miranda?

Her finger beckoned him to come to her. He pushed away from the tree, trotted, then ran to her. How long it had been since he'd seen the woman he loved.

He reached for her. Touched her cheek, and the warmth of her skin fueled a fire within him that he'd smothered for months. Years.

Riley turned his cheek toward Miranda's soft, moist kiss. So many years had passed since she had trickled playful smooches along his jaw. He tried to focus on her face, to see her green eyes crinkling with humor—to feel her velvety skin—but she backed away, her form fading into a wall of smoke and shadows. She turned and disappeared into the haze. "Miranda. Wait!"

Riley opened his eyes, and the hillside where he and Timothy had played as boys took shape. He bolted upright and smacked into something hard. Gypsy squealed and lunged sideways. Shaking her head, she trotted down the hill where she found a clump of grass and started grazing. Riley swiped at his wet cheek then stared at the dampness on his hand. Gypsy's slobber, not Miranda's kisses.

Just his luck.

He stood and stretched, working the kinks out of his back and trying to shake that vivid dream from his mind. He'd often slept on the ground, but never had he passed the night on a grave before, at least not that he knew of. His eyes felt raw and scratchy from the tears he'd shed yesterday, and his heart ached as badly as if Gypsy had kicked him in the chest. His whole family was dead.

As he headed downhill to the creek for a drink, he argued with himself. He still had relatives, but except for his uncle Jud, he hadn't seen them since he moved to Waco. Maybe after he and Miranda were married, they could go visit his uncle and get reacquainted with the rest of the Morgan family. He wasn't sure he could ever live on this ranch again after what had happened, but maybe they could make a fresh start over in the Hill Country, if he could just talk his fiancée into moving that far from her parents.

At the creek bank, he bent and scooped up a handful of water, keeping watch around him, as he'd learned to do those first weeks of war. Only the sounds of nature intruded on the quiet—the gurgling water as it played hide-and-seek among the many rocks lining the creek bed. A colorful cardinal teased his mate, sounding just like Private Boone Perkins from Tennessee rattling on about his gal, saying how she was "Purty, purty, purty." The whisper of wind swished through the dry summer grass. But a man never knew when a birdcall might be an Indian or a Union soldier. Out here in the wilds of Texas, a man never knew when his enemy might creep up on him—

and wasn't his family's demise proof of that?

He needed to get away from this place. Away from the new horrors he'd dreamed about last night—of the fear and pain his parents had endured—horrors that now filled his nightmares alongside those of the war. He doubted he'd ever get a good night's sleep again.

Riley splashed more warm water over his face, wishing there was enough to bathe in. He stood and studied the house where he'd hope to find peace and happiness again. Maybe when he and Miranda were married and she slept curled up against his side, all soft and warm, he'd find that peace again. But then, peace had been elusive, ever since his brother had died so suddenly.

A Bible verse his mother often quoted rushed into his mind as if she were standing right beside him, ruffling his hair and talking softly. "Peace I leave with you, my peace I give unto you: not as the world giveth, give I unto you. Let not your heart be troubled, neither let it be afraid."

He snorted. He wasn't afraid. Never had been. But he couldn't argue that his heart certainly was troubled. He grabbed his canteen from where he'd dropped it last night and filled it with water. From his saddlebag, he retrieved one of the last pieces of jerky he'd bought at a store a few towns back and bit off a hunk.

The loneliness of the place surrounded him like a bunch of Yankees stalking in for the kill. He whistled to Gypsy. The horse whickered and trotted toward him, slowing to snag another bite of grass. He patted the bay's neck, soothed by the animal's companionship, and stared across the valley. What had happened to the dozens of Morgan horses his father had owned? Had the Indians stolen the high-quality broodmares and stallion that his family had raised?

Sighing, he shoved the last bite of jerky into his mouth and wished he had a cup of coffee. He could get some at the Coopers' house. He quickly saddled his horse. He rolled up the blanket he hadn't used last night, piled on his gear, and walked back toward the fenced graves. He bent down to snatch up a handful of wildflowers and carried them to his mother's grave, his heart breaking.

Why hadn't he hugged her the day he'd left?

That day she had lost both sons, not just Timothy. But at least she hadn't known the truth—that he'd been responsible for his brother's death. She would never know now. She would have forgiven him anyhow, being the kind, godly woman she was. His dad would have had a harder time of it, but he would have come around too, sooner or later.

Riley hadn't prayed in years and found the words as hard to swallow as burnt biscuits, but he forced himself. "Take care of them, God. At least they're together with Timothy and the babies now, and Ma no longer has to grieve over them or worry about me."

He took a final look at the five graves, then closed the gate, mounted, and rode out of the yard. His homecoming sure hadn't turned out as expected.

Twenty minutes later, he rode up to the front of the Cooper mansion. He had often teased Miranda about how the house looked like one you would see on a Georgia plantation, and she'd just smile and tell him for the hundredth time how homesick her daddy had been when he first came to Texas, and how he'd wanted a house that reminded him of the one he'd been born in. Four tall, white columns evenly spaced along the expansive front porch rose over thirty feet high, supporting the second-story roof and a fenced veranda that served as the roof to the first-floor porch. They reminded him of soldiers standing guard. The brick house, which had once been a reddish-brown, now sported a fresh coat of tan paint. Evidently, Mr. Cooper had prospered from the war, unlike many of his neighbors.

Riley dismounted. Unease battled excitement. He loped up the steps and pounded on the door, sidestepping from foot to foot. Four long years he'd waited to see his gal again. The large, red door opened, and Jewel, the Cooper's housemaid answered.

She eyed him up and down, her mouth puckering up on one side. "There ain't no work here, if'n that's what you's wantin', but get yourself along to the back door, and I'll have Cook fix you a plate of food."

Riley yanked off his hat and fought back a grin, glad to see that the snappish maid hadn't changed. Jewel always was a crotchety, ol' hen, but she had a big heart, once you got on her good side. "Don't you recognize me, Jewel?"

She scowled and leaned forward, studying him. Suddenly her brown eyes widened and she grinned. "That you, Mistuh Morgan? Why you done growed a foot and shrank that much 'round the middle. C'mon in."

He swatted dust off his shirt and pants, wishing again he had some clean clothes to put on. He stepped inside and his whole world changed, yanking him from his sorrows—from the life of a soldier to the life of the privileged. An elegant staircase with carved spindles curved up to the second-floor landing, its wood gleaming. A huge chandelier reigned overhead like a king's crown, shiny marble flooring spilled out from beneath his feet across the entryway into each adjoining room, and lavish furniture crowded the parlor on his right. He didn't belong here. He never had.

For the first time, he realized he had no place to live. How could he expect Miranda's father to approve of a marriage between them when he didn't have a decent home to take her to? Disappointment weighed down his shoulders.

"Who's there, Jewel?" Mrs. Cooper glided out of the music

room and into the foyer, looking every bit a Southern belle in her fancy dress and coiffure. She gave Riley a brief once-over and scowled. "Why did you let that ruffian in my house? Send him around back this instant."

Jewel hesitated then scurried over to Miranda's mother. She stood on her tiptoes and leaned toward the woman's ear. "Why that's Mr. Riley, ma'am. He done returned from the war."

Mrs. Cooper's eyes widened and her head snapped back in his direction. "Riley Morgan? What are you doing here?"

He stepped forward, squashing the brim of his hat in his hands. He cleared his throat. "Isn't that obvious, ma'am? I'm home, and I've come to see Miranda."

Mrs. Cooper gasped and fanned her face. "Oh, merciful heavens. Didn't she write to you?"

"You wants me to fetch a chair, Miz Cooper?"

The woman regained her composure, and something hardened in her expression. Riley's gut churned. Once again, he wasn't receiving the reception he'd expected. "The last letter I got from Miranda was over six months ago, and it was several months old."

"I see." She turned to her maid. "Leave us, and I'll see Mr. Morgan out."

Jewel nodded then cast him an apologetic glance. Riley swallowed hard. Had something happened to his fiancée too?

Mrs. Cooper stepped forward, clutched his arm, and turned him toward the door. She must have suddenly realized the sad state of his clothing, because she jerked back her hand and covered her nose. She glanced up at him with green eyes much like her daughter's. "Years have passed, and you must realize things change after so long."

The hairs on the back of his neck stood at attention. "What kind of things?"

She glanced behind her and fanned her face again. "Oh,

dear. I do so wish Reginald was here to explain things to you."

"What things?" he asked again.

She nibbled her lip then took a deep breath. "Miranda isn't here. She's uh . . . well, you were gone a long time, and you rarely wrote."

"I penned her a letter every chance I got, ma'am, but I was fighting a war. It's hard to write letters and shoot at the enemy at the same time."

"Oh my." Mrs. Cooper fanned herself faster.

Riley knew he should hold his tongue, but his impatience grew. "Just where is Miranda, ma'am?"

Mrs. Cooper closed her eyes as if steeling herself then looked at him again. "She is living in Austin—with her husband."

As if he'd been shot in the chest, Riley backed up until his spine collided with the front door. A pounding rumble, like the stampeding charge of a Union cavalry brigade, roared in his mind.

Miranda was married?

nnie sat at the table, her head in her hand, supervising the last two girls who dawdled over their breakfast. She'd eaten little herself. Her appetite had fled last night with Laura's declaration that she should find a man to marry. How could she even think of leaving the place she loved so much?

The front door banged open, and Annie jumped. A herd of four youngsters, all talking, surged into the parlor, exhilarated after their morning walk nature lesson. Laura followed, carrying the empty laundry basket. While the children had enjoyed listening for birdcalls and identifying insect and other sounds outside before the sun heated things up, Laura had hung the morning's laundry. She eyed Annie's barely touched plate of pancakes. "You're not still upset with me, are you?"

Annie shrugged and couldn't meet Laura's eyes.

"Tess, please take the basket and put it away, then get the other children settled in the classroom. I'll be there in a few minutes."

"Yes, Miss Laura." The girl took the basket then called to the other children, who followed like ducklings.

Annie watched the gangly girl move with confidence in spite of her lack of sight. At nine years of age, Tess was the oldest girl at the home and had been there the longest of all the children. She was scheduled to return to her family come Christmas, and Annie wasn't looking forward to that day one bit.

Laura clapped her hands. "All right, you two, that's enough dawdling. Take your plates and silverware to the kitchen and wash up. Annie will be there shortly."

The young girls muttered, "Yes, ma'am," in unison and did as they were told, amid the scraping of chairs against the floor and shuffling of little feet and the clattering of a dropped spoon.

Laura brushed back some biscuit crumbs and sat down in the chair Camilla had vacated. Her concerned blue eyes probed Annie's. "Now, tell me what's eating at you."

"As if you don't know." Annie crossed her arms and stared at the ground. How could she leave here? The only home she'd ever had? "Last night, you told me that I should get married."

Laura laid her hand on Annie's forearm. "I didn't say that to upset you, but I don't want you to one day look back on your life and wish you'd done things differently."

Flinging out her hands, Annie huffed a frustrated breath. "I love it here. Don't forget, I traveled most of the southeastern states as a child. I know what's out in this world, and everything I care for is right here." She tried to relax and not raise her voice, when all she really wanted to do was scream, but she'd learned that loud *discussions* made the children anxious. She cleared her throat and leaned toward Laura. "Are you sorry that you've spent so many years of *your* life here?"

The school's director blinked, as if Annie's pointed question took her off guard. "I . . . uh . . . no, I mean . . . sometimes. Oh, I don't know."

Annie's mouth dropped open. In the seven years she'd known Laura, the woman had never expressed a negative remark about spending the best years of her life caring for the children. She couldn't think of a word to say.

Laura was silent a moment before continuing. "Don't take me wrong, I don't regret my work here, but I did have a chance to marry once."

Annie couldn't help it when her eyes widened. Why hadn't she heard this news before? "Honestly? Why didn't you?"

Shrugging, Laura stared past her. "Sean was young then and had his own ideas of what a family was. He didn't want to share me with the children. He wanted a wife at home who cooked every day and was there to greet him after work. He wanted a wife to raise *his* children, not other people's *damaged* ones."

Annie gasped, her heart aching for her friend. "He actually said that?"

Laura nodded and rearranged the centerpiece—a basket of rocks and arrowheads that the children had collected and wilted flowers that had been picked yesterday. "Yes, but I know Sean didn't mean that. He was in love. He was angry and hurt that I chose my calling over a life with him. But I did—I had to. I was completely focused on my dream of helping blind children. Sean never understood that it was so important to me that I'd sacrifice marrying him to help the children. If he'd been willing to wait a few years, things might have worked out, but he was ready to marry then and gave me an ultimatum. Him or the school. I chose the school. I rarely ever see him these days, but once in a while I do wonder how things would have turned out if I had married him."

"Surely you don't mean he lives here in Waco?"

Pressing her lips together so hard they turned a pale pink, Laura nodded again. "He left town for a number of years—went out west, so I heard. He returned a year ago, shortly after his father died and took over his business."

Annie jumped up and paced the room, trying to figure out who her friend was talking about. She'd called him Sean—not a common name in this part of the West. Suddenly, it hit her and she spun toward the table. "You don't mean Sean *Murphy?*"

Laura's stark expression was all the answer she needed. Annie thought fondly of the jovial Irishman she'd seen at town socials. His red hair and teasing green eyes resembled Rusty's. "But he's so nice, and he's funny. How could you not love him?"

Clasping her fingers together, Laura ducked her head. "I never said I didn't love him—just that I couldn't marry him."

For the first time, Annie understood the personal sacrifice her friend had made to help blind children. She rested her hand on Laura's shoulder. "You've been a tremendous blessing to these youngsters and given them a chance to live a better life than they could have otherwise. They may still be locked in darkness, but you've provided them a map—a way to survive and reach beyond the restraints of their blindness. And you've given every one of them a self-confidence they didn't have before coming here."

Laura drew in a slow breath and exhaled loudly. "Thank you. I honestly don't regret my choice, but every once in a while I get to missing Sean, especially after I've seen him in town."

"I'm glad you told me, because it helps me to understand you better." Annie hugged Laura's shoulders from behind and laid her head against Laura's back. "So did Sean ever marry?"

A squeal sounded from the schoolroom, and something crashed against the floor. Annie spun around, and Laura jumped up. "I'd better see to that."

Annie carried her barely touched breakfast to the kitchen. Laura may have avoided answering her question about Sean just now, but she'd have to respond sooner or later, if Annie kept asking—and she would. A soft knock drew her to the front door. Before opening it, she took a steadying breath and prepared her expression. Laura's one condition on her staying at the school when she had first arrived was for Annie to pretend to be blind when others came around. Their school's benefactor had been adamant that no sighted children could stay there, but Laura had desperately needed help and knew how badly Annie needed a home.

Forcing her eyes to relax, she opened the door. "Yes? Can I help you?"

The man's dingy appearance took her by surprise, and she had to work hard not to peer up into his face. Avoid eye contact, Laura had often told her, but one peek at his amazingly blue eyes, and she wanted another glimpse. The man twisted a battered hat in his hands.

"I . . . uh . . . is Laura Wilcox here?"

Amazed that this ruffian knew her friend enough to use her first name, Annie lifted her head. She caught herself and focused on the half-inch of dark stubble on his chin. Cleaned up, the man might even be handsome, though he was terribly thin. Whoever he was, Laura certainly didn't have time to mess with him. "She's busy."

"Oh." The disappointment in the man's voice was almost tangible, but not enough to make Annie waver. For one thing, he smelled too bad for her to invite him in. It would take days to rid the room of his stench.

The hat crumpled more where his large hands crushed it. "I was . . . maybe . . ." He glanced over his shoulder then straightened his stance. "I noticed the fence around the yard had some broken places. Thought maybe I could repair it, so the children won't accidentally get out onto the road where they could get hurt."

His concern for the children softened a small place in her heart, but men rarely expected nothing when they offered to do a favor. She learned that a long time ago. "And what would you want in return?"

He hung his head, as if ashamed to request anything, and shuffled from foot to foot. He shrugged, then lifted his head and sniffed the air. "Something sure smells good in there. If you have anything leftover from breakfast, I sure could use a bit of home cooking."

That was an understatement if she ever heard one. He was tall with wide shoulders, although he could certainly stand to put on some weight. His worn clothes hung loose. Annie didn't want to feel sorry for this man, but she, more than anyone, knew what it was like to go hungry. "I suppose that would be all right."

The man's grateful gaze caught her eye. His were a beautiful deep blue, the color of the sky just before twilight. She realized he was staring into hers, and her heart jolted, and she forced a blank look. "If you'll go around back, I'll have Mrs. Alton bring you a plate, then you can see to the fence. There are some tools in the barn, and I believe there may be some extra fence rails alongside of it."

"Thank you, miss. I'm beholdin'." He backed up, but then paused, standing there facing her so long that she was certain he had noticed her mistake. Finally, he turned and walked across the porch. Annie closed the door and leaned back against it, her heart pounding. Could he tell she could see?

Lying and deceiving folks was the only part of her life that she hated. No one in Waco knew she could see. She despised the looks of sympathy shot toward her and the children from well-meaning folks, but even worse, were the jeers and cruel imitations some of the older boys made. They had walked around, laughing and waving their hands, bumping into things. Several times she'd witnessed their foolish behavior, and it had taken everything within her not to scowl and walk up to those youths and give them what for. But she couldn't.

At least the stranger at the door had respected the need to keep the youngsters safe. She'd better inform Mrs. Alton before the man showed up at the back door and scared her half to death. She crossed the parlor and realized she'd forgotten to ask the man's name.

Oh well, he wouldn't be here for long.

She peeked in the classroom to the right of the parlor. Things were quiet now, and Laura was reading them the morning Scripture.

In the kitchen, she emptied the cart. "Mrs. Alton, is there any food left from breakfast?"

The older woman smiled. "Did my pancakes not fill you up today?"

She glanced at the open back door, not wanting the woman to read the truth in her eyes. Mrs. Alton was the only person besides Laura who knew Annie could see, and although she didn't tolerate lying, for Laura's sake she'd kept the secret all these years. "It's not for me. A drifter came to the door. A soldier, I suspect."

Mrs. Alton spun around. "And you offered to feed him?"

Annie lifted her chin, as if the invitation wasn't so unusual. "In exchange for some work on his part."

"Fine by me, as long as we have enough. Though we do tend to run short at times." The woman shook her head. "I don't understand why Mr. Morrow hasn't sent his monthly draft. I sure hope it arrives soon."

Annie didn't have to ask why. The school depended on the support from its generous benefactor, Charles Morrow, and the occasional donation of food from local farmers and ranchers. At least the kind ladies from Waco and other nearby towns kept the children in clothing, not an easy task for six growing youngsters who had more than their fair share of falls.

The man knocked on the back door, pulling Annie from her thoughts. His face was damp from a fresh scrubbing, and the hope in his hungry gaze as he glanced toward the plate in Mrs. Alton's hand caused a niggle of guilt to slither down Annie's spine. She pretended to feel her way to the coffeepot and poured him a cup, then slowly walked to the door.

He stepped forward. "I can take that, ma'am."

Annie scowled. Did he think her helpless because he thought she couldn't see?

He took the cup from her hand, and Annie nearly leapt back at the reaction that gushed through her just from his fingers touching hers. She covertly glanced down at her fingertips, which felt singed. What in the world?

Mrs. Alton handed him the plate. "You can have a seat there at my worktable."

"Much obliged, ma'am, but I don't mind standing." He downed the coffee in two large swigs, eyes shut and brows lifted. "Mmm . . . you don't know how good real coffee tastes after drinking that nasty stuff the army served us."

"So you're a soldier, eh?"

He nodded, and Annie all but rolled her eyes. Wasn't that obvious by the tattered wool trousers he wore and the belt buckle with CSA embossed on it? She knew the letters stood for "Confederate States of America." Even though many Texans were opposed to slavery, Texas seceded from the Union and entered the conflict as a slave state. She was thankful that few battles had been waged on Texas soil and that the children had never been in danger.

Mrs. Alton cocked her head and watched the soldier wolf

down his pancakes. She tapped her finger against her lips. "Don't I know you, son?"

"Could be." He stopped eating and stared back for a moment, his expression remaining somber. "I'm Raleigh Morgan, ma'am. But most folks call me Riley."

Morgan? Why did that name sound familiar?

Mrs. Alton pressed her hand against her chest. "Of course, I recognize you now. Bless your heart. My name's Bertie Alton, and your mama was a good friend of mine. I'm so sorry for your loss."

Annie turned sideways, dragging her gaze carefully back to Mr. Morgan, who just stood there, staring into his plate. He must be the son of the man and woman who'd been killed in that Comanche attack at the first of the year. Had he known about his parents' deaths before returning home?

He ducked his head, eyes closed, as if struggling to regain his composure. He cleared his throat. "Thank you, ma'am. It was quite a shock to find out they were gone."

Mrs. Alton stepped forward, distress etching her gaze. "Didn't nobody write and tell you about them?"

A muscle in the man's cheek twitched. "No, ma'am. I didn't know until yesterday. Not till I got home."

Annie leaned back against the cabinet, feeling his pain. Imagine returning from war, excited to see one's family again, only to discover they were gone. *Dead.*

Laura strode into the kitchen. "Annie—" She spun toward Mr. Morgan, her friendly blue gaze filled with curiosity.

Mrs. Alton turned, her hands folded in front of her, resting against her apron. "It's Riley Morgan, Miss Laura, returned from the war."

Footsteps tapped across the floor as Laura hurried toward their guest, a concerned look on her face. "Welcome home, Mr. Morgan. I'm Laura Wilcox. I remember you and your folks from church. I attended there too—well, you know, before it burned down."

"I'm obliged for the grub, ma'am." He gave her a tight-lipped nod. "Didn't know about the church."

"I'm so sorry for your loss. Your parents were good people. Your father brought us prairie hens and other game whenever he'd go hunting. He'd leave more with us than he took home for himself."

His eyes blinked, and he stared at his near-empty plate as if he had lost his appetite. But then he shoved in the last big bite and held the plate out to Laura. "Thank you, ma'am. I'd best go fix that fence." He snapped around and marched across the back porch and out of sight.

Mrs. Alton shook her head. "I can't imagine what that boy must be feeling."

"He's not a boy," Annie blurted without thinking. "Why he's got to be in his midtwenties, maybe even thirty."

Laura cast an odd glance her way, a teasing smile dancing on her lips. "He's around twenty-three or four, if my memory serves me right, but the war has aged him. He's lost a lot of weight. You couldn't tell by the look of him now, but he was a handsome youth back when I knew him. Those amazing sapphire eyes of his caught my fancy when I was a girl, but I was always too old for him. I believe he's around six or seven years younger than me."

"We should do something to help him." Mrs. Alton took the plate from Laura, shaking her head. "What a shame he had to come home and learn about his family as he did."

"I imagine it must be hard for him to stay on his ranch with all that's happened." Laura tapped her finger on her lips. "Hmm . . . We could use a man's help around here. The place is falling to pieces. And with the danger from raiders . . . I wonder if he'd be willing to stick around for a time."

Annie's eyes widened. Laura's heart was far too big. "You can't keep him. He isn't a stray dog, you know."

"He fought for us, endangered his life, and missed out on the last few years of his parents' lives. We owe him." Laura moseyed to the back door and looked out.

"No, we don't. We can barely find enough food to feed the children. And besides, you don't even believe in slavery. Wasn't that why that wretched war was fought?" Annie crossed her arms. The last thing she wanted was that smelly man around, messing things up and making her feel peculiar. Watching her with that expressive blue gaze.

Suddenly, Laura spun around, her eyes bright. She snapped her fingers. "I know! He can stay in the tack room in the barn. We can fix it up and give him room and board in exchange for him repairing things."

"I love that idea." Mrs. Alton clapped her hands.

"I despise it." Annie shook her head. "He never asked for a place to stay, just a meal."

"But you saw him." Even though Laura was the director and ultimately made the decisions concerning the school, her eyes begged Annie to be reasonable. "He needs us, Annie—and I think we need him."

"We can't afford to feed a full-grown man. Men only cause problems." Annie stamped her foot. "Have you two taken leave of your senses?"

Mrs. Alton harrumphed and glared at Annie, her disappointment obvious. "Good thing Miss Laura didn't cast you out that day you first came around pretending to be blind and begging for a place to stay. At least Riley Morgan didn't fake nothing." She spun around and slapped two metal plates together.

Annie hung her head, both angered at the situation and guilt-ridden at her selfishness. How could she be so hard-hearted when she had once been in the same boat as Mr. Morgan?

No, he had a home, which was something she never had until coming here.

And men did cause problems—and they bossed women around. They took what they wanted and then left you alone. With nothing. She hadn't thought of her pa in a long while. His abandonment still hurt, even after so many years had passed.

And all the time Mr. Morgan was here, she'd have to pretend to be blind. The charade had long ago grown old, but for the sake of the school and Miss Laura, she had to pretend whenever people were around. She grabbed the milk bucket, intent on returning it to the barn. She'd just have to think up some way to ensure that Mr. Morgan didn't stick around for long.

CHAPTER FOUR

iley led Gypsy to the barn behind the school and dropped the reins, ground-tying the mare. His gaze roved the area that made up the Wilcox School for Blind Children. The white two-story clapboard house was in decent condition, needing only some minor repairs. The barn was another issue. Boards were missing here and there; the top hinge on the right side of the door had broken, causing it to lean sideways; and spots of light dappled the hay-strewn floor where the sun peeked through holes in the walls and roof. He rested his arm across his saddle and heaved a sigh. What was he doing here? Begging work off women wasn't something he'd ever done before.

If he hadn't just wolfed down that plate of food—one of the best he'd had in ages—he'd ride off.

But he couldn't return home. Not yet.

If he worked hard, maybe he'd forget about his troubles and earn another of those delicious meals. He'd worry later about where he would spend the night.

He removed his pistol from his haversack and shoved it in the waistband of his pants then strung the bag over his shoulder. He uncinched Gypsy's saddle and tossed it over a fence rail before removing the mare's bridle and opening the paddock gate to turn her loose. She could keep the lone brown milk cow company and graze on the sparse grass. Maybe the Morgan mare his uncle Jud had given him could be the start of keeping his father's dream alive—a dream of raising quality horses, but Riley couldn't do that with just a single mare.

Shoving away from the rail, he glanced around the yard again. Dreams would have to wait. Right now he had work to do. He removed his gun from his waistband and carried it into the barn. Leaving it behind while he worked would be almost like severing an arm. He'd always kept his weapon close for the past years, but with so many young children about, he couldn't take a chance that one of them might happen upon it, as unlikely as that seemed. He laid it up on a high shelf near the doorway then hung his haversack on a rusty nail. Sighing again, he walked away. He hoped he never had to point that gun at another person again. His eyes closed tight as visions of bloodied bodies filled his mind. The unnatural sound of men's screams echoed through the caverns of his memory. The stench of blood filled his nostrils as it had on so many occasions. Sweat trickled down his temple, and he grabbed hold of the paddock railing with trembling hands. His chest rose and fell with his heavy breaths. *Don't think. Don't remember.*

After a long moment, he swiped his forehead with his sleeve. He forced his feet into motion. Hard work—that's what he needed. Work so hard that he'd collapse at night from exhaustion, and maybe then he'd sleep. He gulped in several gasps of fresh air and moved forward, determined to shove his awful memories aside—once again.

Checking for broken rails, he walked the fence line along

the road, as the warm Texas sun heated his shoulders. He pushed his hat up on his forehead, and looked back toward town. Sooner or later he'd have to ride into Waco and actually stop and talk to folks. He dreaded that day. Dreaded seeing the sympathy in their eyes. Dreaded hearing folks talk about how kind his ma and pa were and how sorry they were about what happened to them. Dreaded them asking about the war. He couldn't talk about that. Not ever.

Grief clenched his heart and a deep longing to see his parents tightened his chest. Calder and Emily Morgan had been good people and didn't deserve what happened to them. He blinked his stinging eyes and swiped them with his sleeves. In all the times on the battlefield and long, difficult days between skirmishes when he ached for home and thought of his family and future, he never once considered that something could happen to his parents. He'd been so focused on keeping himself alive that he hadn't once thought about their mortality.

Or that Miranda would marry someone else.

With his head hanging, Riley returned to the barn and rummaged through a pile of wood until he found enough suitable to repair the fence. Tossing the pieces on the barn floor, he headed for the far wall where a sad array of tools hung. Hens roosting in nests below the tools clucked their disapproval at being disturbed from their morning nap. A huge rooster stood guard on a bale of hay that rested off to Riley's right. The reddish-brown bird stretched up his neck and flapped his wings, looking as though he'd attack at any moment. Riley bent down, scooping up a handful of dust off the floor and flung it at the bird's face and at the same time let out a Rebel yell. The shocked bully fell backwards off the hay, flopped around, then found his feet, and scattered the hens in his frantic effort to flee. Chuckling, Riley shook his head. It felt good to have something to laugh at, even a little bit.

"My word, Mr. Morgan. Have you taken leave of your senses?"

Riley spun around, staring at the pretty young woman who'd first come to the door. She held a pitchfork out as if she meant to stab him. Knowing she couldn't see him, he grinned at the not-so-formidable sight she made. She stood straight as a lodgepole pine tree—all 5'3" of her—ready to take on the world. He yanked off his hat then slapped it back on. "Sorry if I frightened you, miss, but that rooster was standing between me and the hammer."

She scowled and lowered the big fork. Her chin lifted. "I fail to see anything funny. You nearly scared the wits out of me."

Riley ducked his head, tucking in his lips and forcing the grin from his face. She'd obviously heard the humor in his tone. "Like I said, sorry for scaring you, but I learned when I was a boy that if you don't want trouble with a rooster, you'd better let him know right off who's boss."

She set the fork down, leaning it against the wall beside a shovel and several hoes. "You can't let out random yells like that around here. It frightens the children. They can't rely on sight to see what's going on and are extrasensitive to sounds."

The stubborn woman wasn't about to admit that he'd scared *her*, but he did see her point. "I'll try to remember that, miss. I've been living with rough soldiers for a long while. Don't know much about children, especially ones who can't . . . uh . . . see."

Her pert chin inched upwards. The light breeze fluttered the skirt of her dress, and wisps of light brown hair danced around her face. She was a pretty thing, not that he'd noticed.

"They are just like any other children, Mr. Morgan. We all have to learn to live with the hand we've been dealt. Most of the children have been blind all their lives, so it's something they are used to, but we still need to be cautious. It's especially important that you not move things around. A chair left pushed out from a table becomes a dangerous stumbling block to the non-seeing. I trust you'll keep that in mind." Her face lowered, as if she was staring at the pile of wood he'd left in the middle of the floor.

He winced. "I understand, miss, and I'll be careful. The last thing I'd want to do is hurt a child."

She nodded but didn't leave. His curiosity rose. He searched the crevices of his memory, trying to figure out if she'd been at the school before he left, but how would he know since he hadn't paid an ounce of attention to the place back then. All he had cared about was himself. He kicked at a stone, sending it rolling along the ground. It *plunked* against the wall, and the young woman's head turned toward the noise. Such a shame that a pretty, spirited gal like her had to be blind. Riley cleared his throat, not liking the direction his thoughts had taken him. "Did you need something, miss?"

"Oh, uh . . . Miss Laura sent me out to tell you that you're . . . uh . . . welcome—" she coughed, as if the words were distasteful "—to stay overnight in the tack room, if you want. Of course, it's not much of a place. Just a hot, little room."

He cocked his head, intrigued with her obvious dislike of him. What could she have against him? Glancing at his dusty pants, he frowned. Probably his rank odor offended her. Scent was about all she had to judge him on, since she didn't know him or his family. He peeked down at his stained shirt then sniffed his underarm and rubbed his hand over his bristly whiskers. He needed a bath—bad. But hygiene wasn't exactly at the top of a soldier's list of chores.

She took a step toward the boards and pointed past him. "The tack room is back there. Behind that closed door."

Riley strode forward and grasped her arm. Her brown eyes widened, and she yanked her arm from his hand and backstepped. "What do you think you're doing?"

"There's boards, miss. On the ground." He waved his hand at them, then realized the futility of his action. "I didn't want you to stumble on them."

She crossed her arms over her chest. "See! That's just what I was talking about. I could have fallen flat on my face and gotten hurt."

"That would be a shame."

Scowling, she sniffed and hiked her chin, but she then grimaced and lifted a hand to cover her nose. He ought to get to work, but he hadn't been around a woman in so long that he just wanted to stand there and gawk at her. Long, light-brown hair was pulled back and tied with a blue ribbon. Her skin, lightly kissed by the sun, had a smattering of freckles dotting the bridge of her nose and sprinkling her cheeks. She barely reached his shoulders, but she wasn't in the least intimidated by his size, if she was aware of it. "I'm afraid you have me at a disadvantage, miss."

She lowered her hand and licked her lips, drawing his gaze downward. Her thin brows scrunched together. "How so?"

"You know my name, but I don't know yours."

Those pretty lips pursed, as if she was deciding if he was worthy of knowing her name. "It's Annie. Annie Sheffield."

He lifted his hat—an action wasted on her but too much of a habit to skip. "It's a pleasure to meet you, Miss Sheffield."

←— ★ —→

And just how was she supposed to respond to that? He tipped his hat even though he thought she couldn't see. The small, respectful action was unexpected, especially from a man who seemed so uncouth. Few men had ever tipped a hat to her. "Uh . . . thank you, Mr. Morgan."

Why did he have to be so nice? She suspected that he'd be quite handsome once that layer of dirt and grime was gone. Her gaze kept lifting to his intriguing eyes. "Well, I just needed to tell you what Miss Laura said. There's plenty of work that needs done around here, so if you're of a mind to stay for a bit, she said it's all right."

"That's kind of her to offer." His gaze dropped to the ground, and he nudged aside one of the boards with his boot.

Annie just wanted to say what she had to and then get away from him. His stench was turning her stomach, and the fact that she hadn't eaten much of her breakfast wasn't helping. She shook her head. Why had Laura insisted in offering this man a place to stay when he had a home not far away? Yeah, the house had been damaged, from what she'd heard, but it was still standing. How could someone have a home and not want to live there? She couldn't comprehend such a thing.

"I reckon I should get to work fixing the fence."

Annie nodded. "All right. Let one of us know if you need something and can't find it." She turned to walk away then stopped. "Just so you know, we can't pay you anything, but Mrs. Alton will see to it that you don't go hungry."

He nodded, then his ears turned red as if he just realized she couldn't see him. Annie grimaced. Even after seven years, she still didn't like deceiving folks, but the charade was necessary, for the sake of the school.

"That would be nice, miss. It's been a long time since I had food as good as that breakfast I just ate, and even longer since I've had three good meals a day."

He could definitely use some fattening up. The man was as thin as the hayfork handle she'd grabbed and aimed at him earlier. "I'll get some bedding for your room."

"Much obliged, miss, but don't go to any trouble on my account. I've got my bedroll, and to tell you the truth, I don't even know if I can sleep inside." His ears reddened again, as if he'd said more than he meant to. "But I do appreciate the offer, miss."

She nodded and spun on her heel, needing to get away from him, but she purposely slowed her pace. *Yes, miss. Much obliged, miss.*

And what did he mean that he couldn't sleep *inside?*

Having him around would make things so much more difficult for her. She'd have to stay on guard, always careful not to look into his eyes or walk too fast or do anything out of character for a blind person. Keeping an eye on the children would be a hundred times harder, as would gathering eggs and milking Bertha. Why had he stopped *here?* Why hadn't he kept riding or asked some rancher for work?

And why had Miss Laura insisted that she invite him to stay when they could barely feed the children?

She flung her hands out to her side as she walked around the side of the house. Since her birthday celebration, everything had gone downhill faster than an empty barrel. First Laura hinted that she find a man and get married, and now a grungy man showed up at their door, and Laura suggested they keep him. Annie stomped up the steps and reached for the back door, then suddenly halted, the blood rushing from her face as a chilling thought galloped across her mind.

No. No. No! Surely not.

Surely Laura was just being neighborly.

Annie dropped down onto the steps and wrapped her arms across her churning stomach. Could Laura have matchmaking plans?

No, it wasn't possible. And yet, she'd seen how Laura's eyes had lit up when she talked about Mr. Morgan. How she'd said he was a good man from a good family.

Annie picked up a rock and flung it clear to the garden. She had no interest in Mr. Morgan or any man for that matter. She'd seen man's cruelty as far back as she could remember. Men who made women do horrible things. Men who beat women and even children. Men who'd grabbed hold of *her* and would have forced her to do things she hadn't wanted if she hadn't been able to connive herself out of their hands with empty promises and fast feet.

How could she ever trust a man when her own father had run off and left her when she was just a child?

⟵ ★ ⟶

Riley smashed another nail into the board then straightened and attempted to wobble the gate, but it held steady. He nodded, satisfied with the job he'd done. Once the fence surrounding the schoolyard was fully mended, Miss Laura would no longer have to worry about the children accidentally slipping through a gap and getting lost or hurt.

Picking up the top board on the pile, he sidestepped to another section of the fence. Glancing down the road to where the fence ended, he calculated how much time it would take to repair the whole thing. He'd need more boards, and finding them would take more time than repairing the broken sections. There were probably some around his folks' place.

He stood and pressed his fists against the small of his back as he stared off to the west. Could he go back there? See his parents' dreams reduced to nothing but the skeleton of a house and crosses on a hill?

Heaving a heavy sigh, he rubbed the back of his neck. There may be things at the house he could use. Things he'd want besides his ma's teacup. His gut churned at the thought of returning to his ravaged home, but his mind was made up. He'd go back once, make a good, thorough search of the place, and then he'd find out who he needed to talk to about selling the land. There were too many memories—too many broken dreams—too many reminders of his failure for him to ever live there again.

CHAPTER FIVE

Swinging the milk bucket in one hand, Annie squinted at the brilliant light of the sun just peeking its head over the hills to the east. The air smelled fresh—free of the perpetual Texas dust—after last night's thunderstorm. The trio of barn cats, one black with a white chest and paw, one pure white, and a striped gray tabby, greeted her with their eager meows. The gray leaned against her skirts and gazed up, scolding her with a long fussy cry for being late. "I'm sorry, Penelope, but I didn't sleep well last night and was a bit late getting up. Come along. I'll have your breakfast soon enough."

Halfway to the barn, Annie spied something wadded up just outside the entrance. Stopping beside it, she glanced around then snatched up the heavy blanket. The pungent scent of mildewed wool overpowered those of the new day. "Pee-yew. Where did you come from?"

Could the storm have blown it clear to their house from one of their neighbors? Wrinkling her nose, she tossed the grimy coverlet over a fence rail and slipped into the barn, blinking at the shadows. She glanced around, hoping not to encounter their new handyman. The knot in her stomach uncoiled. Maybe he was already out working somewhere. She scanned the yard, taking in the newly mended fence but didn't see him. Maybe the man wasn't an early riser, but with him having been a soldier, she expected the opposite.

Mr. Morgan's horse lifted her head over the gate and nickered, as if she hoped Annie had brought her breakfast. Annie walked to the stall and scratched the intelligent-looking horse between the ears. "You've sure got a pretty face, gal."

Startled by her own words, she peered over her shoulder, glad to see the door to the tack room was closed. Talk like that could reveal her ruse.

The white cat and the black, a pair she called Salt and Pepper, sat back several feet and meowed, as if complaining that she wasn't supposed to make a stop before the cow's stall. Bertha's nose appeared between two slats and she bellowed, low and deep. Several of the hens that were pecking the barn floor flapped their wings and hightailed to the back of the barn, squawking. Were all the critters upset with her today?

"Sorry, girl," Annie said to the mare. "Miss Bertha doesn't like to wait for the morning milking."

She set the milk pail down and grabbed an armful of hay from the small stack in the corner, carried it into Bertha's stall, and dumped it in the feed bin. The eager cow shoved her face down, grazing Annie's hand with her damp nose. Annie jumped but then giggled, wiping her hand on her apron. "Hold your horses, old cow, before you eat my hand."

She fetched the bucket and milk stool, and settled down beside the brown cow. Her hands made a swishing sound as she rubbed her palms together to warm them and then began milking. The familiar *psst* echoed against the bottom of the empty bucket, sending the scent of fresh milk spilling into the air. The bold tabby stood on her back legs and leaned a paw against Bertha's hind leg. Her cries joined those of the other two until Annie laughed at the pitiful spectacle they made. "You critters are more demanding than the children when dinner is late."

She squirted the milk from one teat at the tabby. The cat's tongue went into action, quickly licking the white liquid off her face. Annie grinned and gave the other less friendly cats a squirt, then resumed filling the bucket. She enjoyed their plaintive begging each morning. Laying her head against Bertha's warm side, she remembered how thinking about Mr. Morgan had kept her awake much of the night.

How would she keep her secret from him?

She'd already made several careless mistakes. Stiffening, she realized if he'd been watching her milk, he'd have figured out she could see because of how she'd given each cat a drink. Her stomach clenched. His being here made everything more difficult. If he discovered her secret, would he tell others? If the townsfolk found out, they might toss Miss Laura out on her backside for deceiving them all these years.

Being dishonest and sneaky had been the only way of life Annie had known until she came to Waco and learned that she and her pa were the oddity. But Miss Laura wasn't like her. She had made a rash decision and only deceived people to protect a starving and abandoned thirteen-year-old. Miss Laura was good and decent, and decent folks worked hard. They didn't steal. Or generally lie. She searched the corners of her mind but couldn't remember her daddy working a day of his life, unless you counted gambling. Playing cards was hard work, so he'd said, but she suspected he just plain enjoyed trying to win coins away from the other players.

Bertha swung her head around, eyed her, and uttered a

deep bawl. Annie stopped milking, knowing thoughts of her daddy must have caused her to tug too hard. She sat up straight and placed her hands on her knees, pushing back the anger and hurt that tended to well up like a building thunderstorm whenever she thought about her father. After seven years, her heart still hurt that he had abandoned her. Did he ever think about her? Regret his decision? Was he even alive now?

Annie sighed. What did it matter? She loved having a place to call home. She loved having clean clothes and a place to take a bath at least once a week. She'd never return to that other way of life, no matter what.

Pepper waved his paw in the air, drawing Annie's attention. He sat on her left side next to Salt, both felines watching her like a pair of starving orphans who longed for a meal but were afraid to ask. On her other side, Penelope finished licking her paw before she stretched and crept toward the pail. She glanced up at Annie and meowed.

"Oh, no you don't." Annie waved her hand, scattering all three cats. Penelope darted to her right, between the slats and into the next stall scattering a pair of nesting hens. The cat stopped and looked back. Annie grinned and started milking again. From the corner of her eye, she saw Penelope's head jerk around, her back arch, and the fur on her tail lift.

Suddenly, the pile of hay Penelope stood on moved. Something—or someone—groaned. Annie's heart jolted at the same moment the gray tabby hissed. Screeching, Penelope dashed back in her direction and flew past the cow. Annie grabbed the pail just as Bertha sidestepped. She fell backwards off the milking stool, and the pail flew up, showering her with warm milk. She gasped and lay on the hard-packed ground for a moment, and then her gaze zipped back to the stall beside Bertha's. Had some wild animal hidden in the hay?

Suddenly a huge form rose up, and the hay fell away.

Annie's stomach lurched. It wasn't an animal. It was a man—a man with a blanket covering his face.

She rolled sideways and attempted to crawl across the barn floor toward the pitchfork, but her knees kept snagging the skirt of her dress, impeding her progress. She glanced over her shoulder, then stood up and ran the rest of the way. Who would stay in their barn without permission? Was he a raider? She'd read in an Austin newspaper about how soldiers with no homes to return to were riding across the state, stealing, killing people, and doing unimaginable things to women. Snatching up the big fork, she spun back around, hoping with all her heart that the man just wanted a place to sleep and would move on.

But if the man had more nefarious ideas, she was prepared to protect Miss Laura and the children, no matter the cost.

———— ★ ————

Someone held Riley tight. Something covered his face. Hot, stale air did little to fill his lungs. He was going to suffocate if he didn't get his face uncovered. His arm broke free, and he fought against the cloth trapping him, his hands clawing at the coarse fabric. Sweat rolled down his cheek, and his heart thundered like the hooves of a charging cavalry regiment.

He gave another hard yank and broke free. Sucking in precious air, he blinked, and his mind sharpened. His blanket hung over one shoulder, a corner of it in his hand. He snorted a laugh. A dream—that's all it was. He hadn't been captured. His frantic heartbeat slowed and he looked around. Last night, he'd lain down on the bed in the tack room, but how had he gotten out here? He plucked strands of hay off his shirt, trying to make sense of things. Had he been sleepwalking?

A shadow darkened the barn entrance, drawing his gaze. He squinted against the bright light and stood, dusting off his clothes. "Miss Sheffield?"

The poor woman looked as if she'd been caught in a downpour—at least the top half of her did. Strands of her wet, light brown hair had turned darker and hung limp across her shoulders. She had that pitchfork pointed at him again. What had he done this time?

She frowned, and he'd swear she was gawking at him if he didn't know better. "Mr. Morgan?"

"Who else were you expecting to be here this early?"

Her chin lifted and her pretty lips puckered. "I sure wasn't expecting anyone to be buried under a mound of hay. You scared me half to death." She ducked her chin. "Your unexpected presence frightened the cow and caused me to spill the milk—all over myself. And now I doubt we'll have enough for the children's breakfast."

His gaze fell on the upturned bucket and stool, lying on the dirt floor in front of him. He scratched his head, the fog of sleep still muddying his thoughts. Just what had he done to cause all that?

"What in the world were you doing in that stall?" She walked over to the barn wall and leaned the hayfork against it then strode back to the center of the walkway and shoved her hands to her hips? "Well, are you going to answer me?"

He knew exactly how one of the children must have felt when she scolded them for doing wrong, but at the moment, she looked more like an irritated hen that had dishwater dumped on her than a teacher. He sure had a way of ruffling her feathers. Riley couldn't help grinning.

She blinked and her expression changed from anger to something he couldn't quite decipher. "Never mind. I don't want to know anyway."

She dipped her head and plodded forward slowly. Holding up her skirt, she took a step then swung her foot around in front of her from one side to the other and back, then she took another step, and swiped her foot again.

Riley stood there, intrigued, by her odd actions.

One more swipe, and her foot connected with the pail, making a hollow *thunk*. So she was searching for the bucket. He'd never considered how difficult such a simple task must be for people who couldn't see. How did she manage to feed and milk the cow then carry the pail back to the house without stumbling under its weight? He bent down to pick it up for her, but she leaned down at the same time, and their foreheads conked together.

"Ow! Oh!" She held one hand to her head and hauled back and clobbered him on the arm with her fist. "You've got to be the most infuriating man I've ever met."

"Sorry, ma'am. Just trying to help." He felt bad for hurting her, but a chuckle slipped out in spite of his trying hard to hold it back. He'd been miserable and had shoved down his emotions for so long that her being so upset over something so petty as a little spilt milk just hit him funny.

She scowled and continued to rub the red spot over her left eyebrow. "Are you laughing at me?"

He tucked his lips together and shook his head, trying extrahard to contain the amusement making his shoulders bounce. "Uh . . . no, ma'am."

She stomped her foot, pressed her hands against her hips, and lifted her face to his. For being so useless, her pretty brown eyes bore straight into his, or so it seemed. She huffed out a sound, something between a cat hacking up a hairball and a horse's whiffle, spun around, and marched out of the barn.

Bertha mooed, long and deep, as if scolding him too.

Riley's chest bounced as he attempted to not laugh. For someone who was so gentle with the children, Miss Sheffield sure had a short temper and no patience with him. It made no sense that her actions would tickle his funny bone, but they did.

He shook his head, righted the stool, and stuck the pail under the cow. Maybe he could offer an apology for scaring and embarrassing her by finishing the milking. He hoped the old cow had enough left so the children didn't go without.

Resting his head against the cow's side, he let his thoughts drift to Miss Sheffield again. He'd seen some women during the war, but most of those had been haggard from the exhausting duties of nursing wounded soldiers or doing laundry from sunup to sundown for more men than he could count. They'd been thin from the lack of good food and most times covered with grime. No, he'd rarely seen one with Miss Sheffield's wholesomeness, or one whose skin looked as soft as a horse's muzzle. Or whose big, brown eyes lit with fire in spite of their ineffectiveness. Her spirit reminded him of Miranda's.

Riley stiffened. He didn't want to think of Miranda and the pain she'd caused. He shook his head. He had no business thinking of Miss Sheffield either. He was a man with nothing to his name except a piece of property he didn't want. Soon, he needed to go into town and see about selling it.

CHAPTER SIX

*L*aura loved teaching the children, but she coveted the few moments that she was able to get away each week. As she and Annie approached the edge of town, she lifted her nose and sniffed, catching a sweet fragrance on the warm breeze. "Someone's baking today."

"Yes, and if I wasn't so nervous about going into town, I'd be hankering for a bite even though we just finished our noon meal." Annie's steps slowed. "Maybe I should go back and stay with Mrs. Alton in case one of the youngsters won't take a nap."

Shaking her head, Laura chuckled. "I don't know why you get so anxious every time you go to town."

"It's not the townsfolk that concern me but the strangers. The men who gawk at me and even try to start up a conversation."

Laura wrapped her arm through Annie's, slowing her pace. "You're a pretty young lady, and it's only natural that they study you. Men like to watch women. It's just how they're made."

"Well, it makes me feel like there are ants crawling all over me." Annie shuddered, but her lips twitched and a grin broke out on her face. "I have a hard time not laughing sometimes when they learn I'm blind. You should see their expressions. Some are saddened, but most are horrified and back away as if I have some disease they could catch."

Laura understood how Annie felt. Most men looked at her the same way since she was generally in the presence of a blind student or Annie whenever she came to town. "I know, but I don't think it's funny at all. It makes me angry. People need to be educated. A blind person can live a good life, as long as they learn some crucial skills."

"You're preaching again."

Laura glanced sideways at Annie, biting her lips to keep from grinning. "My apologies. I do get on my soapbox at times."

"Yes, you do." Annie peered out from under her bonnet, smiling.

Love for the younger woman flooded Laura's heart. How would she have managed all these years without Annie's help and companionship? The feisty orphan had blossomed into a pretty woman—a bit headstrong at times, but a responsible hard worker and the best of friends, in spite of their age difference. She dreaded the day Annie would leave, yet she knew that day was coming, even though Annie would argue the point.

She still wasn't certain she'd done right by the ragtag orphan who'd appeared on her doorstep seven years ago. Yes, she had learned manners and proper etiquette for a female and she'd forsaken pick-pocketing, but Laura never should have forced Annie to pretend to be blind. That was the only thing she'd lived to regret, but how else would it have been possible for the girl to stay at the school? Mr. Morrow was a kind, generous benefactor, but he had made it clear that only blind children were to live at the Wilcox School for the Blind. She could argue the point that at thirteen, Annie had been more an adult than a child, but regardless, she didn't have it in her heart to turn the starving girl away. She knew how hard it was to grow up without a father—and poor Annie had neither father nor mother.

"What are you going to do if Mr. Morrow's letter isn't there?" Annie nibbled on her lower lip.

Laura glanced across the field beside them, taking in the blanket of multicolored wildflowers swaying in the breeze. In the nine years that she'd run the school, Charles Morrow had never been late with a payment, and the fact that he was this month more than worried her. What would happen to the school if something happened to Mr. Morrow? With all the expenses from the war, the town wasn't able to support them, and the small monthly fee that only half the parents could afford to pay wouldn't keep them in food for a week.

As much as she loved the children and helping them, there were times she longed to be married—to share the experience of carrying a child of her own with a husband she adored. She laid a hand against her flat stomach. The image of the one man she almost married filled her mind, but no, it was far too late for a life with him. She was already thirty-four, and if she didn't marry before long, her dream would fade into dust. But was she being selfish? Wasn't helping the children more important than her own desires?

Annie's irritated voice yanked her out of her thoughts.

"And how am I supposed to weed and water the garden with Mr. Morgan around all the time? And what about keeping an eye on the children when they are outside? How am I supposed to do that if I can't watch them?" Annie stooped, snatched up a rock, and flung it across the field. "Why did you have to hire that—that—man?"

Laura bit back a smile. She'd never heard the girl go on about a male before, but then the only men she encountered were generally those they saw in town or at church. The few men Annie's age hadn't shown any interest in the young woman they perceived as blind, even though she was pretty. But Annie hadn't seemed to be bothered by their lack of interest.

"Are you ignoring me? I've asked you something like a dozen questions and you haven't answered." Annie stopped and stared into Laura's eyes.

Lifting her eyebrows, Laura tapped the girl's nose. "Ah ah, no eye contact, remember? And don't exaggerate."

Scowling, Annie started walking again. "Why did you hire him? Don't you realize how difficult it makes my life to have him around?"

"We need him, at least for a little while. We don't have the time or physical strength to tend to all the things that need fixing. And besides, with all the raiders and carpetbaggers around, I feel safer having a man on the property."

Annie stomped down the road. "But you don't even know him."

"I knew his family, and I remember Raleigh from when we were younger."

"Raleigh? I thought his name was Riley." Annie peered sideways then darted her gaze straight ahead again.

Laura slowed her steps as they drew near the general store at the end of Waco. "His given name is Raleigh, but his younger brother never could say it correctly and called him Riley, and the name stuck."

"Can't see as they're all that much different. So did his brother die in the Indian attack with his parents?"

Shaking her head, Laura watched a wagon stop in front of Sean Murphy's blacksmith shop at the far end of town. She hoped he would come out of the building so she could catch a glimpse of him. "No, his brother died before Riley left for the war. On his birthday, in fact."

Annie caught her breath and turned to her friend. "That's awful. What happened?"

Laura pressed her lips together and shook her head. "So sad. Timothy was only ten, and was playing with another boy when he stumbled across a rattlesnake. The poor child got bit and soon died. Riley loved him dearly, and was so upset that he rode off. The war had just started and Riley joined up, and as far as I know, never saw his folks again."

"That's so sad."

"Yes. I can't imagine how he felt to come home and find them gone."

"So sad." Annie took hold of Laura's arm, allowing her to lead her into the store as they commonly did when in town. The scents a person normally expected to greet them when entering a store, like spices or leather or pungent pickles, paled to the overpowering scent of gardenia perfume, which the storeowner's wife applied with a lavish hand. Laura just hoped Mrs. Petree didn't go off on her tirade about how she smelled like her store again. She'd heard it more times than there were rocks in Texas.

"Phew!" Annie whispered loudly in Laura's ear.

"Shhh." Laura fanned her face.

"Good afternoon! I was wondering if you two would come in, being as this is mail day." Mrs. Petree bustled from behind the counter and gave Laura a quick hug, enveloping her in an almost visible cloud of floral fragrance. The friendly woman next touched Annie's shoulder and then the two embraced.

Annie held her hand in front of her nose, coughed, and moved a few steps away.

Lifting her handkerchief to her nose, Laura tried hard to avoid gagging at the strong floral odor permeating the air around her. As far as she knew, not another lady would dare touch the gardenia fragrance, because they all had their fill of it whenever they entered the store, and not another soul would sit on the same pew as the Petrees at church.

"How are you doing, Mrs. Petree?" Annie asked, staring blankly ahead, playing her role well.

"Just fine and dandy." Mrs. Petree raised her voice as she normally did when talking to Annie or one of the children, as if being sightless meant one also had hearing problems. "How are those poor, misfortunate children? Are they all well?"

Laura nodded, cringing at the woman's snide reference to her students. "Yes, thank you." She glanced past the woman to the mail slot, relief flooding her to see a letter lying cockeyed in her box. Mr. Morrow had come through again.

Mrs. Petree smiled. "I suppose you're wantin' your letter from that kindhearted Mr. Morrow."

"Yes, please. I confess I was getting a bit concerned that it hadn't arrived yet. It's generally here by the first of the month."

Turning her back to them, Mrs. Petree pulled the envelope from the slot and spun back around, handing the missive to Laura. "Odd, though. It's not the usual handwriting. Perhaps Mr. Morrow has hired a new clerk."

"Hmm . . . I suppose he could have." The letter felt lighter than usual. Laura turned the envelope over, and her heart flip-flopped. The scrolling initial on the wax seal was an R, not the usual M. She shoved the envelope in her handbag, hoping Mrs. Petree had missed that detail. Laura liked the friendly woman, but if there was anything newsworthy, everyone in the county would know about it within a week.

"I heard that you had a man working out at your place." The woman's graying brows lifted.

Laura noticed Annie stiffen, but then the young woman reached out her hand and walked forward, touching the closest display table. Laura breathed out a tight breath. She hated deceiving their neighbors, but they'd played the ruse for so long that there was no turning back now. "Yes, Riley Morgan has agreed to stay for a little while to fix a few things around the school."

Mrs. Petree shook her head in disapproval. "It's not right for a man to live at the same place as two unmarried women."

Laura lifted her chin. "There's nothing improper about it. Mr. Morgan is staying out in the barn's tack room. And it's only temporary." More temporary than she wanted if the school's financing wasn't included in the envelope in her handbag.

"Well, I'm just sayin'. You know how people talk."

Laura worked hard not to react to Mrs. Petree's remark.

Behind her, Annie snorted then coughed. "Uh . . . pardon me. I must have gotten some dust in my throat."

Laura reached behind her to give Annie a gentle nudge, but she was out of reach. "I should get the thread I need and get back to the school before the little ones wake up from their nap." She turned and grabbed hold of Annie's arm. "Come along, dear."

Mrs. Petree grabbed her ever-present bottle of perfume and dabbed the gardenia scent behind her ears. "I'd heard that Morgan boy was back. I'm surprised that he hasn't been into town yet. It's a cryin' shame about his folks. Wonder if he got word about them bein' gone or if he just found out after he got home. They was nice folks, Calder and Emily." She clicked her tongue and shook her head. "Too bad their son ran off and left them the same day that younger boy died. We 'bout lost Emily, too, that day." She shook her head.

Footsteps echoed down the boardwalk, and two women entered the store. Mrs. Downy, the wife of the town's barber, who also served as the dentist when needed, entered with her mother, Mrs. Black. Both women's eyes brightened when they noticed Laura and Annie.

"Afternoon, Miss Wilcox. Miss Sheffield." The barber's wife smiled broadly as she helped her mother to a chair that sat beside the stove that hadn't been used in months.

Laura walked toward them, thankful for the timely opportunity to steer the topic away from Riley Morgan. "How nice to see you both."

Mrs. Black tapped her cane on the floor. "Next time we have our sewing bee, we oughta be able to finish up that new set of clothes we've been stitching for them blind children." A pensive look crossed the woman's wrinkled face. "You don't have any newcomers, do ya?"

Laura shook her head. "No, ma'am, just the same ones we've had for a while. The children will be delighted to have some new clothes. You women are such a blessing. I don't know what we'd do without your generosity." She spoke the truth. The townswomen worked hard to keep her students clothed, not to mention the quilt they stitched for each new child who came to the school.

Annie had wandered out onto the boardwalk, most likely needing a breath of fresh air. Laura longed to join her and to read the letter that was fanning a wildfire of questions in her mind. "I need to get my thread and be on my way. You ladies enjoy your day, and if you can let me know what day you plan to deliver the clothing, I'll ask Mrs. Alton to prepare something special for our tea time."

While Mrs. Petree informed the two women that Alice Samuels had run off with the Higgins boy and how dreadful that must be for her parents, Laura selected her thread, dropped the coins on the counter, and made a quick exit before the woman could mention Riley Morgan again.

Annie stood at the end of the boardwalk facing the school. The warm afternoon breeze ruffled her skirts and long hair that was tied back with a blue ribbon that matched her new dress.

The colonial blue calico had been a wise choice, and the stylish cut of the waistline emphasized the girl's womanly shape. Laura sighed. Annie was no longer a coltish tomboy, although she did still favor outside chores over household duties.

One of these days, she would catch a kindhearted man's eye, and then Annie would leave. What had she been thinking to have suggested that very thing to Annie on her birthday? How would she manage without her?

iley strolled out of the bathhouse, feeling—and smelling—a far sight better than he had in a long while. Thanks to the inexpensive set of clean, but used, clothing he'd bought from Mrs. Braddock, the proprietor, he hadn't needed to put his dirty clothes back on. That set should probably have been tossed in the fire that heated the water he'd washed in, but since it was his only other set, he'd taken Mrs. Braddock up on her offer to wash them.

He untied Gypsy from the hitching post and headed down Second Street, observing again how the place had changed. Waco had only been about ten years old when he had been conscripted, and the town had changed little over the past four years.

A high-pitched voice that reminded him of a mosquito whizzing past his ear pulled his attention to the open door of the general store. He'd caught a glimpse of Miss Laura and Annie entering the store when he'd peeked out the curtains of the bathhouse while he was buttoning his shirt. The woman chattering on and on sure wasn't either of them.

He dismounted at the smithy and glanced at the rickety wagon sitting out front. Two small colored boys chased each other around the front of the wagon, making a wide arc around the sad-looking mule hitched to it. The animal's ribs stuck out, resembling his ma's washboard. One of the boys squealed and jogged backwards in Riley's direction. Riley could see the child's mother's eyes grow wide. She snapped her fingers. "Eli, Isaiah, git in the back 'fo' I fetch my switch."

One boy skidded to a halt, but the other kept coming, unaware that Riley stood behind him. Riley held out his hand, and the shorter boy banged into it. "Whoa, there."

The child spun around, eyes wide, and fear etching his face. "S–sorry, mistah."

"It's all right, but you'd best listen to your ma."

The child raced back to his mother, who took hold of his shoulders and stared at Riley as if he might do the child harm.

He hated ruining their fun, but the boy should be more careful. There were still plenty of white men who would have the boy severely beaten for running into them. Riley wasn't one of them, but they didn't know that.

A thin black man hurried out of the livery with a huge red-haired man lumbering behind him. The black man's eyes went wide when he saw Riley. "Uh . . . pardon, sir. I hope my boys ain't botherin' you."

"Eli, he done bumped into the man." The mother glanced at her husband then hung her head, as if already accepting her child's punishment. Riley pulled his gaze from her to the father who also hung his head and wouldn't look at him. Beside the colored man was the broad-shouldered livery owner, who stood only about as tall as Riley's shoulders, but his upper arms were bigger around than Riley's thighs, and his face covered in freckles. He nodded, albeit a wary nod.

Riley parroted his action and smiled. "The boys weren't bothering me. I was just enjoying their liveliness."

Both men seemed to visibly relax and grinned. "They be that, fo' sure. Don't know how we gonna keep them cooped up in that wagon fo' so long."

"Where you headed?" Riley asked, hoping his question came across as friendly and not nosy.

"That General Sherman, he done issued a special order and set aside some land fo' us freedmen. Somewhere in Georgia fo' folks like us. That be where we's a'goin'."

"Special Field Order 15," the blacksmith stated.

Riley nodded. "I read about that. He's giving forty acres to colored families on some of the Sea Islands, if I'm not mistaken."

"You aren't." The blacksmith scratched the curly red hair on his chest that peeked out where the top button of his shirt was missing. "You look familiar. You from these parts?"

"Name's Morgan."

The blacksmith grinned and held out his hand. "Riley Morgan?"

Nodding, Riley couldn't help the smile that tugged at his lips. He'd wondered if anyone would recognize him, considering how much he'd changed.

"I'm Sean Murphy. I knew your pa." The man's twinkling eyes dimmed. "I'm sorry for what happened. Calder and Emily were good folk."

Riley dipped his head in agreement. "Thanks."

Sean clapped him on the shoulder so hard, Riley nearly lost his footing. "Let me see Peter's family off, and I'll get right back to you." His eyes narrowed. "That is, if you don't mind waitin' a wee bit."

"I'm in no particular hurry."

Acceptance brightened Sean's eyes.

Peter held out the bag. "This is fo' you. Much obliged to you fo' looking over my wagon and mule."

Sean eyed the sack then took it. The critter inside flopped around as if trying to get free.

Peter ambled to his wagon then turned back to the blacksmith. "I thank you for yo' kindness to Issie 'n me."

Sean waved his hand in the air. "Think nothing of it. And safe travels."

Peter climbed in the wagon, and Riley watched them drive off. The boys dangled their feet over the back of the tailgate, their eyes gleaming as if they set off on a big adventure. Behind them sat a forlorn collection of rolled-up ragged quilts, a few boxes, and a crate with three chickens in it.

As they turned the corner, Sean swung around, his lips pressed tight. "I sure hope they make it. I tried to give them some food, but Peter was too proud to take it." He shook the burlap bag, and the critter within chattered. Sean's lip curled up.

"A squirrel?"

Sean nodded. "Not my favorite thing to eat."

"I've eaten a few of those in my day," Riley said.

"You want it?" Sean held out the bag. "Think those blind kids would like some fried squirrel?"

Riley lifted one shoulder. "One wouldn't be enough to feed half of them. Why don't you just turn it loose?"

"Good advice." Sean chuckled and glanced at Gypsy. "Nice horse. Looks like a Morgan. So what can I do for you today?"

"She needs a new set of shoes."

"I can take care of that. But first, let me get rid of this." The blacksmith walked through the smithy and out the back door. He returned a moment later with an empty bag and tossed it across his anvil as he came back toward Riley.

Hearing raised voices, Riley turned and studied two men

walking in his direction. One man waved his hand in the air. "It'll be the ruin of Texas, I tell you."

Sean leaned toward him. "That's the barber. He's also our dentist, Kirk Downy. The other man is John Barnsdall, the local gunsmith. He's new to town since you've been gone. Lost his oldest son in the war."

Both men stopped as they approached. The barber glanced up. "You there, what's your opinion of this Freedman's Bureau?"

Riley shrugged, unsure just what the man was hoping he'd say. "Don't know all that much about it. Just that it's an organization Congress established to help feed and clothe the freedmen."

"They're giving confiscated lands to slaves."

"They're no longer slaves, Kirk." Sean crossed his brawny arms over his chest.

The blacksmith may have been shorter than the other three men, but Riley didn't doubt the others were aware of his strength.

"'Forty acres and a mule' is what they're calling it in the newspapers." Mr. Barnsdall scratched his cheek. A black armband encircled his right arm, indicating the death of a family member. "Don't quite seem right to be giving free land to coloreds when so many white folk are going without."

"What white folk?" Sean cocked back his head.

Mr. Barnsdall's ears turned red, and he glared at Sean. "I don't know. We've got white men becomin' raiders and stealing our horses and breakin' into our homes. If those men had land, they wouldn't be raiding."

Sean took a step forward. "Those men raid because they're too lazy to find work."

Riley's admiration for the blacksmith grew.

"Well . . ." Mr. Downy swatted his hand at Sean as if shooing away a pesky fly. "We're just having a friendly conversation, Sean. Reginald Cooper and some of the other cotton farmers came to see me today. They don't intend to release their slaves unless they are forced to." He shook his head. "I don't know what this county will do without the income from selling cotton. We're already scraping the bottom of the barrel with all the money we've had to pay out to help fund the war. Who's going to harvest the cotton if all the slaves are gone?"

"Maybe it's time the big plantation owners try a new crop."

"That's what I've been saying." Mr. Barnsdall pointed his index finger at the sky. "Cattle, that's the future of Texas."

"Bah! Cattle." Mr. Downy shook his head. "Cotton has always been king in Texas and always will be." He looked at Riley, crinkled his forehead, and his fuzzy eyebrows merged into one. "Who'd you say you were?"

"Riley Morgan."

"Morgan?" The dentist stroked his chin then his eyes widened. "Not Calder and Emily's son?"

He nodded, preparing himself once again, but the consoling words didn't come.

"You got taller, boy." Mr. Downy wagged his finger at Riley's belly. "And you've lost weight, if I'm not mistaken."

"I reckon most every man who fought in the war is thinner than he was when he left home, maybe except for some of the officers."

Mr. Barnsdall shook his head. "That war was somethin' awful. We're mighty lucky we didn't have any skirmishes around Waco."

All four men nodded. Sean looked down the street and stiffened. Riley glanced past the other two men and down the road that headed out of town to see what had caught Sean's attention, and his gut clenched. Miss Laura and Annie were walking home, and it looked as if they might be headed straight into a passel of trouble.

Annie watched a russet-colored rabbit hop onto the road in front of her. It froze, only its nose twitching, then darted off into the brush as if just realizing people were around. Up ahead near the school, three men on horses rode in their direction, but she didn't recognize any of them. She lowered her head and sighed as she walked beside Laura on the road leading home.

Though she'd never had a strong desire to own fancy doodads, she took pleasure in looking at the new things that passed through the store. She longed to pick up a lace handkerchief or a new bonnet and really look at how it was made, but the most she could do without making someone suspicious was to run her fingers over them.

Pretending to be blind had ceased being interesting a long time ago. Maybe one day she could visit another town, where people didn't know her, and she would be free to walk the streets at a regular pace and watch all the goings-on without worrying about anyone noticing. Maybe then folks would treat her as if she were normal and not cast pitying looks in her direction and shake their heads. She'd overheard, "Poor thing" and "She's so pretty. If only she wasn't blind . . ." more often than Mrs. Petree dabbed on perfume.

"I declare, that Alvia Petree could talk the ears off an elephant." Laura fanned her face with her hand. "Pardon me for being so blunt, but that woman sure tries my nerves."

"At least she smells like a flower." Annie gently nudged Laura's side with her elbow and snickered.

"You mean a whole flower garden, don't you?"

Annie laughed out loud, and Laura did too. At least she had one friend who knew her as she truly was. Keeping her head down and holding on to Laura's arm, Annie peered out from under the brim of her bonnet as the three men stopped their horses in the road, blocking their path. She felt Laura stiffen.

"Well, now, if that ain't the prettiest sight I've seen in a coon's age," one of the men said.

Annie's heart skipped a beat. While there had been on occasion adolescent boys who poked fun at the blind children and her, most men they encountered were polite and respectful, but this man's tone left no doubt that he had tomfoolery on his mind. She lifted her head a smidgen, being careful that her bonnet brim shielded her eyes from the men's view. All three wore the faded and raggedy gray trousers of the Confederate army and rode horses as thin as Mr. Morgan's. She tightened her grasp on Laura's arm. Could they be in any danger this close to town?

"Just go on your way, gentlemen. You've no business with us." A person unfamiliar with Laura's voice probably wouldn't have noticed the slight warble that Annie detected. "I'm the administrator of the Wilcox School for Blind Children, and we must be getting back. The children will be waking from their naps soon."

One man dismounted, dropped his reins, and walked toward them. "Them kids won't even know you're not there. Now us . . . well . . . we haven't been in the company of two such lovely womenfolk in a long while. What say we all go somewhere and have some fun?"

Miss Laura gasped and backed up, dragging Annie with her. "We're not that kind of women. I am offended at your insinuation, sir."

"My what?"

"Your *suggestion*, Garth." Another man dismounted and stopped in front of Annie. "You smell like a bouquet of flowers. How come you're so quiet, missy?" The man stank like rotten eggs and tugged on the brim of her bonnet. Annie made her eyes go blank and slightly cross-eyed. The raucous smile fled his unshaven face, and he stepped back as if he had encountered someone with smallpox.

"She's a purty thang, ain't she?" a younger man, still on horseback, said.

"What's wrong with her?" Stinky backed up all the way to his horse and smacked into it. The animal jerked its head and side-stepped, as if it, too, was repulsed by the man's stench. Did soldiers never wash?

A memory slithered through her mind—of the dirty, young pickpocket who longed to be clean.

The leader of the group waved his hand in front of Annie's face, and she tried not to blink. He muttered a curse. "She cain't see nothin'."

The man on horseback chuckled. "Maybe that's a good thang. Then she cain't see how ugly you are."

Garth's hand went to his gun. Laura sucked in a breath, and grabbed Annie's arm so tight it pinched her skin. She pulled her back two paces. Annie stepped on the edge of her skirt, flailed her arm loose from Laura's hand, and fell hard on her backside. The men roared with laughter. Laura bent to help her up, and while her friend's body shielded her view from the men, Annie grabbed a large rock off the ground and held it behind her dress.

"Pray," Laura whispered as she helped her up.

"Just take the old one," Stinky said over his shoulder, as he chased after his horse.

A huge fist gripped Annie's heart. *No!*

She wrapped her arms around Laura and held her tight. She had listened some in church, but mostly spent her time shushing wiggly children. Could a God so far away really care about her—about Laura? Would He even hear her if she cried out to Him?

Garth pried at Annie's hand—the one without the rock. Laura's whimpers sounded in her ear. *God, if You're up there, please don't let these men take Laura. Do something!*

Garth grabbed Annie's wrist, digging his fingers into the tender underside. A sharp pain forced her to loosen her hold. She couldn't overpower the man's strength, and he pulled her arm away from Laura's waist, giving her a shove backwards. He yanked Laura to his side, a leering grin spreading across his pockmarked face.

"Let's go," he said, dragging Laura beside him, her fists pounding his chest and back.

Stinky caught his horse but still hadn't mounted. The younger man had already turned his horse in the other direction and glanced back to watch the events, his eyes gleaming.

Annie couldn't stand by and do nothing. It didn't matter if they figured out she could see. She wouldn't let Laura be taken without a fight.

She let out a war cry that would frighten a Comanche and charged forward, lifting the rock as she ran. Garth spun around, dragging Laura with him, and his gray eyes widened as Annie lobbed the weapon at him.

He jerked back, but the rock smacked into his cheek. He howled, pressing his hand to his face, and when he pulled his hand away, his fingers were covered in blood. He growled, his lips pulling up in a wolflike snarl, then hauled back his arm. Annie closed her eyes and swerved, bracing for his fist.

Gunfire pierced the air, and she jumped. Garth sobered and lowered his arm. He released Laura, spun around, and ran for his horse. A rider whizzed past her and chased the men past the school, then swung back around and galloped toward them. *Riley!* He pulled to a stop so fast his horse nearly sat down. He dismounted, his concerned gaze going straight to hers.

It took every ounce of her control not to stare into his

beautiful eyes. She forced her head down, blocking her view of him. Another horse pounded toward them from town, but she stood still. Laura, she noted, had mostly regained her composure though her hands still trembled.

"Are you two all right?" Riley stepped toward them but then dropped his hands to his side, the right one still holding his gun.

"Yes. I can't thank you enough for coming to our rescue, Mr. Morgan. I don't know what would have hap—"

"Laura!"

Annie knew without turning that Sean Murphy had arrived. No other man in town had ever called the school's director by her first name.

"Sean." Laura turned and disappeared from Annie's view. She heard them walk away as Laura recounted what happened.

Mr. Morgan cleared his throat. "Uh . . . did I see you throw a rock at one of those men?"

She lifted her hand to her chest, hoping he couldn't hear how hard her heart was pounding. What could she say that wouldn't be another lie? "Did I hit him?"

"Sure did, but how could you know you wouldn't hit Miss Laura?"

"I . . . uh . . . did you know that blind people have an abnormally sharp sense of hearing?"

"No, I don't guess so, but it does make sense. Soldiers wounded in the war learned to adapt when they lost an eye or a limb. I reckon it makes sense that people who can't see would depend on their other senses more."

Annie exhaled a loud breath, grateful that the conversation had steered away from the rock throwing. She stared forward, her gaze resting at his top button and realized he wore a different shirt. Not new, by any means, but at least it was clean and didn't smell like rotten onions. He smelled nice, in fact. Like bay rum.

She hadn't noticed during the hubbub if he'd shaved or not and tilted her head just enough to see his tanned chin, free of whiskers. She longed to glance up and see if he was as handsome as she suspected, but she didn't dare. Surely he was suspicious of her after seeing her lob that rock at the horrible man.

"You mind if I walk you home, Miss Sheffield?"

Annie shook her head. "Thank you, but I'll walk with Miss Laura."

"Guess you weren't listening. She and Sean are halfway back to the school already. She must know that you're safe with me." He picked up Gypsy's reins and stuck out his elbow toward Annie.

She was so flustered that Laura had gone on without her that she started to lift her hand. When he halted suddenly, she bypassed his arm and raised her hand to her cheek, tucking a strand of loose hair behind her ear.

His hand gently latched on to her wrist then placed it around his arm. She held still, unsure if allowing him to escort her was proper or not. She could have done fine without him, but she relaxed. The muscle in his upper arm tightened, and she realized that though thin from his army diet, he was a man used to hard work.

And he'd saved her from a bashing by that vermin. And saved Miss Laura from being kidnapped and much worse.

Maybe she needed to treat Riley Morgan a bit nicer in the future.

CHAPTER EIGHT

W ith her arms crossed over her chest, Laura stared out her bedroom window, watching the deep navy sky fade to black. Stars flickered overhead, as numerous as bluebonnets in spring. She rested her head against the window frame and thought about how close she had come to being taken captive by those heinous men. If Mr. Morgan and Sean hadn't come along . . . She shivered just thinking about the awful things she might be enduring this night if not for them. Never had she felt so vulnerable.

Sean had done a lot to alleviate her fears. He'd been so courteous and truly seemed worried about her. He had insisted on walking her home after the horrifying incident and even sat on the porch with her until she'd stopped shaking. She hadn't seen him up close for so long other than at church and an occasional town gathering, and then she was always busy keeping an eye on the children. In his work clothes he looked so . . . manly. He'd been so attentive and concerned that she could almost pretend he still cared.

Too bad he had never married and had a family. She wanted to ask him why he hadn't but couldn't bring herself to do so.

What if she was the reason?

But he hadn't looked at her as if he blamed her for his solitary life. In fact, she thought she'd seen interest in his green eyes, but she was afraid to believe it. Could he possibly still have feelings for her?

Regardless, she'd chosen a different path years ago, and there was no going back.

"What was that sigh for?" Annie asked.

Turning, Laura wondered how much to say. The young woman had become her best friend, but nearly fifteen years separated them in age. In truth, she was almost old enough to be Annie's mother, but their relationship was more like sisters than parent and child. She watched as her friend, seated at the small desk in her chemise and drawers, applied blacking to her Balmoral boots. Though Annie had grown up street-tough, she was ignorant about men and their desire for power and women, but today she'd had a rough glimpse of what self-centered men could do. "Are you all right?" she asked, ignoring Annie's question.

"I'm fine. I'm more worried about you." She glanced up, a boot on one hand and a blacking rag in the other. "I was so scared those men would take you. What would happen to the children if anything ever happened to you?"

Laura crossed the small room and sat on the edge of her bed. "I suppose we should make plans in case that should ever happen."

"I wouldn't have a clue what to do, other than watching over the children. I suppose I'd need to write to their parents and Mr. Morrow." Annie straightened and looked past Laura. "Speaking of him, Mrs. Alton made up a list of supplies we need, now that we have received his draft for the month. The list is over there in my apron pocket." She nudged her chin toward the back of their door, where her apron hung on a peg.

Laura stiffened. "I completely forgot about the letter after nearly getting abducted." *And spending a glorious time—albeit too short of a time—with Sean.* She opened the dresser drawer that held her handbag and fished out the missive. She hesitated opening it, hoping it didn't contain bad news, but she feared it must. Why else would someone other than Mr. Morrow or his agent be writing her?

Carrying the letter back to her bed, she sat and broke the seal. The strong odor of smoke made her wrinkle her nose.

> *Miss Wilcox,*
>   *I regret to inform you that my uncle, Charles Morrow, has died.*

Oh, no. Kind Mr. Morrow was gone? She glanced at Annie, glad she was still engrossed in her polishing, then continued to read.

> *As I am his only living heir, the Waco property in which the blind school resides now belongs to me. I will be arriving on or near July 23rd to view the property and arrange with an agent to sell it.*

"No!" Laura jerked, as if someone had stabbed her. Pain squeezed her heart. July 23rd was just four days away.

Annie's gaze shot straight to hers and she straightened. "What is it?"

Shaking her head, Laura scanned the rest of the short but devastating note.

Please make plans to vacate the school within thirty days from the date of this letter.

Otis Ramsey

Her hands dropped to her lap, as she no longer had the strength to lift them. Tears burned her eyes. Losing the school was too much to face in light of how her nerves were still pulled taut after the day's events. She swiped at her cheek, afraid that any second she would start blubbering.

What would they do? How could she continue the school without a building or finances?

She tossed the letter on the floor and hurried to the door. She couldn't let Annie see her fall apart.

← ★ →

What in the world? Annie stared out the empty doorway after Laura. Her friend was normally stalwart and not easily shaken. She wasn't one to fall apart easily, but then today had been out of the ordinary.

The letter Laura had tossed aside beckoned her. Dare she read it? If it had been all that private, wouldn't Laura have tucked it away somewhere?

She slipped out of the chair and tiptoed to the door, looking out into the sitting room, half expecting to find Laura in one of the upholstered wingback chairs or the rocking chair where she enjoyed reading after the children were in bed. But there was no sign of her. Annie quietly shut the door then hurried across the room and stared at the note on the floor, her heart pummeling her chest as if it sought to escape.

Before she could change her mind, she bent and scooped up the letter. The blacking from her fingertips marred the edges of the fancy paper, leaving clear evidence of her snooping, just as the shocking words she read tainted her security.

They were losing the house?

Her gaze roamed the bedroom she'd painted herself with milk paint, the only room she'd ever had. She loved this house—this room. This home.

Tears stung her eyes, blurring her view of the cherished room. What would happen to her? To the children?

And what about Laura? She'd sacrificed the possibility of having her own family in order to care for their students.

Crossing her arms tight around her, she rocked back and forth. She had nowhere else in the whole world to go. This town was her home, and every single person believed her to be blind. No one would take her in if they knew the truth. No one would hire her to work. What would she do?

One thing was certain—she'd never return to her old ways. She could never again be a pickpocket, even if she faced starvation. She wadded up the paper and tossed it across the room, then hurried downstairs to find Laura.

———— ★ ————

Riley guided the wagon across the dry creek bed and onto his family's property. He had to admit that he was thankful to not be returning home alone this time. Instead, a wagonload of giddy children sang a jaunty song about butterflies and bumblebees, while Miss Annie sat beside him, uncharacteristically quiet. Her shoulder bumped his as the wagon dipped into a deep rut and scrambled back out, but she made no effort to slide over on the seat.

He hadn't seen much of her after the raiders' attack yesterday, except at supper, and she'd seemed in fine spirits then. Miss Laura, though, who'd recruited him to escort her and the children on an outing, had deserted them, saying she had important business in town.

He closed his eyes and tilted his head back. The morning

sun warmed his face, but did little to remove the apprehension he felt at seeing his home in disarray again. When he'd requested off to return home for the day, Miss Laura had asked if they could use his land for an outing. Had she known it would make things easier on him to not return alone? And with the children being sightless, they wouldn't be upset by the looks of the place.

He glanced sideways at Miss Annie. She sat with her arms crossed, and every so often she'd sigh without realizing it. A light-green gingham sunbonnet that matched her dress shielded her pretty face from view, but he was sure he'd find a scowl there if he could see it. He wanted to pretend it didn't bother him that something was wrong, but he couldn't. "You care to say why you're so quiet?"

Her head jerked toward him. "What?"

"I can tell something's upset you. Don't try to deny it."

She shrugged and turned her ear toward the children. "Are you-all sitting down?"

"Yes, Miss Annie," they responded in unison.

"Anybody hanging over the side of the wagon?"

"No, Miss Annie."

"That's good, because it's a long walk back if one of you should fall out."

"Not too far for me," Rusty shouted. "Hey, let's sing 'John Brown's Body' next."

"No, let's not," Miss Annie said. "Sing the Bingo song."

Cheers rang out, then young voices filled the air.

Riley enjoyed sitting close to Miss Annie. He leaned toward her to be heard over the din. "They sing real nice."

She nodded. "Music is one way they can express themselves. Many blind people are especially talented in playing an instrument or singing."

"What about you?"

"Me?" She gave him a small smile and shook her head. "Can't carry a tune. Miss Laura is the one with the musical talent. She can sing like a songbird."

"I bet you could do about anything you set your mind to."

Her face turned toward him but he leaned his elbows on his knees, holding the reins loosely between his fingers, and watched a fly buzzing around one of the horses' ears. He felt as if she were studying him, but that was nonsense.

"Why would you say such a thing? You hardly know me."

He shrugged. "I figure any blind person who can find a rock and conk a raider on the head with it, can do about anything." She could also milk a cow, hang laundry, and scurry around the yard better than most people he knew.

Her cheeks reddened. "That was rather impulsive of me."

"Don't know how you avoided hitting Miss Laura with that rock. I'd sure hate to rile you. Could be dangerous."

She was quiet for a moment, and then a sweet sound poured from her—a giggle. She shook her head. "I don't know what got into me—and I certainly don't know how I hit that awful man. It was probably stupid of me, but I just had to try to do something to help Miss Laura."

Riley grinned. "And what was that howl you bellowed? It would rival any Confederate soldier's."

Her cheeks flamed, making her even prettier. "I was angry."

"See, I knew that was a dangerous thing." He chuckled, enjoying bantering with her.

"I imagine you must have looked like a warrior charging down the road on your trusty steed. You certainly sounded like one. You're lucky I didn't throw that rock at you."

He leaned back in the seat, liking the image she portrayed of him as a warrior instead of a battered soldier. He was getting used to coming to her rescue, whether she liked it or not. During the war, he'd known many men who thought themselves invincible, and most were now dead. Miss Annie needed to learn she had limitations that a person with sight didn't, whether she believed it or not. He didn't want her getting hurt.

Riley took slow breaths, bracing himself as they crested the hill and his family home came into view. At least this time he didn't have to deal with the shock of the unknown, although the sight still created a twisting ache in his gut. What was he going to do? How could he ever live here again?

CHAPTER NINE

nnie sat on a blanket under the shade of a huge pecan tree, packing up the last of their picnic. Camilla and Lissa lay fast asleep at her feet, exhausted and red-cheeked from playing in the sunny field and frolicking in the shallow creek. Tess and Becky sat quietly chatting on the far corner of the blanket, attempting to string together chains from the daisies they had picked earlier with Mr. Morgan's help. While Rusty wriggled at the edge of the creek, allowing the water to soothe a bee sting, Mr. Morgan and Henry waded nearby, collecting rocks.

If not for having to remember all day that she was supposed to be blind and being careful to not slip up, things would have been perfect. She'd never spent so much time in a man's company and hadn't known it could be enjoyable. Riley Morgan was gentle and patient with all of the children, and his smiles for them told her he was enjoying their company. But she hadn't missed the sideways glances he'd shot toward his house and how it saddened him to see it in such a state of disrepair.

How dreadful it must be to know his parents perished there, fighting for their lives. She was glad that he hadn't had to return alone. She and the children weren't much comfort, but she hoped they were a little.

She lifted her hair off her neck, allowing the breeze to cool it. What would it have been like to grow up in such a peaceful place? To have a father and mother who loved you and doted on you? She could barely remember her mother. They hadn't had much back then, but at least she didn't have to run the streets, stealing from good, law-abiding citizens.

Sounds of laughter emanated from the creek as Henry and Riley held a splashing contest. She admired the way Riley stood still, taking the brunt of the splashes and allowing the boy to be the victor. Rusty hollered to join in, and then the three were splattering each other.

Finally, Henry plopped down beside the younger boy, and Riley walked toward her, carrying his lithe, muscled physique on his long legs. He raised his hand, smoothing his hair, a satisfied smile replacing the lost look that so often encompassed his expression. He was a fine-looking man, even while hobbling on his tender bare feet over the rocky bank. She swallowed hard, and forced herself to look away before he caught her staring.

He stopped right beside her, and she could feel his eyes on her. She focused on his pale feet—so white compared to his tanned face and hands that they looked as if they could belong to another person. Her gaze traveled to his long toes. She was barely able to contain her giggle at seeing the tuft of dark hair on the three biggest ones. Who knew men had hairy toes?

"Looks like you could do with a cooling off, Miss Annie."

She lifted her head so that her gaze landed on the creek without moving her eyes. A dip in the water would feel wonderful, but it would most improper to have her dress clinging to her as Mr. Morgan's shirt was stuck to him like a second skin. "I . . . uh . . . no, I'm fine. Thanks."

"No, I don't think you are." He bent down, and the next thing she knew, he shook his head like a dog, sprinkling drops of water on her.

She squealed but quickly lowered her voice so as not to awaken the girls. "You beast," she hissed teasingly, even though the water felt refreshing. "Be careful, or I'll lob a rock at *you*."

He chuckled then dropped down beside her. "After living in a world filled with tension for so long, I can't tell you how good it feels to relax and play with those young'uns."

"Was it horrible? The war, I mean?"

He stared off in the distance. "Yeah. Most times it was."

"I'm so glad the war didn't reach Waco. I don't know what we would have done."

He gazed off and sighed before turning his eyes toward his house. A different kind of war had played out here. She'd have to be more careful of the things she said. The last thing she wanted was to cause him more pain.

Becky yawned and leaned her head on Tess's shoulder.

"Girls, go ahead and lie down and rest for a bit. Being out in the sun tires out a body."

"Aw, do we have ta?" Lissa yawned again, her eyes drooping.

"Yes. You'll feel much better for taking a short nap," Annie said.

Lissa slipped down like melted butter, but Tess, being older, wasn't so ready to give in. Annie recognized the defiant set to the nine-year-old's mouth.

"If you're not sleepy, Tess, why don't you lie down and just rest and see how many different birds you can hear?"

"All right, Miss Annie." The girl lay down, her feet hanging off the end of the blanket and her hands behind her head.

"Can you see the boys?" she asked Riley. "Are they all right?"

"They're fine. Just sitting at the edge of the water."

"Thank you for spending time with them. They need a man's influence, but rarely get it."

"What about their fathers? Do they ever come to see them?"

Annie shook her head. "Both boys are orphans." And she didn't know what would happen to them if the school closed.

They sat there in silence for a while, the children's soft sleeping sounds rising up around them. Riley squeezed the water from the ends of his untucked shirt. Annie almost suggested he take it off so that it would dry quicker, but then she realized how improper such a suggestion was. There'd been a time not so long ago that she'd have just spouted out the first thing that came to her mind, but she was finally learning to think before she spoke.

"A wagon's coming." He stood, reached up into the tree where he'd hung his gun belt before going in the water, then strapped it on.

Annie stood too, making sure she stayed behind Riley. She cast a quick glance toward the wagon that held two people then looked back to check on the boys. Henry had already heard the wagon because he stood and turned toward the sound of jingling harness.

Riley stepped back and patted Annie's shoulder, his hand lingering for a moment. "It's all right. Just Miss Laura and Sean Murphy."

She exhaled, unaware she'd been holding her breath. She hadn't really expected trouble from someone moseying along in a wagon, but after yesterday, her nerves were coiled tighter than Alvia Petree's bun. And if something were to happen, there was no place close for the children to hide.

"The boys are doing fine. Just sitting in the shallow water," Riley said. "Let's walk out and meet the wagon, so we don't wake the girls."

Before she could object, he gently took her hand and looped it around his arm. Shivers coursed through her, but not from the dampness of his shirt. She had never understood the lure of a woman to a man, but there was a security she'd never before experienced in walking at a kind man's side, knowing he'd protect her. Hadn't he proven that yesterday? And yet, how could she trust this man she'd only known a week when her own father hadn't protected her?

As they drew near the wagon, she tugged her arm free. She glanced at Laura, hoping to see her looking happy and successful in her attempt to secure another location for the school. Instead, she looked resigned. Sad.

Mr. Murphy stopped the wagon and set the brake then assisted Laura down. She glanced past Annie to where the children rested then she turned her gaze on Riley. "I know you wanted to spend some time at your home, Mr. Morgan, and I do thank you for indulging me this day and helping Annie oversee the children."

He touched the brim of his hat. "It was my pleasure, ma'am."

"Why don't you go on up to your home now—and take Annie along with you? It would be good for her to get away from the children for a while. Sean and I can watch them."

Annie had a hard time not looking at Riley. She was sure he wouldn't want her tagging along, and when he didn't respond, she offered the excuse he probably wanted. "I'm fine. I don't need a break."

"No, you go on." Miss Laura waved her hand, fingers down, shooing her off like she was a pesky gnat.

"It's fine if you want to come," Riley said, although his tone didn't sound all that convincing.

She was curious about him and his family, and she really wanted a peek inside his home. Every so often, while he'd been engaged with the children, she'd cast a look over at the house, but it was too far away to tell much about it. She'd never seen a place that Indians had attacked before, but she didn't want to intrude. And why was Miss Laura pushing her to go? Did she just want to be alone with Sean for a while longer? She turned back to Mr. Morgan. "Are you sure you don't mind?"

"It's fine. Here, take my arm." He took her hand, his fingers warm against hers, and once again wrapped her arm around his. "It's not far, but the ground is rocky and dips in places."

Sean was checking his horses and had his back turned, so she flashed Laura an irritated look. Laura ignored her and started walking toward the children.

As they strolled the short way to Riley's house, Annie kept her head tilted away from him so that he wouldn't notice her staring at their surroundings. Her dress swished through the foot-tall grass and wildflowers, sending a disturbed grasshopper leaping away to a quieter spot. Bald cypress and live oaks hugged the creek bank, offering cherished shade from the hot Texas sun, but few stood in the fields where she could imagine cattle and horses grazing in the wide valley. "It's so peaceful here," she said. "Even though we live a bit outside of town, sometimes we can hear the noise from one of the saloons or even Sean's hammering. It just depends on which way the wind is blowing."

He gave off a snort. "I used to hate this place because of the quiet. I was miserable when we first moved here."

"Why? I think I would love living someplace like this." Out of the corner of her eye, Annie saw him glance at her, his surprise evident.

"Well, because I missed my friends mostly. And I knew ma didn't want to move any farther from her family, so I suppose

I was angry at my pa for not listening and upsetting her."

"I can understand that. Laura is the only friend I've ever had. I can't imagine how I'd feel if she moved away."

Riley stared at the pretty, young woman at his side. How was it that she'd only ever had one close friend? Had she been locked away all her life, separated from others because of her blindness? How sad that she'd never known the friendship of girls her own age.

But then hadn't his life been much the same? He'd not made many close friends after his family had moved to the Waco area, but at least he had more than one. He'd been busy working, helping his pa get this place established, and had been afraid that if he formed close relationships, his father would pack the family up and move them again. Still, he had some friends—and local acquaintances. "Where is your family?"

Annie bent her face toward the ground, but not before he noticed her wincing.

"What's wrong?"

She shook her head. She'd left her bonnet on the quilt where the girls slept, and her light-brown hair gleamed in the afternoon sun, looking almost blonde. "I have no family. My mother died when I was young, and—" her voice caught, and she turned her face away. "I don't know where my father is— or if he's even alive."

"I'm sorry. I shouldn't pry."

She glanced back and offered a timid smile. "Don't feel bad. It was all a long time ago, and I don't regret coming to Miss Laura's school for one moment. It's really the only home I've ever had."

His brows pinched together. He couldn't help wondering where she'd lived before coming to Waco, but he wouldn't ask, knowing it bothered her to talk about her past. He stopped a few paces in front of his old home, and the muscles in his body tensed, as if he were headed into battle. He didn't want to go in there again. To see his mother's always tidy house in such disarray. But he needed to see what else there was of his past that he could salvage.

"Is something wrong, Mr. Morgan?"

Riley didn't know what to say. How could he explain his hesitancy to go into his own home when he didn't fully understand it himself? He was thankful that Annie couldn't see what the Comanche had done. He grabbed one of the arrows sticking in the side of the house and rocked it back and forth until he could pull it free, then he bent the despised weapon, snapping it in two.

Annie's head jerked toward him. "What was that?"

"Um . . . nothing much. Just an old stick I broke." And it was—a potentially lethal stick.

"If it bothers you to have me here, I can go back." She hiked her pert chin. "I don't need any help."

He smiled at her spunk then sobered. "Maybe I do."

"Hmm?" Her eyes darted up, almost locking on his but not quite. "Help with what?"

He yanked off his hat and forked his fingers through his hair then smacked the hat on again. "I, uh . . . it's hard to see the place deserted like this. Ma should be here."

Annie touched his arm. "I'm so sorry for your loss. I can't imagine how difficult it must have been for you to come home from the war and discover what happened here."

Her concern touched him. During the war, he'd shoved aside as many emotions as he could. He didn't want to think of all the buddies he'd lost—buddies who'd been at his side one moment and gone the next. So many that he'd lost count. And why them, and not him? Why had God spared him at Shiloh—at Gettysburg—and during countless other battles, only for him to come back home to nothing?

His throat clogged from the sudden lump that formed. Allowing himself to feel now only meant pain. He couldn't let this snip of a woman into his heart. He'd done that once, but it wouldn't happen again.

"I'm happy to go inside with you if it would make things easier."

"I can do it myself. I don't need help."

Annie stiffened at his terse words. "Fine then." She turned back toward the picnic area. "I'll just leave you to your business."

She walked away so quicky that he just stood there and watched. But between here and where the children were was rocky, slanted ground. Surely she'd stumble without his help. He kicked his feet into motion and caught up with her and reached for her arm. How did she even keep her balance with her nose held up so high?

"Just hold your horses." She stopped and spun around so fast the he nearly collided with her.

"I didn't ask to intrude on your business, if you recall. Miss Laura forced me on you, and I don't blame you for not wanting me here. What could I do anyway? Hmm?"

Riley hung his head. Now he'd gone and hurt her feelings. His ma would have taken a switch to him for the harsh way he'd said he didn't need her help. He sighed regretfully. "I'm sorry for being gruff. It's just that being here brings out a lot of emotion—and for so long I've stuffed those feelings down, packed tight like my belongings in my haversack." He stared up at the pale blue sky. "I don't know how to deal with feelings anymore."

When she didn't say anything for a few moments, he glanced down at her pretty face. The irritation had faded, replaced by wistfulness and something else he couldn't decipher.

Annie licked her lips. "Sorry for getting upset. I understand what it's like to push your pain aside. I was so angry and hurt at what my pa had done for so long. One day I realized that I was only hurting myself by staying mad at him, so I decided to put all that anger in a box and close the lid."

"Did it work?"

She shrugged. "Sometimes. But there are still days when I start thinking about what he did, and it still hurts. Even after seven years."

Riley longed to ask her what had happened, but he didn't want to intrude on her privacy or cause her more pain. "If you want to go in the house with me, you can."

She tilted her face up and she smiled. "I'd like that, if you don't mind."

He wasn't sure if he minded or not, so he kept quiet as he guided her back to the house. "Just let me go inside first and clear the floor so you won't stumble on anything."

Maybe having her at his side would make things easier.

CHAPTER TEN

nnie hoped her presence would make it easier for Riley to return home, but he'd plunked her down on a kitchen chair and disappeared into one of the bedrooms. She could hear him rummaging around. Rising, she hurried to the window and peered out at the broken Indian arrow he had tossed aside. She couldn't imagine the pain involved in one of those sharp arrowheads piercing one's flesh. How dreadful to know that his parents must have been terrified and he wasn't here to help defend them. What horrors had they faced at the hands of the Comanche?

She shivered at the awful thoughts racing through her mind and tried to focus her attention on the cabin. Slivers of sunlight spotted the kitchen floor, shining through the holes in the log cabin's chinking. The far side of the room served as a parlor with one rocker shoved up against the cold fireplace and another dumped over onto its side, with a broken bottom rung. A dusty rose-colored settee and a small writing table sat along the bedroom wall. How odd that the peg lamp sat there undisturbed by time or the heinous events that had occurred.

The kitchen was less than half the size of the one at the school, and the scent of dirt and wood ash from the cast-iron stove, whipped up by the light breeze, caused Annie to sneeze. Dabbing her nose with the handkerchief she kept up her sleeve, she tried to imagine the place filled with the sweet scent of pies baking as Riley's mother bustled around, preparing a meal for her small family. Had she been a good cook? Had she been tall with the same blue eyes as Riley? The same dark hair?

Her mother's hair had been light brown like her own, but she could no longer remember the color of her mother's eyes. And her features had long ago faded in Annie's mind. She rested her cheek in one hand and drew circles around a dusty knothole on the table. How different her life might have been if her daddy had worked a real job or owned a ranch like this one. She would never have been forced to pilfer scraps of food from people's trash heaps, or steal clothes off some hard-working woman's clothesline, or lift watches from proud young men. That last feat still bothered her.

She couldn't return to her old ways—she wouldn't. But what would happen to her if the school were forced to close?

She looked around the room again. If Mr. Morgan didn't want this place, maybe he'd let her live here—but then if the school closed and he lost his job, he'd have to return home, most likely. Could he make this place into a home again?

A few minutes later, after his quick search through the house, Riley guided Annie back outside. He carried a crate he'd found in one of the bedrooms under one arm, but all she could see was a quilt lying on top. His lips were pressed together so tight they were nearly white, a deep crease marred his forehead, and his eyes blinked over and over, as if he were trying hard not to weep. Did men actually cry? She dropped her gaze before he caught her staring.

If she'd ever had her own home, it would bother her, too, seeing it in such disorder. While he was still in the back of the house, she had picked up the tablecloth from the floor, folded it, and laid it over the dusty table. She had wanted to do more to tidy up, but thought it might arouse his suspicions.

"My ma never let her house get dirty like that," he said. "I ought to come and clean it one of these days out of respect for her."

"It will be hard to keep it clean unless you repair the broken windows first."

He shot a glance her way. "How'd you know the glass was broken?"

Annie's heart tumbled, as if rolling end over end, down a steep incline. She had to be more careful with what she said. Mr. Morgan was no fool. She faked a tiny cough to clear the tightness from her throat and thought quickly. "Simple. I could feel the wind blowing in the opening—and glass crunched under my boots when I walked past the window."

"I suppose that makes sense."

"I could help clean up things, if you'd like." As soon as the words left her mouth, she realized how dangerous such a situation would be.

He shook his head. "Thanks, but I'm afraid you'd just be in the way."

Annie gasped. She gave him a quick punch in the side with her elbow then dropped his arm and crossed hers over her chest. "I can cook, clean, and do laundry just like most women, Mr. Morgan. Blind people are not incapable of doing common chores."

"That's not what I meant."

"What *did* you mean?"

He shifted from foot to foot, as if he were searching for an escape. He shrugged. "I know you're an extraordinary woman, Miss Sheffield, but you must admit you have limitations."

She lifted her chin in the air. "No, I don't."

He shook his head. "I knew people in the war who felt the same way." He pinned a look on her, and she forced her eyes to focus on his top button. "Most of them are dead now."

She opened her mouth, but slammed it shut. Of course she knew a blind person couldn't do everything that a seeing one could.

"I apologize for snapping at you, and I don't mean to hurt your feelings, ma'am, but honestly, it would take more time and effort to show you what needs to be done than it would to just do it myself." He didn't wait for her to respond but walked over to the chopping block and set down the crate. "I need to check the root cellar, and then I should be done here."

Even though his argument made perfect sense, she didn't have to like it. Besides, she wanted to help him.

He rounded the side of the house, and she heard a creak and the thump of a heavy door being dropped open. She glanced at the crate, then moseyed toward it and lifted up the edge of the heavy quilt. She peeked back toward the side of the house and then looked into the crate. He'd salvaged precious few items—a family Bible, two books, a shoebox, and the colorful but dirty quilt. She was starting to peek into the smaller box when she heard the cellar door thud closed. Jumping back, she slid over to where Riley had left her and tried to look innocent—an expression she'd cultivated when she was young but had rarely used of late.

He came around the side of the house with several items of men's clothing draped over one arm.

Her heart softened. His pain must be incredible. He'd gone off to fight in the war and returned to find his family dead. She'd never known a man well, except for her father, and he didn't count. Riley Morgan seemed like a decent man most of the time, but she didn't dare drop her guard with him. Could they possibly become friends?

And why did she even want to?

⟵ ★ ⟶

Riley left the house, wishing he never had to return, but he knew his mother would be rolling in her grave if he put the ranch up for sale and brought folks to view the house without it being clean and in good repair. He'd come back just one more time. He'd buy the supplies, fix up the place, then never return again. It hurt too much.

And besides, he wasn't too likely to sell the place with those other arrows still stuck in the front of the house.

Miss Sheffield stood in the same spot he'd left her, but she turned as he approached. He stopped beside the crate he'd filled earlier and added his pa's clothing to the pile. With all the weight he had lost, they'd probably be baggy. But then again, if he kept eating Mrs. Alton's delicious cooking, he'd bulk up quickly. The thought brought a small smile that quickly vanished. How many times during those long nights away had he dreamed about eating his ma's chicken and dumplings again or her beans and cornbread—her apple pie. Never again would he taste them.

Miss Sheffield kicked a rock and sent it skittering in front of them as she hurried to keep up with him. He peered down at her, realizing he'd forgotten to offer her his arm. Still, she walked quickly beside him, keeping up with his long-legged pace. He slowed down. "Here, take my arm and forgive me for neglecting to offer it sooner."

She batted her hand until it connected with his arm. Years had passed since he had a pretty woman walk beside him. The last woman to make him feel any longing had been Miranda.

His heart constricted at thoughts of her betrayal. But he could not honestly blame her. She may have been a bit persnickety at times but she was young and desirable—a lovely woman from a wealthy family. He was just the son of a rancher who owned a tenth of the land her father did. Why should she wait for him to return from the war?

Because she had promised she would.

The thing that irritated him the most was that she didn't have the decency to write and tell him that she'd married. He never again wanted to let a woman have such control over his emotions that she could cause him such pain.

He forced himself to find something good to think about. He glanced up at the cloudless sky, thankful the day remained comfortable despite its being midsummer. Birds in the trees lining the river chirped cheerful tunes while a roadrunner streaked across the path in front of them. Bad things happened, but life always managed to go on. That's what he needed—a reason to continue on. A purpose for his life.

"Could I ask you a question, Mr. Morgan?"

He liked the soft tone of her voice—low, with a slight huskiness. "I reckon so, ma'am."

"Please don't call me that. It makes me feel old."

His gaze shot to her face, and he wondered how old she really was. Not much more than twenty, if he had to guess. Her cheeks looked as soft as peach skin, and his fingers twitched wondering what it would feel like to touch them. He cleared his throat. "Sorry, miss. What is it you want to know?"

She turned her head up toward him, as if to look at him. "Why do you live in the tack room at the school when you have such a nice home here?"

Riley winced. His home was no longer nice, but she couldn't see what he saw. Namely, the devastation to his house and the graves atop the hill. She didn't know how it pained him to be here. Didn't know how he'd run out on his parents when they had needed him the most. How his brother had been alive one moment—running and laughing with his friends—then scared, writhing in pain, and dead a short while later.

"I'm sorry. I shouldn't have asked such a personal question."

"No, it's all right." He clenched his jaw. Being here was hard enough, but talking about it was another thing. He sighed before answering her. "This place has too many memories. I could never live here again. I plan to sell it."

Annie gasped. "How can you turn your back on your family home? If I had a place like this, I'd never leave it."

Her words cut straight to his heart. Was he making the wrong choice? Should he wait and reconsider selling after he had more time to think about it?

No. He shook his head. There was nothing left for him here. The sooner he left the better.

←——— ★ ———→

Laura peeked at the mantel clock. Only five more minutes before Mr. Otis Ramsey arrived. Her stomach had been churning ever since she'd received the note last night saying that he would visit the school promptly at ten the next morning. The back door tapped shut, footsteps sounded, and Annie entered the parlor

"Where are the children?" Laura asked.

Annie smoothed her apron. "They're all out behind the barn. Mr. Morgan is giving them rides on his horse, and Mrs. Alton is keeping watch on the others."

"Good. I sure don't want any of them to overhear our conversation with Mr. Ramsey."

"I don't mind telling you that I'm worried. What will we do if he says we can't live here any longer?" Annie clutched her fingers in front of her.

Laura reached out and squeezed her arm. "Don't give up yet."

A hard knock echoed through the unusually quiet school, and both women turned toward the door. Laura took a strengthening breath, hurried toward the entrance, and opened the door. Though she knew kind Mr. Morrow well since she'd been his daughter's best friend, she'd never met his nephew. A plump man with odd, purply-pink lips that reminded her of the plum wine she once drank gazed at her with narrowed hazel eyes.

He sniffed and brushed his finger across the lower edge of his nose. "Miss Wilcox, I presume?" His eyes studied her approvingly from her head down to the last button on her shoe. Then his gaze flicked past her to where Annie stood, and his brows lifted. A sensual smirk tugged at his mouth.

Any hopes she had that this man might reconsider and be sympathetic to her cause sank clear to Laura's boot tips. "Mr. Ramsey?"

He lifted his chin. "Who else were you expecting? Or are you normally in the habit of interrupting your so-called school teaching by accepting callers at this time of the morning?" His brow lifted in disdain, and without waiting to be invited, he pushed past Laura. His gaze roved the parlor, as though he were mentally measuring its dimensions. Laura wondered if he was appraising the property, planning what furniture would be his to sell as well as the house itself.

Passing Annie, he ambled to the kitchen doorway, tsked and shook his head, then spun around, staring at the young woman's backside. The impudent man had uttered only a few brief sentences, and Laura already disliked him.

"Would you care to take a seat in the parlor, or would you prefer to sit at the table?"

"Yes, I believe I would." He brushed past her back into the

parlor, looking over the furnishings as though assigning a price tag to each lovely piece. "It's far smaller than I expected. My home in St. Louis must be five times more spacious than this one."

His disdain for her home sent Laura's blood boiling. If he disliked the place so much, maybe he'd give her time to figure out a way to buy it herself. But how was that possible?

He plopped down hard on the settee, making it creak under his weight. He ran his hand over the round end table as if checking out the quality of the walnut wood.

"May I offer you some tea, Mr. Ramsey?"

"I'd prefer coffee. And some petit fours, if you have them."

Of all the nerve! She pressed her lips closed to keep from saying something she'd regret, and caught Annie's expression. The girl was struggling hard to keep her mouth shut. Laura looped her arm through Annie's and hauled her toward the kitchen.

"She can stay here and keep me company," Mr. Ramsey said.

"I'm sorry." Laura shook her head. "Annie has duties to be done."

Annie followed Laura into the kitchen, and lifting a hand to her throat, made a face and a gagging sound. Fortunately, Laura had pulled her into the kitchen so she hoped Mr. Ramsey hadn't heard her.

"What a lecher!" Annie whispered and gave an exaggerated shiver. "Ish! I feel as if spiders are crawling all over me."

Laura pulled the teakettle off the stove, glad that she'd had Mrs. Alton warm up some water a short while ago. "Shh . . . You don't want him to hear you."

"I don't care if he does. It's obvious that he means to sell the place. Didn't you notice how he was gawking at everything?" Annie flung her arms in the air then dropped them to her side so hard they made a loud flap. "And can you believe he had the nerve to ask for petit fours? What are those, anyway?"

"Little cakes."

Annie snorted. "Oh sure. We have plenty of those lying around." She opened the breadbox and pulled out several pieces of cornbread leftover from last night's dinner, and placed them on a plate. "Too bad we don't have a whole sack of sugar in the pantry so I could whip up some frosting for these."

Annie's sarcasm brought a smile to Laura's lips. "Be nice."

"I think I'll go outside with the children. Even Mr. Morgan's company is preferable to that horrible man's." She turned as if to leave.

Laura quickly set down the teapot and clawed at Annie's sleeve. "Oh, no . . . no, you don't. You're not leaving me alone with him."

Annie's shoulders dropped. "I know. I wouldn't do that even though I'd like to. Besides, I can't wait to see his expression when he sees the cornbread." Both women snickered.

"Just don't let him notice you watching." Laura poured the tea then placed the saucers and plate of cornbread onto the tray. She place a tiny amount of sugar in a bowl normally used for salt then carried the tray to the parlor.

Mr. Ramsey frowned and waved his handkerchief in front of his nose. "This place reeks of children."

Laura set the tray down a bit harder than normal, rattling the teacups. The man was insufferable. How could he possibly be related to kindhearted Mr. Morrow? She handed her guest a teacup then gave one to Annie before taking her seat.

As expected, Mr. Ramsey turned up his nose at the cornbread. Laura wished she had something better to serve her guest, but with the lack of money and many food items in short supply because of the war, this was the best she could do on short notice. Her Southern-born mother would cringe if she were still alive.

Mr. Ramsey sniffed his tea and looked up at her.

"I apologize for not having coffee to serve, sir."

His brow puckered. "It's in short supply everywhere, but I had hoped for a cup." He sipped the tea and winced then added several of the tiny spoonfuls of their precious sugar to his cup. He downed the whole cupful in one long drink then set the teacup down with a loud *clink*. "I should get to the point of my visit." The man, far closer to her age than Annie's, gave her a passing glance then gawked at Annie.

Laura cleared her throat, drawing his gaze back to her. She'd been trying hard to remember if she'd ever heard mention of him before. He must be the son of Mr. Morrow's sister since he had a different last name than their kind benefactor.

He leaned forward in his chair and whispered. "Why won't that girl look at me?"

Laura tightened her grip on the chair's arms. "This is a school for the blind, you know."

Disgust replaced his appreciative gaze. "You mean a pretty thing like her can't see?" He shook his head. "What a waste."

Laura coughed a warning at Annie as the girl scowled. "You do realize she isn't deaf, sir?"

He waved a dismissive hand in the air. "As I mentioned in my letter, my uncle, Charles Morrow has died. As I am his heir, this property now belongs to me, quaint as it is. I do believe I'm being quite generous in allowing you thirty days to vacate." He puffed up like her old rooster.

The mangy polecat only cared about himself and padding his pocket, not the welfare of innocent, misfortunate children. It truly irked Laura to ask anything of him, but for her students' sake, she must. She scooted to the edge of her chair and leaned toward the miserable excuse of a man, holding out her hands. "Please, sir, I implore you to give us more time. I will need to contact the parents of the children who have families in the area and have them come for their children. It will take time to find someone to deliver the letters. I also need time to figure out what to do with the orphans who have no other place to go. Surely you can understand that thirty days isn't nearly enough time."

Mr. Ramsey glanced at the cornbread, pinched off a corner and tasted it, then he lifted the square, dropping crumbs all over himself and the settee. He shoved the whole piece into his mouth. After a few quick chews, he stared at her and shook his head. "I apologize, but I need to be finished with this whole affair as soon as possible. Thirty days is the most I can allow." Crumbs flew through the air like a dandelion puff.

Laura bit back the unladylike scolding she was tempted to give him. She glanced at Annie, knowing the worrisome thoughts that were surely running rampant across the girl's active mind. Neither of them had anywhere else to go. She stared at Mr. Ramsey and stood. "Please, sir, I beg you to reconsider. Couldn't you give us at least six weeks? There aren't many places suitable for us. We may even have to move to another town."

Mr. Ramsey shook his head. "I can't take that much time away from my business. I'm being generous as it is, since it's within my power to take possession immediately. But I understand your need to find another place."

Laura's mind raced. There had to be something she could do. "What about selling it to me? May I inquire how much you want for it?"

"I will need to get the place appraised, but I doubt you'd be able to afford it."

"I see. Well, forgive me for being rude, but we have our work cut out for us. I must start looking for a new location right away, so if you'll be on your way, we'd appreciate it."

His chin hiked, but he had the courtesy to rise. He started

for the door, then turned back and snatched up the last two squares of cornbread and plodded outside, without so much as tipping his hat.

"What a horrible man." Annie hauled back as if to slam the door.

"Please don't give him the satisfaction of knowing he upset us," Laura begged.

Annie's lips twisted up on one side but she shut the door only a little bit harder than usual. "Fine. But what are we going to do?"

Laura took her hands. "I honestly don't know, sweetie." She pulled the girl into a hug and held her tight, not at all liking the look of their future.

CHAPTER ELEVEN

*A*nnie trudged outside, her heart dragging along with her feet. She'd promised to help keep an eye on the children so Laura could run into town to see if they had any other options and Mrs. Alton could return to her kitchen and prepare their noon meal. The older woman only needed to fix enough food for the children and Mr. Morgan, because Annie was certain she and Laura would have no appetite.

As she rounded the far corner of the barn, she noted the boys on the horse Mr. Morgan was leading toward the back of the property. Since his back was to her, she quickly surveyed the serene scene. Mrs. Alton was sitting on the picnic quilt, rolling a rag ball to Lissa and Camilla. Becky and Tess were several paces away, tossing clothespins into a bucket.

"Ah, good. Annie's back. You two young'uns play ball with each other." Mrs. Alton pushed up from the quilt and stood there for a minute. "Oh, my. I'm getting far too old to be sitting on the ground."

Annie smiled, albeit a bit melancholy, and walked over to the cook. "You're not getting old."

Mrs. Alton swatted her hand in the air. "Annie Sheffield, now don't you go telling fibs."

"Annie, I rided a horsie." Camilla rose up on her knees, her face turned upward. "It was fun. *Mi padre* lets me ride his *caballo*—his horsie, but Mama, she does not like it."

"Go and talk with the girls." Mrs. Alton patted Annie's shoulder. "I'll head back and get lunch started."

Annie nodded and dropped down onto the quilt beside Camilla. She caressed the girl's dark hair. "And just what did you like about it so much?"

"We went fast," Lissa said.

"Fast?" Annie's gaze shot to where Mr. Morgan had reached the far fence and was turning to head back this way. "How fast?"

"Bouncy fast." Camilla sprang up and down on her knees.

"And you weren't scared?" Annie focused her irritation with Mr. Ramsey on Mr. Morgan instead. He had no business trotting the horse while the girls were riding.

"It's all right, Annie." Tess turned away from the bucket, holding a fistful of clothespins she'd just collected from the ground. "Mr. Morgan had the person in front hold on to the saddle horn, and he held on to the one riding in back. He made sure we didn't fall. I like him."

"Thank you, Tess. That makes me feel better knowing you weren't in any danger." She turned her gaze back to Riley Morgan. He was clean shaven this morning, and he was wearing the clothes that he'd found in the cellar. She liked seeing him in something other than his army pants. Scowling, she turned away. What should it matter what he wore or if he had shaved? He would soon be gone too. At least he had a home to return to—if he didn't sell it.

She plopped down beside the younger girls on the quilt, folded her legs in an unladylike manner, and rested her elbows on her knees, her face in her hands. Her world was turning upside down, and she didn't know what to do about it.

How could that odious Mr. Ramsey be so selfish that he would turn out blind children? He mentioned having a home in St. Louis, and he must have also inherited Mr. Morrow's home, which means he owned three houses. She shook her head, hardly able to comprehend such a thing. Did the man not have a heart? A conscience?

All the girls had family to return to, but what would happen to sweet Rusty and quiet Henry? Who would want to care for two blind orphan boys? Sure, they could help some family out, but they would never be able to do as many things as a boy who could see. And how would they continue their education? So many people were struggling to get by after supporting the war efforts and having difficulties getting their crops to market the past few years. And with the slaves set free, who would pick all the cotton grown in the area? Nobody would want to care for boys like Rusty and Henry.

Her heart ached, not just for herself but for them all. Change for their children came a lot harder than it did for other children. A fly landed on her hand, and she swatted it away. It buzzed her face, and she jerked back, waving her hand around her head.

"Are you all right?"

Annie froze. "I'm fine. A fly pestering me, is all." She kept her back to him, but she heard him set Rusty on the ground. The saddle creaked as Henry climbed down. The pungent scent of horse wafted toward her . She wasn't fond of the smell of cattle and sheep, but for some reason, the smell of horses never bothered her.

"I rode Mr. Morgan's horse, Miss Annie. Could you hear me?"

Annie smiled. "Yes, Rusty, I always hear you."

The boy grinned so wide his freckles almost sparkled. He trotted over to Tess. "I rode Gypsy. I was way up high."

"We rode her first," Becky said.

Henry followed the younger boy, but had a proud look on his face that Annie rarely saw there.

"It's your turn now," Mr. Morgan said.

Rusty spun around and hurried back. "Can I have another ride? Huh, Mr. Morgan? That Gypsy is the finest horse I ever rode."

Mr. Morgan tousled the boy's hair. "You're right. She's a good horse. But as for the ride, it's Miss Sheffield's turn." He took hold of Rusty's hand and guided him to the quilt. "Have a seat, and you can continue your game of ball with the girls."

Annie jerked her head in his direction, his words just soaking into her mind. "My turn?"

"Yes, ma'am. I have orders from the boss lady to see that you get a ride, too." He bent down and claimed her hand. "C'mon along."

Though she had no plans to climb aboard his horse, she allowed him to pull her to her feet. It wouldn't do for the children to think she was afraid. Right off, she noticed Mr. Morgan's fresh scent. Had he actually bathed in the middle of the week? Her cheeks warmed at such a thought.

"It's perfectly safe, I assure you."

Annie could hear the humor in his voice. Did he think she was frightened? "It's not that. I can't leave the children alone."

"They're not alone." He tugged her hand, and she allowed him to lead her off the quilt. "We won't go far, and I'll keep an eye on them."

"Yes, go on, Miss Annie." Tess smiled. "It's a lot of fun."

"And you feel so high up," Becky said.

Annie dipped her head, focusing on her hand resting in Riley's. Highly inappropriate, but she rather enjoyed the feel of his hand wrapped around hers.

"But you'd better hold on to the saddle horn or Mr. Morgan will hold your leg." Lissa rolled the ball to Camilla, unaware of how her words affected Annie.

The thought of a man holding her leg, even through the padding of her skirt and petticoats, made blood rush to her cheeks.

Mr. Morgan leaned in toward her ear, chuckling. "Have no fear. You're perfectly safe with me. I won't let you fall off."

Even though she believed him, she longed to look into his eyes, to see his assurance. He'd proven to be gentle with the children and he treated the women with respect, but why was he teasing? Had he sensed her embarrassment?

Turning toward the horse, she reached out her hand and walked forward until she touched Gypsy's side. The mare's skin quivered, and she turned her head back to look at Annie. Could the horse tell she was nervous? The few times she had ridden, she had always sat in front of or behind her daddy—on a stolen horse.

She was tempted to go ahead and take Mr. Morgan up on his offer, but what about her skirts? Would they cover her legs properly? This was one time she wouldn't mind donning her old trousers. She lifted her hands to her cheeks at the thought of Riley Morgan seeing her in men's pants. She could feel herself blush. It was something she hardly ever did.

"If you're ready, I can lift you up. You could sit sideways in the saddle, if you would prefer."

"That would be the wise thing, I suppose. You promise to keep an eye on the children?" Not that she wouldn't do so herself.

"I promise. Now, turn around, please."

She did as requested, and her heart caught in her throat. He stood so close that if she even hardly moved she would touch him.

He took hold of her wrists and lifted them. "Put your hands on my shoulders."

She paused a moment then did as bid. His shoulders were so solid—broad—not at all like her slight ones. His hands wrapped around her waist, and she shot up into the air like a cannonball. A squeal slipped out, but in the next instant, she was plopped onto the saddle. If her hips had been any wider, she would not have been able to sit sideways, but it wasn't altogether uncomfortable. She grasped hold of the saddle horn on her right and the back of the saddle with her other hand and held her breath. If she fell, it certainly was a long way down. Clenching her teeth, she scolded herself. She never used to worry about such things when she lived on the streets.

Mr. Morgan held out his hand as if to catch her if she fell. His eyes gazed up at her, his face tan from the many hours he spent outside as a soldier. She could even see his long, dark lashes, as she made a passing glance. The hollowness in his cheeks was disappearing, and he was beginning to look healthier, thanks to their cook's wholesome meals. "Are you settled, Miss Sheffield?"

She was anything but settled. She slowly took a deep breath and nodded. The light breeze tickled her sweaty neck, and her heart pounded. Being nervous wasn't a feeling she'd experienced for a long while—and she didn't like it. But riding the horse was fun, as Tess had said, although she would prefer riding astride. Too bad that was socially unacceptable for a woman.

He walked her around the field three times, and she marveled at his patience. How many times had he gone in the same circle, escorting the children on their rides? The grass was smashed down and a trail was forming already. She peeked at the children, glad to see they were all keeping busy with their games.

Tears pricked her eyes at the thought of being separated from them. Of never seeing them again. They were her family. She would miss them far more than they would ever miss her.

"You're awful quiet today. Got something on your mind?" He peered back over his shoulder.

He had no idea. And she sure wasn't going to divulge any information. "I suppose I do."

"Whoa, girl." He pulled the horse to a stop beside the children, dropped the reins, then held up his arms to her.

Annie released her tight grip on the saddle horn and placed her hands in her lap, pretending that she hadn't seen his. The thought that he would hate her if he ever learned the truth of how she had deceived him ate at her nearly as much as the prospect of the school closing down.

He cleared his throat. "Uh . . . I can help you down now, if you'll hold out your hands."

She complied, and he stepped close, his chest bumping the toes of her shoes. He took her hands and guided them to his shoulders. His breath caressed her cheeks, making her breath catch in her throat. His hands connected with her waist, and he lifted her down to the ground as if it were no effort at all. His hands remained at her sides for a moment longer than proper, and she ached to glance up and read his eyes, but didn't. Maybe he was just waiting to see if she lost her balance.

For all practical purposes, they were alone. The children could hear them, but it was obvious they were engaged in their own activities and paying them no mind. "I . . . um . . . thank you, Mr. Morgan, for that ride on your horse. I actually enjoyed it."

He stepped back and nodded. "My pleasure, ma'am."

Before she realized what she was doing, she reached out and smacked him on the arm. "I told you not to call me *ma'am*. My name is Annie. Just call me that."

"It would be my pleasure, Miss Annie."

"Just plain *Annie* is fine." She tilted her head up high enough to see the lower half of his face.

"Then you must call me Riley—or Raleigh—if you'd rather. It's my actual Christian name."

She nibbled her lower lip. She'd never referred to a man by his first name, except for when she and Laura had talked about Sean Murphy. But what harm could it do? She bit her lip as if making a crucial decision and nodded.

"Good. I reckon I should get back to work." He tipped his hat, gathered his reins, and walked back toward her. Leaning close, he whispered, "You're not the least bit plain—Annie."

⟵———— ★ ————⟶

While Tess and Becky washed and dried the supper dishes, Annie put away the clean silverware. On the far side of the kitchen near the back door, Laura washed Camilla's hair in the round basin, while Lissa fidgeted beside them, waiting her turn. Today wasn't their usual bath day, but Laura had discovered that a traveling minister was in town, and they'd all be going to the tent meeting the following evening.

"Ack!" Laura squealed. "Hold still, girl, you're getting me all wet!"

Annie snickered, but immediately sobered. *Before long, these pleasant evenings with the children would be a thing of the past.* She knew the girls would adapt to being home again easily enough and probably preferred being with their parents, but what would happen to the boys? To her and Laura?

A teardrop rolled down her cheek, and she swiped it off with her sleeve. *This was foolishness.* Crying had never accomplished anything except making her nose stuffy and red. She needed to get away before Laura noticed and became concerned. With the silverware all put away and ready for tomorrow's breakfast, she walked back to the older girls. "I have . . . uh . . . something I need to do, so finish up here then go upstairs and prepare for bed."

"Yes, Miss Annie," they said in unison.

She hung her towel on a peg to dry then hurried from the room, feeling Laura's questioning eyes on her. Outside, her feet propelled her toward the barn—the place where she'd often sought sanctuary when she needed to be alone. At least that's how things had been before Riley Morgan moved in. She was thankful he was presently gone to the Brazos to help the boys wash up.

At the last minute, she turned from the barn, slipped through the gate, and walked out to the pasture to get Bertha. *What would happen to the old cow when the school closed?*

Annie's throat tightened and her lower lip wobbled. She didn't want anything to change. Why couldn't things just keep going the way they had the past seven years? She'd been so happy and contented, and for the first time in her life, she'd had a real home. Tears poured down her cheeks, and she stopped, lifted the edge of her apron, and wiped them off. She'd never been one to give in to tears, but her heart was breaking.

Bertha plodded toward her, eager for her supper and ready to be relieved of the milk she'd produced all day. Annie patted the cow's head then wrapped her arms around Bertha's neck. The deep moo from the complaining creature vibrated against Annie's chest, bringing out a giggle in spite of her melancholy. "All right. I can take a hint. C'mon."

Bertha followed her to the gate then plodded into the barn and into her stall. She stuck her head in the empty bucket then looked back at Annie with sad, pathetic eyes. Annie grinned and shook her head. Leave it to the cow to cheer her up. "You look so pitiful."

From out of their hidey holes, the three cats hurried to her side, meowing. She filled Bertha's feed bucket then settled in to do the milking. Ever since arriving, Riley had taken over the job, but she found the rhythmic motion soothing, and if the cow didn't cheer her up, the cats surely would.

The scents of hay, animals, and fresh milk surrounded her, filling her with contentment as the milk level rose in the bucket. Maybe she could move away from Waco to a place where people didn't look at her as if she were only half a person, and find a job working for some rancher or helping his wife. She was a passable cook, having helped Mrs. Alton and even filling in for her when the woman was unable to work or was ill. But she hated leaving all that was familiar to go to another place, as she had so many times as a child—a place where there were nothing but strangers. At least strangers wouldn't see her as a blind woman who was incapable of doing anything and had no value. *Why did people have to look down their noses at others who were different?*

Salt and Pepper licked their paws while Penelope crept toward the bucket. "Oh, no you don't." Annie pulled down on one teat and aimed it at the tabby, shooting her with milk. The surprised cat jumped and darted through the slats of the stall at the same time Salt and Pepper dashed away.

"Who are you talking to?"

Annie jumped at the sound of Riley's voice near the barn entrance. She'd been so engrossed in her thoughts that she hadn't heard him return with the boys—and not hearing Rusty wasn't an easy feat. Her heart thumped, and she scrambled for a response.

He walked toward her then stopped right behind her. "You

should have left the milking for me. I'd planned to do it."

She shrugged, grateful for the change of topic. "It's no bother. I actually enjoy the quiet here."

"I guess it is pretty noisy at the house. Henry's fairly quiet, but that Rusty can jabber like a magpie."

Annie nodded. "That's so true, but he's a dear boy."

"Why don't you let me take over there?"

She sat up, stretching her tense back and arms. Even though only a bit over a week had passed since she last milked, her muscles complained as if it had been months. Besides, if she quit milking, she'd be free to leave and not have him hovering over her. "I just might take you up on that offer. Laura could probably use my assistance inside."

He helped her up and back from the cow, hung his hat on a post, then took her place. At least he didn't belittle her by offering to escort her back to the house. With his strong hands and arms, he made the milk splash in the bucket at a much quicker pace than she had. She stared at his wide shoulders, her eyes following the line of his body, which narrowed to a trim waist. A few times she'd spied young lovers at church socials or town events off by themselves. Once, a girl had laid her cheek against her beau's chest and his arms had wrapped around her. She'd never understood why a woman would want to let a man hold her like that. Had never been tempted to allow a man such liberties . . . until now.

He peeked over his shoulder at her, and stared for a moment. She worked hard to keep a straight face and to keep her gaze focused on a fly walking across Bertha's side. Riley scowled, and without warning, shot up from the stool, forcing her to take a backward step to avoid being in the very position she had earlier pondered. What was wrong with him?

"What's the matter?"

She blinked. "What do you mean?"

He lifted his hand, pointed it at his face, and wagged it up and down. "Your nose is red. Have you been crying?"

Her cheeks warmed, as if she'd been standing over the stove cooking in the heat of a summer's afternoon. She covered her nose to hide the evidence, but he tugged her hand away. "Tell me what's wrong."

She shook her head, moved that he was concerned for her. "I can't."

"If someone bothered you—"

Her gaze darted up but she jerked it back down, noticing that his sleeves were rolled up to reveal his tanned arms. "No, it's nothing like that."

He relaxed his stance and ran his hand through his hair. "Well, I'm a good listener if you ever want to talk about it."

She'd never had a man overly worried about her, and didn't know how to respond. Shifting from foot to foot, she struggled with what to say.

He leaned his hip against the stall gate. "Is this about the school closing?"

Her gaze shot up to his, but again, she stopped before looking into his eyes. "How do you know about that?"

"Miss Laura came out onto the porch and told me when I brought the boys back. It's a crying shame that Mr. Ramsey is so selfish. Makes me want to . . ." He punched his fist into his hand. "Never mind."

Annie nearly smiled at the image of distasteful Mr. Ramsey sitting on his backside in the dirt after Riley had clobbered him. She sucked in her lips until she got control. "So what are *you* going to do?"

He lifted one shoulder and dropped it. "Miss Laura said I could stay here until the thirty days were up, if I want to—for room and board."

"And do you?"

A smile twittered on his lips. "Could be. I'll have to wait and see what happens."

"With what?" She noticed Penelope peeking at the abandoned bucket from between the stall slats. "I should go and let you finish the milking, since you were kind enough to offer."

"It can wait. If you want to stay and . . . and talk some more."

"Thank you, but I—I'm not sure I can talk about it just yet." Not without breaking down, and she wasn't about to do that in front of him.

Penelope stepped between the slats and crept toward the bucket of milk. "I'll just head on inside."

"You don't have to always run away, you know. I don't bite."

She smiled. "I can honestly say I never once thought that."

"Whew!" He swiped his hand across his forehead in an exaggerated motion and grinned.

She'd never had a man tease her in a nice way. They'd always made catcalls or poked fun at her because they thought she was blind. If they had enough time, maybe she and Riley could actually become friends.

Penelope took another step and glanced at Annie, as if daring her to do something. Two more steps and the cat would have free access to the milk. As if sensing Annie's dilemma, Bertha swished her tail, spooking the cat so badly that she jumped straight up into the air. Penelope let out a howl that made Riley jump. The cat dashed right across his boot tips, sending him reeling backwards into Bertha, arms pumping. Annie had to turn away or he'd for sure see her laughing.

Working hard to keep the humor from her voice, she asked, "Did something happen to one of the cats?"

"You wouldn't believe me if I told you." He chuckled. "We almost lost the bucket of milk, though. I reckon I should finish the milking, then I need to bring the horses in from the pasture."

Annie was relieved that he found humor in the situation

rather than letting such a thing embarrass him and make him angry like her father would have.

"Would you like me to walk you to the house first?"

She frowned. "I think I can handle that on my own. That's what the guide ropes are for, you know?"

"Hey now, don't take things the wrong way. It has nothing to do with you being . . . uh . . . well, you know." He crossed his arms for a moment, dropped them to his side, then crossed them again. "It's just a polite thing for a gentleman to escort a lady. That's all."

"Oh. Um . . . I appreciate that, but I know you have things you need to do."

"Nothing that can't wait."

"What about the milk? You can't leave it or the cats will get into it. Trust me, I know."

His face brightened. "We can take it with us. It will only take a minute or two to walk you back."

A sensation, like drinking hot tea on a cold night, trickled through her insides and down to her stomach. She knew she shouldn't open the gate and allow Riley Morgan into the small world of people she cared about, but there was something about the man that made her want to unlatch it and let him enter. Sometimes she didn't think her feigned blindness bothered him in the least, but other times, she was sure it did. The man was a puzzle that she'd like to figure out.

He approached, holding the bucket in one hand, and held out his other elbow. "Here's my arm."

She took it and glanced upward, staring at his lips.

He gazed back at her for a long moment. "Has anyone ever told you that you have pretty eyes?"

His unexpected compliment took her off guard. She'd grown up suspicious of people and hadn't known what it was like to be able to trust anyone until she'd come here. She wondered if he could have some reason for telling her such things. *Could he want something from me?*

"Um . . . sorry. I didn't mean to embarrass you. It's just that your eyes are so dark—they remind me of Bertha's."

Annie gasped. "A cow? My eyes remind you of a cow's?" She jerked her arm free of his then reached out with both hands and shoved him sideways.

He held out the milk bucket and shuffled sideways in his effort to not spill any. "Hold on! That's not what I meant. And besides, cows have pretty eyes."

She lifted her nose in the air to give him a good look at her cow-eyes. "I'll just find my own way home, Mr. Morgan."

"Annie! Wait."

She didn't stop or turn but marched out of the barn. "It's Miss Sheffield to you."

CHAPTER TWELVE

*L*aura unpinned her blonde hair, and it cascaded down around her shoulders as she shook it out.

Annie sighed. If only she had such pretty hair—and eyes the color of the sky. But no, she had *cow eyes* and mousy brown hair. She might as well be an animal. She blew out a loud breath and lay down on her bed, resting her chin in her hands.

"What was that for?" Laura asked.

"You wouldn't believe me if I told you."

Laura set her hands in her lap and stared at her. "Try me."

Scowling, Annie crunched her lips together, dreading to hear those horrible words voiced again. "Oh, fine then. That—that Mr. Morgan said I had eyes like Bertha."

Laura's eyes widened, and she snorted in her struggle to not laugh. "Oh, surely not."

Pushing up, Annie perched on the edge of her bed and crossed her arms. "Yes, he did."

Losing the battle, Laura fell back against the wall, cackling.

Tears ran down her eyes, and she mopped them with the sleeve of her nightgown.

"It's not funny." Annie didn't like her friend laughing at her, but she was glad to see her not frowning. Laura hadn't smiled once all day—until now. If Annie hadn't been so devastated, she might have found humor in the situation herself, but honestly, what was there to laugh at when the man you've barely started liking says you resemble a cow. Tomorrow, she'd start taking a smaller amount of food on her plate, lest she be called a pig next.

Finally, Laura got control of herself. "My goodness. I haven't laughed like that in ages."

Annie leaned back against the wall and stared out the window at the blackened sky. "I was so mortified."

Laura snorted again, but managed to regain control. "I believe he meant that as a compliment."

Annie leaned forward. "Don't defend *him*. And if that's a compliment, I'd sure hate to hear what he thinks of people he *doesn't* like."

Laura pulled the soft locks away from her face and said, "Men often have trouble saying what they mean. They're not as good at communicating as women are. What exactly did he say?"

"I'd rather not repeat it," Annie replied loftily. She stared at the sampler she'd made during her first years at the children's home. The alphabet stitched in bold, black script covered the top quarter of the fabric, and below that was a row of meticulously sewn flowers in various colors. Centered at the bottom was a replica of the Wilcox School for the Blind. She had painstakingly worked on the sampler an hour or so each evening after she'd come up to her room, and their room was the only place Laura would allow her to hang it, for fear someone would ask questions about who had stitched it. At least when she looked at it in the future, it would remind her of this place and Laura's continual patience in teaching her to sew.

Laura rose, crossed the small room and sat on Annie's bed. Still vexed with her, Annie refused to look at her.

"I apologize for laughing, but I think I understand what Mr. Morgan was trying to say."

Annie's gaze snapped to Laura's. "You *do?*"

Nodding, Laura reached for Annie's hand. "Yes, Sean once told me my hair reminded him of melted butter. I thought he meant it was too oily since several days had passed since bath day. I was angry with him for weeks and refused to talk to him."

"Oh, dear. That sure isn't very romantic." Annie tried to imagine big, ol' Sean trying to say sweet words of love to her friend, but it was hard. "At least he didn't say you reminded him of a four-legged barnyard animal!"

Laura patted her hand in a patronizing manner, and Annie was tempted to pull away, but she didn't. The gentle contact reminded her of how her mother used to touch her, so many long years ago. She laid her head on Laura's shoulder, trying not to think of how lonely she would be once they parted.

"Don't take me wrong or get upset, but I can see why Mr. Morgan compared your eyes to Bertha's. Most people think cows have pretty eyes. Yours are a beautiful deep-brown shade, and you do have long lashes."

"But certainly not like a *cow's.*"

"No, not that long, of course. I do believe you caught Riley Morgan's eye, though."

Annie pushed away. She was tired of how she felt whenever she thought of Riley or when he came near. She just wanted everything to go back to the way things used to be. "Well, I don't want any part of him. And why would you say such a thing? Attracted to me? Humph."

Night sounds serenaded them—crickets in the grass and

tree frogs that liked to climb up the side of the house chimed in, too. Far off, a horse whinnied. Annie rose and walked to the window, staring at the dark silhouette of the barn. She wondered if Riley was sleeping in there. She leaned forward, eyes searching for his lean figure.

"I see him watching you when he thinks no one's looking," Laura whispered. "And he told me he thinks you're amazing."

Annie's chin dropped, and she couldn't do a thing to stop it. After a moment she realized how she must look with her mouth hanging open and shut it. "You can't possibly be serious. He's never given me the impression that he liked me. In fact, quite the opposite."

Cocking her head, Laura studied her. "What has he done to make you think he doesn't like you?"

Annie shook her head and flung her arms out to the side. "I don't know. He always tries to walk me back to the house—as if I'm incapable of finding it, even though I've walked to it a million times. And he always tries to take over the milking if he sees me doing it, when I've been doing it for years. And he wouldn't let me help clean up his house. He must think blind people aren't capable of doing anything."

Laura smiled and turned her head away, but not before Annie saw it.

"What?" Annie crossed her arms over her chest.

"Annie." The bed creaked as Laura pushed to her feet and walked over to where Annie stood. "He's just trying to be a gentleman."

"Huh, well, he has a funny way of showing it." Annie paused, looking Laura in the eye. "And you know what else he does that drives me loco? He tips his hat to me—even though he thinks I don't see it. Isn't that just plain silly?"

Laura lifted her hands to Annie's cheeks and stared into her eyes. "You like him, don't you?"

"What! No! That's absurd. How could I like him when everything he does annoys me?" Annie wanted to wipe that knowing smile off her friend's face. *Was Laura completely daft?*

"Methinks thou doth protest too much." Laura cast a wily look over her shoulder as she walked to the table. Tiny insects scattered as she lifted her hand to the lantern's globe, and blew out the flame.

"Methinks you don't know what you're talking about." Glad for the darkness, Annie turned back and stared out the window. Lightning danced across the far horizon in zigzag lines that didn't touch the ground, and she waited for the thunder to boom, but it never came. Sweat trickled down her back, and she longed for a cooling rain.

"Annie."

If she'd been lying in bed, she'd be tempted to feign sleep, but she could hardly do that from the window. "Yes?"

"Riley Morgan comes from a good family. He's kind to the children and polite to women. He's just spent the last four years away from home fighting in that dreadful war, risking his life as a soldier. From what I've read, the soldiers lived in squalid conditions much of the time, and he came home to find his parents dead and his fiancée married to someone else, yet Riley doesn't seem bitter or hardened. A woman could do far worse than a man like him."

"Good night, Laura."

Morning would come far too soon, but with so many things on Annie's mind, sleep would not come easily. If only she could take a pallet outside and sleep on the porch where the breezes were stronger. Moisture beaded on her forehead, and she leaned farther out the window, looking toward the barn where Riley lay sleeping.

Laura's words drifted through her mind. Could Riley have designs on her? *What if such a ridiculous thing were true?*

She'd never once had a man—or a boy, when she was younger—show the least bit of interest in her—at least not once they discovered she was blind. They could never see past her supposed disability. She rested her elbow on the windowsill and placed her chin on her hand. It didn't matter if Riley liked her. In a few weeks she'd be gone from here—unless a miracle occurred. And she had never seen a miracle.

———— ★ ————

Annie climbed into the front of the wagon as Riley lifted the last child into the back. Each youngster's face had been scrubbed clean, and each was dressed in Sunday best.

Miss Laura clapped her hands. "Quiet down and give me your attention, children. I need to tell you something." She waited for the din to silence then continued. "I have a surprise. I talked to the minister who is holding tonight's revival, and he told me that he was riding past the school this morning and overheard you singing during music class. He invited you-all to sing tonight."

Excited cheers spilled forth. Annie turned on the wagon's bench seat and saw Riley standing behind Laura, with a broad smile. He sure was handsome when he smiled—which he seemed to be doing more and more lately.

"So I want you to be on your very best behavior. Reverend James will start the service with several hymns. Then we will go up front and introduce you-all. Mr. Morgan and I will help you get lined up, and then you'll sing 'All Creatures of Our God and King' and 'Amazing Grace', just like we've done at home. Any questions?"

Rusty's hand shot up, which didn't surprise Annie in the least. "Will there be food afterwards?"

Riley chuckled and shook his head.

Laura smiled. "I don't think so, but if you-all perform well and sit quietly during the service, I imagine we could have a snack before bedtime."

Cheers from the children rang out.

Riley escorted Laura to the front of the wagon and helped her up to the seat. Annie realized that getting in the wagon first would put her in the middle, sitting next to Riley. She tucked her skirts under and crossed her arms, holding them tight in her effort to make herself as thin as possible on the seat. Laura sat down and leaned toward her ear. "He doesn't have anything contagious, you know."

Annie frowned and poked her friend in the side with her elbow. Laura chuckled and straightened her skirt.

The other side of the wagon dipped and creaked under Riley's weight. Annie hadn't spoken to him since the previous night, and she dreaded being so close to him now. She was half embarrassed and still half angry. It was beyond her how saying someone's eyes resembled a cow could be construed as a compliment.

He clicked out the side of his mouth at the same time he snapped the reins, and the horses plodded forward. His arm pressed against her shoulder. She leaned toward Laura, but her friend pushed back as if purposely trying to force her closer to Riley. Annie sat straight as a broom handle and kept her eyes straight forward. She would endure the short ride into town and try not to think of the clean-shaven, fresh-smelling man next to her.

A few long, uncomfortable minutes passed, and the public square came into view, the courthouse rising up tall and proud at the far end. Wagons and a number of saddled horses lined the streets surrounding the square. A canvas shelter had been erected over a temporary stage, where a makeshift pulpit had been erected. Rows of benches—some newly made of fresh wood and others borrowed from the Baptist church—were spread out before the small stage. Behind the benches, people sat in clusters on their quilts with their families. Annie was tempted to smile at several grannies who sat in rocking chairs that family members had hauled in their wagons, but she caught herself.

How many similar events had she attended here? Town gatherings and celebrations were frequent, shopping among the local farmers selling fruits and vegetables out of the backs of their wagons, and buying cotton. The one that stood out most in her mind was when Sam Houston came to town and gave his antisecession speech to a crowd in front of the courthouse. Texas seceded anyway, but the speech sure had stirred up the townsfolk for a long while.

She couldn't miss the number of women clothed in various stages of mourning dress, from solid black to gray and lavender, and the men with black armbands. So many people had lost loved ones in the war.

Riley pulled the wagon to a halt, set the brake, and wrapped the reins around it. He hopped down and held up his hands to her, but she kept her face straight ahead. He cleared his throat. "Miss Annie, if you'll scoot over to the left, I can help you down."

Oh fiddle. She hadn't even thought about having to get down.

"Go on, Annie. We need to get seated before the service starts. The reverend is saving us places on a couple of the benches he borrowed from the area churches, but if we're not there before the meeting starts, we'll lose them."

Annie scooted over on the seat, wondering why they hadn't come earlier if Laura was so worried about losing their seats. She held out her hand, and Riley took it and placed it on his shoulder. When she'd settled her other hand, he took her by the waist and lowered her to the ground.

"There are a lot of folks milling about here this evening. If you'll wait until the children are unloaded, I'll help you get to your seat."

She wanted to snap back that she didn't need his help, but the tone in his voice conveyed concern rather than condescension. Annie nodded.

Turning slightly, from the corner of her eye, she watched Riley help Laura to the ground. He didn't lift her down but rather held up his hand to assist her, and though he smiled, it was a different kind of smile from the one he gave her. She fell back against the wheel, trying to grasp hold of the idea that maybe he did like her.

The children's excited chatter invaded her thoughts. She was grateful for this happy evening. The youngsters would soon be informed about the changes ahead, if Laura couldn't find a way to keep the school open.

Riley helped the children to form a line behind Miss Laura, and she walked toward the seating area, looking like a mother mallard with her ducklings. People stared as usual, but most were kind glances. Riley stopped beside Annie and stuck out his elbow. "Here, take my arm."

Her cheeks warmed at the thought of allowing him to escort her in front of so many people. Since Laura had gone on ahead, there was really no other option. She reached for his arm and looped hers around it. If she was completely honest with herself, she had to admit she liked the man. He was just as Laura had said—kind, helpful, courteous, handsome—and now that she had thought about it some, she realized her anger with his helping her stemmed from her need to be independent and not needy.

She'd never had a beau before, but for this one moment, she pretended he was hers.

She took her seat, and this time didn't fuss about sitting

next to him, but she did bemoan the fact that she'd led most everyone to believe she was blind. If not for that, she might actually consider attempting to win Riley's heart. But why would a man like him allow himself to be attracted to a blind woman? Not that he was—but she was starting to hope he might be.

CHAPTER THIRTEEN

Riley glanced at Annie sitting more relaxed on the church bench than she had in the wagon. She hadn't yet talked to him—not since he'd made that stupid remark about her eyes resembling Bertha's. He shook his head just thinking about his careless words.

He'd only wanted to compliment her—to tell her how pretty her eyes were—dark like Bertha's, fringed with long lashes. It didn't sound all that bad to him, but she sure had taken offense. He leaned forward with his elbows resting on his knees and glanced at the children. The oldest three sat on the bench with him and Annie while Miss Laura sat in front of them, in the middle of the younger ones.

A large crowd had already gathered. People squeezed closer together on the benches while others spilled out around the outskirts. Any kind of a gathering always brought out people eager to visit with neighbors, but they seemed especially glad to get together now that the war was over. People could relax once again and go about the business of life. The buzz of conversation filled the air as farmers and ranchers, merchants and businessmen, all speculated on the future and how things would change now that the slaves had gained their freedom.

He suspected cotton growing would probably wind down now that the workforce wasn't there to harvest it, but how would that affect the economy of Waco? Several men to his left raised their voices in differing opinions until one man's wife shushed him. His neck and ears turned red, but he settled in his seat and faced the front. Riley grinned but then sobered. The action reminded him of his parents. Everyone thought Calder Morgan was the boss of the family, but most of the time his ma ruled the roost. His heart clenched. He missed his parents. If only he'd had a chance to see them one more time—to tell them how much he loved them.

Ducking his head, he widened his eyes when they started stinging then blinked away the unwanted tears. With his head down, he noticed Annie's hands folded in her lap. Her nails were not the clean, polished nails of a debutante but rather chipped and even had a bit of dirt under them. He wanted to take hold of her hand—to tell her not to worry about things at the school, but how could he make such a promise? He couldn't even decide what he wanted to do himself.

And he certainly didn't want Annie to think he was interested in her. He'd learned his lesson where women were concerned.

Keeping his head down, Riley stared at the dirt and crumpled grass at his feet. A spot in his heart still ached at Miranda's defection from their betrothal. She had always been a bit of a flirt—a pretty woman who seemed to crave the attention of men, and he'd fallen under her spell. He was dimwitted to think she'd wait for him, especially after he found her in the arms of Nate Watson that time. But he'd believed her story that Nate had corralled her and forced his attentions, and he had defended her honor with a fistfight. Now he wondered . . .

Riley shook his head. What did it matter now? It was part of the past. Miranda was married, and there was no sense pining over her. Besides, Annie wasn't Miranda, and it wasn't right to compare the two. Annie was sweet, loved the children and Miss Laura dearly. Yes, she had a temper, but he was sure she could never be deceptive like Miranda had been. *Lying wasn't in her nature.*

Out of the corner of his eye, he saw a tall, slim man stepping toward the front. Riley leaned toward Annie. "When he calls up the young'uns, I'll help Miss Laura. Why don't you stay seated?"

She made a face as if she were annoyed by his suggestion, but after a long moment, she nodded. Her need for independence resonated as loud as cannon fire. How difficult was it for her to know that many young women her age were already married and some even had children? A physical pain pierced his chest. If he could give her his own sight, he felt sure he would do so. She ought to have a chance to live a normal life, not one where she was trapped in darkness. All of the sweet children deserved that too, but it was not the hand they'd been dealt in life. Still, if he hadn't lived near them and watched them doing chores, dishes, and other daily tasks for the past few weeks, he'd never have believed how capable they were.

"Welcome, ladies and gentlemen. Thank you for coming tonight. I want to welcome back all of our soldiers and offer my condolences to those families who lost someone during the war." He paused in respect for the families whose soldiers had not returned. Then he leaned forward on the pulpit, his eyes smoldering with excitement. "And thank the Good Lord, the war is over."

Claps and loud cheers rang out all around Riley, and several of the children jumped at the sudden ruckus. He started to comfort them, but they didn't seem overly worried, so he settled down on the bench again.

The minister lifted his hands to quiet the crowd. "My name is King James."

Murmurs and chuckles echoed through the crowd. Behind Riley, Rusty shouted, "Did he say he was a king?"

Miss Laura hurried to shush the precocious boy who'd set the crowd heehawing.

The minister laughed too, but lifted his hands again. "My parents had no idea how much trouble that name would cause me. My Christian name isn't a whole lot better than my brother's though. Most folks call him Jimmy or J.J., but his full name is James Josephus James."

"James James," a man in back repeated. "What a hoot!"

The reverend waited for the laughter to die down again, then continued. "I'd like to start this evening in prayer. Would you please bow your heads with me?"

He thanked God for the nice weather and the town's hospitality, and then he offered a prayer of praise to the Good Lord for seeing the nation through the war. He prayed again for unity and for God to comfort those left homeless or injured and for those in pain over their lost loved ones.

After all his shocking news when he'd first come home, Riley hadn't thought to thank God for protecting him during the four years of war. At first, he'd been so angry and hurting over Timothy's death that he'd just wanted to die himself. But then he witnessed his fellow soldiers dying, one after another, and he realized how much he wanted to live—to return home and make up for deserting his family in the time of their greatest need. For so long, he'd been angry at God. Why should God listen to his prayers now that he was safe?

Riley sat up and stiffened his back. He had only agreed to come to help Miss Laura with the children, but he would have been better off saying no. A long time ago when his brother died, he'd decided God had turned His back on him—even after Riley had pleaded with God to save Timothy. It was too late for him to change.

←— ★ —→

Annie liked the minister right away. His kind eyes seemed to look straight into her heart. His gaze roamed the crowd, as if he were concerned that someone might need a special word from the Lord. And whoever heard of a man named King James—a preacher no less!

He leaned against the pulpit, as if trying to get closer to the congregation. "We've been through hard times, folks. Some people much harder than others. There are women in the South who have lost their husbands and sons. Their daughters have been mistreated by cruel men, and their homes destroyed. I'm saying this so that we can be thankful things aren't worse here in Texas than they are."

He pushed away from the pulpit and walked around to stand in front of it. "I'm asking you to set aside your opinions of the war and what the next steps for our country should be. Let's put aside for now the debate over whether or not Texas should rejoin the Union. Let's don't be worrying about what's to become of your cotton farmers whose slaves have been set free—farmers who have acres of crops to be harvested and no workers. No, I'm asking your thoughts to dwell on your heavenly Father now. Open your hearts to Him and hear His word to you tonight."

He beckoned the musicians, two fiddlers and an accordion player, who joined him onstage. "We didn't want to move one of the heavy pianos outside, on the off chance it might rain, so I've asked these gentlemen to join me as we sing several hymns to our Lord."

The fiddle players looked to Casper Hornsby, who pulled his accordion apart on a wheeze, and nodded his head. The minister lifted his face toward heaven and sang the chorus of "Crown Him with Many Crowns," followed by "All Hail the Power of Jesus' Name" and "Rock of Ages."

Annie closed her eyes and joined in singing the familiar hymns she often sang at Sunday services. Riley Morgan's deeper voice stayed surprisingly on key. Just one more thing to like about the man, especially since she herself couldn't hold a tune.

Soon the accompanists left the stage and the minister waited for them to take their seats before addressing the crowd again. He smiled, the hair on his moustache dancing. "We have a very special treat tonight. Today I met Miss Laura Wilcox, who is the administrator of the Wilcox School for the Blind, as most of you-all know. We had a nice talk, which led me to offer an invitation to have the children sing tonight."

Soft gasps and pleasant *oohs*! echoed across the square, and a smattering of applause built to a loud rumble. Annie glanced sideways, and Tess, Henry, and Becky all three had wide grins spreading across their faces.

"Miss Wilcox, would you please bring your exceptionally talented children up front and sing a few songs for us fortunate people?"

Miss Laura rose and tapped Rusty on the arm. He stood and the other small children followed. Riley hopped up, squeezing past her, and he whispered to Becky, who stood. Annie wanted to go along and help get the children lined up, but she would only be in the way, and besides, she didn't deserve to stand up in front of all these good churchgoing people and pretend a lie. She was so tired of it all.

Closing her eyes, she let the words of the children's songs wash over her like a gentle spring rain. Their voices rose sweetly as the words floated across the audience. "I once was lost, but now am found, was blind but now I see."

Annie's eyes shot open. Her heart pounded. She was once lost, but then she found a home. *She* was blind—sort of—but what did those last words mean to her? She'd never before considered how the words of that hymn modeled her life. What did the rest of the song say? She must have sung it a hundred times, but the words muddled in her brain like thick molasses as the crowd's thunderous applause for the children pounded in her ears. Riley guided the children back to their bench, and each one's face beamed with pride. Bless that minister for giving them this chance to stand out.

Taking his seat beside her, Riley leaned close. "They did great, huh?"

She nodded, and leaned toward his ear. "I'm not deaf, you know."

He chuckled and faced forward, duly scolded. Annie found herself grinning with him.

"Glory be," Reverend James said, shaking his head. "The Good Lord has surely blessed those youngsters with the voices of angels." He glanced down at his worn Bible. "I'm opening my message tonight with a verse from the book of Romans. 'For the wages of sin is death; but the gift of God is eternal life through Jesus Christ our Lord.'" He snapped his Bible shut so fast several people on the front rows jumped.

"Just what is sin? Do you really know?"

"It's when you don't obey Miss Laura," Rusty shouted.

Out the corner of her eye, Annie saw Laura's hand shoot out and cover Rusty's mouth as she quieted him again. Laughter rippled around them.

"That can be one form of sin, young man. Sin is a willful or deliberate desecration of a religious or moral principle. That means if you murder someone, you've sinned. If you dishonor your parents, you've sinned. If you disobey God's Word, you're a sinner."

As if someone had shoved a knife in Annie's heart, a sudden realization stabbed her—*she* was a sinner. She had lied—stolen. Ducking her head, she hid her face, sure that everyone around would see the blackness that marred her heart.

"The truth is, every single one of us is a sinner." Reverend James held up his Bible. "God's Word says: 'For all have sinned, and come short of the glory of God.' All—not some." He kept silent for a long moment as if to allow his words to soak in.

Annie sucked in a silent sob, and Riley glanced at her. She turned her head away, not wanting him to see her struggle. Never before had a preacher's message knocked her upside the head with a huge dose of reality and made her feel so convicted. Most times she barely heard what the preachers said, because she was so busy keeping the children still.

But this man didn't mince words. She was a sinner. Not even God would want someone like her. She squeezed her eyes shut but the unwanted tears streamed out. Riley leaned away from her and pulled something out of his pocket and nudged her with his handkerchief. She took it, glad it was at least clean. Wiping her eyes, she caught a brief splash of Riley's scent—manly and clean. How different he was now from the filthy beggar who'd first come to their door.

"I see the worried expressions on some of you-all's faces. Let me tell you that you're not without hope. Don't forget there are two parts to that verse I first read. 'For the wages of sin is death—but the gift of God is eternal life through Jesus Christ our Lord.' Yes, we are all sinners, folks, and each of us will face death for our ill deeds, whether slight or heinous, but I'm here to tell you that there's more. You can be forgiven. You can be set free from your sin. That's the second part of that verse—'the gift of God is eternal life through Jesus Christ our Lord.'"

Hope soared in Annie's heart like a bird set free from a snare. She could be forgiven.

"Scripture says: 'For God so loved the world, that he gave his only begotten Son, that whosoever believeth in him should not perish, but have everlasting life.'" Reverend James stepped off the stage, Bible tucked under one arm. "All that is required is that you believe on the Lord Jesus Christ and repent of your sins, and God will welcome you into His fold."

Annie relived all the horrible things she'd done. From her earliest days, she'd been taught to steal—fruit from the street vendors, a loaf of bread, wallets, watches, even rings right off people's fingers. She'd done it all to earn her daddy's approval and had never known such deeds were wrong until she'd overheard a street preacher one day saying that stealing was a sin. After that, she'd been uncomfortable taking things that didn't belong to her, but her daddy had forced her to do so in order to eat.

And then she'd pretended to be blind—just to have clean clothes and a home.

She was a sinner.

She didn't deserve God's forgiveness.

"So how does one become saved? God's Word says: 'For by grace are ye saved through faith; and that not of yourselves: it is the gift of God: Not of works, lest any man should boast.'" He patted the top of his Bible then held it out to a man on the front row. "Salvation is a gift, folks. Just like if I was to give my Bible to this man. It's not something you can earn, no matter how good a person you are. The kindest, most generous people in this world will spend eternity in hell unless they repent of their sins and accept Jesus into their hearts. I'll say it again. Salvation is a gift. Yours for the taking."

He pointed his finger at the crowd. "Will you accept God's gift?" He moved his hand, pointing toward people farther back. "How about you?"

The long, thin finger swept sideways, and Annie was certain it was pointing straight at her. Heart pounding, she licked her dry, dust-coated lips.

"And what about you? Will you receive the gift? Or will you refuse it?"

Annie wanted the gift—more than she'd ever wanted anything. Just as she no longer stole things, she longed to be free of her lying—her deceit. But would God accept her—a terrible sinner? Hadn't the preacher said God loved everyone?

She searched her mind for his words. So much of the meeting she'd spent time stewing over her past, that she'd missed much of what he'd said. But didn't he say God was no respecter of persons? Maybe He would accept a reformed pickpocket.

"I need to close so you folks who have long rides can get home before the sun sets, but I don't want anyone to leave here who feels God calling them." He motioned to the musicians, who gathered their instruments, came back up front, and began quietly playing. The preacher held out his arms. "If God is calling you, don't ignore Him, folks. Eternal life in heaven is at stake. One last thing. I'm sure you noticed I didn't take up an offering. In case you haven't heard, the Wilcox School for the Blind has fallen upon hard times. As you leave tonight, there will be men with baskets at the end of the aisles, and if you feel led to drop in a few coins to help these children, I know it would be appreciated. Every penny donated tonight will go to the school, and please, no Confederate bills." Soft ripples of laughter echoed around the town square as people stood.

"Thank you-all for coming tonight. As you head home, let me leave you with one final exhortation from Micah 6:8. 'He hath shewed thee, O man, what is good; and what doth the Lord require of thee, but to do justly, and to love mercy, and to walk humbly with thy God?'" The preacher lifted his hand and blessed the people. "Go in peace, and I hope all you-all will come back tomorrow evening."

"We can go now?" Rusty jumped up, bumping into Annie's back.

Annie stood and spun toward Riley, who also rose. "I can't leave yet. I've got to go talk to that preacher. Will you take me up there?"

CHAPTER FOURTEEN

iley was ready to run down the aisle but not toward the preacher. He just wanted to get out of there and away from the emotions that swirled through him like a flash flood. The man's sermon made him think too much. Remember too much. And remembering only caused pain.

He picked up his hat from the bench and placed it on his head. People were crowding the aisles like cattle, all trying to get through the same few openings.

"Did you hear me?" Annie asked, tugging on his sleeve. "I want to know if you'll take me up front so I can talk to the minister."

Riley shook his head. He was plenty close enough to the preacher already. "Sorry, but I need to help Miss Laura get the children to the wagon."

Annie's hopeful expression sagged. "Of course. It's getting late, and they need to get home. Go on, then. I'll just wait until things are less crowded, then make my own way up front." She backed up to the bench and sat.

Riley pushed his hat back on his forehead, feeling as low as a toad's belly. She couldn't stay here alone. He glanced at Miss Laura. Though people crowded past her, she had the younger children in the aisle, already lined up, and was gathering the older ones to finish up the row. Should he leave Annie here, alone and unprotected, to help Miss Laura, who seemed to have things under control? He scratched his temple. Could Miss Laura even drive a wagon?

He glanced down at Annie, sitting there so straight, looking pretty, even though her hair, which she'd coiled into a bun, listed to the left a bit. It only made her more charming. Pulling his gaze away, he started for Miss Laura. "You stay right there," he called back over his shoulder to Annie.

"Look out, comin' through." Sean Murphy barreled his way through the crowd toward the front. He got to the line of children at the same time Riley met Miss Laura. She glanced at him over Becky's head, then her gaze swerved to Annie's. Love and concern emanated from her eyes.

"She wants to go up and talk to the preacher." Riley quirked his mouth to one side and shrugged a shoulder.

"I can help you get the children home, Laura." Sean's deep voice boomed over the chattering of the crowd.

Laura looked at Sean, and after a moment, she nodded. She looked back at Riley. "I'd appreciate your staying here and seeing Annie home safely."

Great, just great. He took a deep breath, gave Miss Laura a curt nod, and then turned back to Annie. The last place he wanted to be was closer to that man of God. The guy actually had him squirming on the bench with his pointed statements, but there were too many issues unsettled in Riley's mind for him to make things right with God just yet.

And then there was Annie, the woman who kept him awake at nights and stirred up things he didn't want to feel. He'd best just see her to the front and get it over with. He hiked back to her, dodging around a couple of women blocking the aisle as they chatted. He held out his hand to Annie. "All right, I'll take you up front."

Her head jerked up, and she lifted tear-stained eyes that almost reached his, but then lowered. Her nose and cheeks were red and splotchy. His gut tightened. What could she possibly be so distressed about? Was she upset with him for refusing to take her to the preacher?

No, she wasn't one to get upset over something so trivial. More likely, she was worried about the school closing. Of course, that was it. As far as he knew, she had no family, so what would become of her? He sat down beside her, wanting to take hold of her hand and reassure her things would work out, but he couldn't. "Care to tell me what's wrong?"

Her chin quivered, and she shook her head. "I need to talk to the minister."

"All right. Things are clearing out, so let me help you up there."

She took his hand and allowed him to help her up and lead her to the front. They waited while the preacher prayed with three others, and then Reverend James stepped in front of Annie. Riley realized he still held her hand and released it. "The lady would like a word with you, sir. She . . . uh . . ." He waved his index finger at his eyes. "She can't see."

The minister studied Riley a moment then nodded and turned to Annie. Stepping back, Riley got the distinct feeling that the man saw right through him—to the struggle going on inside him.

⟵ ★ ⟶

"It was kind of you to loan us your wagon tonight and to see us home, Sean, especially since Riley stayed to walk Annie back." Laura rearranged her skirt and peeked over her shoulder at the quiet children. As she turned back, her gaze collided with Sean's, sending her heart pounding like the children's footsteps at mealtime.

"Those young'uns are plumb tuckered out, aren't they?" he said.

"The excitement of singing, I suppose. They don't get many opportunities to show their talents." Laura faced forward, bemoaning the fact that her voice had wobbled. She placed her trembling hands in her lap. She was feeling like a silly schoolgirl with her first infatuation.

Maybe because Sean had been her first—and only—beau?

"Mrs. Alton baked pie for us to eat after the service, although I don't know how many of the children will be able to stay awake to enjoy it," she said. "Would you care to stay and have a slice?"

"I'd like to, but I don't think I should. Sure wouldn't want to give anyone a reason to gossip."

Warmth rushed to Laura's cheeks, but she appreciated Sean's concern for her reputation. "I should have thought of that. People do talk, you know. It's just that I'm so used to having Annie and now Mr. Morgan around that I didn't think—" She realized she was rambling and forced herself to be quiet. She wasn't one to get nervous most times, so why did being around Sean make her so antsy?

"Beautiful, isn't it?" Sean nudged his chin toward the horizon.

The sun had already sunk below the horizon, but fingers of light painted the clouds a pinkish-lavender shade that reminded her of purple coneflowers. Twilight settled across the land, turning the sky to indigo. Crickets chirped all around them, welcoming them back home. Evening was a peaceful time, when most of the day's chores were done and she could relax and do some reading or mending.

The school rose up before her as they drew nearer, reminding her that their days there were numbered. She'd all but talked her tongue off trying to find another benefactor or to get the city to support the school, but all her efforts had been in vain. Reverend James's kind offer to donate the evening's collection to the school was a blessing she hadn't anticipated. She hoped there would be enough donations to pay off her creditors and be able to refund money to the parents who had paid several months in advance for their children's care. She didn't want to close the school owing anything to anyone.

"Whoa, there." Sean pulled up the wagon in front of the house and then helped her down. The girls slid out of the wagon and plodded up the stairs.

"Rusty's asleep, Miss Laura," Henry whispered.

"I'll carry him upstairs if you'll show me where to put him," Sean said to the older boy, but then he glanced at Laura. "That is, if it's all right."

Laura nodded and followed the girls inside. "There's pie in the kitchen, if you're not too tired," she said as she lit the parlor lantern.

Lissa yawned loudly and rubbed her eyes. "I'm tired."

"I'll take her up," Becky offered. "If you'll save me a slice of pie."

Laura ran her hand down the girl's soft cheek. "You go ahead and help Lissa. I'm going to run up and light a lantern for Mr. Murphy."

"He's a nice man." Becky smiled, her faded blue eyes pulling inward in an unnatural slant. She pawed the air until she located Lissa sitting on the bottom step, then she helped the younger girl up the stairs.

Laura lit the lantern then hurried back downstairs.

Henry held the front door open for Sean, and the big man carried Rusty inside. His gaze latched on to hers, and for the briefest of moments, she imagined they were married and Sean was carrying in their own child. She swallowed the lump clogging her throat. She'd thought that dream was long dead and gone. "Henry can show you where to put Rusty. I'll go cut a slice of pie so you can take it home."

Sean's warm smile reached inside her and twisted the key to the lock on her heart. She spun around and scurried into the kitchen. Camilla sat at the table, while Tess had found the pie and carefully began slicing it.

Laura walked up behind her and touched her shoulder. "Why don't you get a cloth and help Camilla wash up? I'll take care of this."

Tess smiled over her shoulder. "All right, Miss Laura."

Tears burned Laura's eyes. Oh, how she'd miss these sweet children when they returned home. She needed to tell them soon, before they heard from someone else about the school's closing, but that would be one of the hardest things she'd ever done.

Blinking back the tears, she sliced the pie and placed the slivers onto plates. "Tess, could you please set these on the table?"

"Yes, ma'am."

"Lissa and Rusty went on up to bed, but Becky and Henry will be back down in a minute. I'm going to take a slice to Mr. Murphy. You-all eat your pie, and if I'm not back when you're done, go on upstairs. Annie and I can take care of the dishes."

Laura dished out a generous slice for Sean and set it on one of the older, chipped plates, then covered it with a towel. She wished they could sit down together and enjoy each other's company, but she saw the wisdom in being cautious.

She found him outside, leaning against the porch railing.

"Sure is a pretty evening, even if it's a wee bit hot still," he said.

"Such is life in Texas."

He chuckled. "True enough."

"Thank you again, for helping us tonight."

He turned, leaning back against the post, his features illuminated by the light streaming out the open front door. A smile tugged at his lips, and the intense look in his green eyes branded her heart. "My pleasure. Anytime you need something, Laura, you only have to ask."

She handed him the pie. "I need to tell you something, before you hear it from someone else."

Concern dipped his eyebrows and he straightened. "What is it? You're not sick, are you?"

"No, it's nothing like that." The tinny noise of a saloon's piano already littered the peaceful evening. She stared off at the lights of town, summoning the strength to tell him.

He reached down with his free hand and clasped hers. "Tell me, and put me out of my misery. I'm imagining all kinds of things."

Her hand seemed tiny compared to his brawny, callused hand. Such a strong, capable man. She licked her lips and glanced up at him. "Unless a miracle occurs, the school will be closing in a few weeks."

His eyes widened. "Closing? Why?"

She relayed the story of Mr. Ramsey's visit, and Sean scowled.

"How could that sidewinder do such a mean thing?"

Laura shook her head. "I don't know, but he did. He gave us thirty days. I've been all over town, trying to get alternate support for the school, but I've had no luck, except for whatever Reverend James collected today."

Sean released her hand and set the pie plate on a nearby

rocker. Then he took hold of her shoulders. "I'm so sorry, Laura. I know what this place means to you."

She shook her head. "It's not the place, but the children. When I have to send them home, each one will take a piece of my heart with them. And I don't know what I'll do with the boys. Neither of them have families."

"The Good Lord will work out something. I can't believe He'd let a tyrant close your school after all your hard work. But what will you do if that does happen?"

She shook her head. "I don't know. I have no desire to leave Texas. Maybe I can find a position as a schoolteacher, although most schools still prefer male instructors."

Sean stared up at the porch ceiling for a long minute, the warmth of his hands still heating her shoulders. Finally, he looked down. "I never stopped loving you, Laura. I want you to know that. It's not too late to marry me—that is if you might still be interested in me."

CHAPTER FIFTEEN

On the walk home with Riley, Annie felt as if a huge burden had been lifted from her shoulders. And she couldn't quit smiling. God had forgiven her—for all her stealing, for her lies and deception. She was a Christian now, washed clean by the love of God. Jesus Christ, God's own Son, died on the cross to set her free from her sin—and free she was—except for one remaining issue.

Her bogus blindness.

She hadn't had the nerve to tell Reverend James about that, partly because Riley was so close and would surely have overheard. That's not how she wanted him to find out. Her heart pounded harder just thinking about how she would tell him that she wasn't blind. And she had to—sooner or later. She liked him a lot, but would he even cast her a second glance once he learned the truth?

The glow of the thin moonlight illuminated the road just enough that they could see the well-traveled path, and in the distance, the lights of the school beckoned them. Riley's heavier footsteps plodded along next to hers. He'd been awfully quiet since they left the public square. Had the minister's message touched his heart too?

"What did you think of the service?"

His pace slowed, as if her words had taken him off guard. Well, what else could she expect when she hadn't said a word to him all day?

"It made me think a lot," he said shortly.

"Yes, me too. It's like the blinders have been taken off my eyes, and for the first time I can fully understand Christ's sacrifice for me. I've heard lots of sermons about being a sinner, but not until tonight did it really hit home. I've done a lot of bad things in my life."

He stopped and turned to face her. "You? Like what?"

A rock-sized lump lodged in Annie's throat. What could she say? Tell him that she'd been a pickpocket? A thief? She shrugged. "Don't you have things in your past that you regret doing?"

He hesitated, as if disappointed in her response. "Sure. I imagine everyone does."

Lifting his face to the sky, he stood there for a long moment, as if studying the stars. He took a breath then glanced down. "Annie, I'm sorry if I offended you yesterday. I don't have much of a way with women. I just wanted you to know that I think you have beautiful eyes."

Beautiful like a cow's? she wanted to ask, but the seriousness in his voice held her back. In the distance, she could hear the ruckus of the saloons, and to her left, some creature splashed in the water of the Brazos, while a bird's lonely cry rent the air. Crickets sang all around them, and lightning bugs flickered, as if helping them find their way home. She and Riley were completely alone, and she wasn't the least bit concerned. He would take care of her.

Suddenly, tears filled her eyes, and she ducked her head. Somehow, without her knowledge, this man had crept into her heart, and she didn't want to have to say good-bye to him. But soon she would.

"I didn't mean to upset you again. Please, Annie, don't cry."

She sniffed. "I'm sorry. I guess I'm just extra emotional today."

"I understand. I know you're worried about the school closing."

"Yes, that's part of it." That, and how she was going to tell everyone who knew her that she'd lied to them and tricked them. Everyone would hate her.

Riley lifted his hand, and held it right beside her cheek. "You have a tear here."

She swallowed hard, as his index finger gently swiped across her flesh.

"Your skin is so soft."

She blew out a laugh, and turned her face away. "Don't tell me it feels like duck down or something."

He chuckled, then gently grasped hold of her chin and turned her toward him. "All right. How about if I say it's as soft as a flower petal?"

She shuffled her feet, quelling her sudden urge to run away. Talking like this with a man—with anyone, actually, but especially Riley—well, she'd never done it before.

"Um . . . several of the children have asked to touch my face so they could know what I look like." Riley cleared his throat. "You can do that—if you want to, that is."

Annie felt her mouth drop, but she snapped it shut, she hoped before he noticed. The children had done the same thing to her, many times, but it seemed so inappropriate for her to touch Riley's face—and yet she wanted to. She started to look around to see if anyone was near, but she knew they were all alone.

Riley moved from foot to foot, just as she had a few moments earlier.

Annie lifted her hand. Her fingers trembled as they drew close, and then she touched his chin. She couldn't help the giggle that broke forth. "It's prickly."

"Sorry. I didn't get a chance to shave before tonight's service. I had to go to Sean's to see if I could borrow his wagon and mules." His voice trembled a smidgen, and his breath sounded ragged.

Annie moved closer so she could reach higher. His warm breath caressed her hand as her fingers brushed the softer skin of his cheekbone. With her arms stretching up so high, she found it hard to breathe, but she rather enjoyed exploring his face. She ran her fingertips across the stiff hair of his eyebrows and then brushed them down the hair at his temples. He sucked in a breath, as if her touch affected him. Her hands trembled as she lowered them, again feeling the bristle of his chin whiskers.

Her hands dropped to her side, as if all the bones were suddenly gone from them. How could touching a man make her feel so—so feminine? She swallowed hard. "You . . . uh . . . have a very nice . . . uh . . . face."

He coughed and cleared his throat. "My hair is dark brown, and my eyes are blue."

Blue as the sapphire ring for sale in the mercantile.

"I—" She caught herself before saying *I know.*

He cupped her cheeks with his hands, his breath warm on her face. Then he lowered his lips to hers, hovering just above them. Annie's eyes widened, but his were closed. Then he sucked in a shaky breath and suddenly dropped his hands, leaving her feeling limp.

"I . . . uh . . . suppose I should get you home before Miss Laura calls out the Texas Rangers.

Annie stared at Riley's dusty boot tops, half relieved, half disappointed. "I thought the Rangers all left to fight in the war."

"All right, a posse then."

He took her hand and led her back to the house, then he opened the gate and walked her up the porch steps. He tipped his hat. "Good night, Annie."

"Thank you for waiting for me."

"You're most welcome." He smiled then hurried down the steps and disappeared into the darkness.

She closed the door then leaned back against it. How much her life had changed since she last walked through that door!

———— ★ ————

The rooster crowed, loud and annoying, from his favorite spot in the hayloft. Annie pulled the pillow over her head, but soon the lack of air forced her to push it away. She stretched, yawned, and glanced at Laura's already made-up bed. How did she almost always manage to wake up first and get dressed without Annie hearing her?

Letting out a long, satisfied sigh, she realized the reason she hadn't heard Laura today was because she'd been dreaming of a certain man. Pushing up from the bed, she hurried to the window and looked over at the barn. The wide doors already hung open, but Riley wasn't in sight. She rested her elbows on the windowsill and remembered last night. First and most important, she'd made peace with her Creator. Her heart had filled with warmth after her brief talk and prayer with Reverend James, and now her sins had been forgiven. She was a child of God.

And that thrill didn't even include Riley. He held her hand

yesterday and had come within a hairsbreadth of kissing her, and she had actually wanted him too.

She rushed through her morning ablutions and hurried downstairs to help Mrs. Alton finish breakfast, while Laura roused the children, as she normally did. Half an hour later, Annie's excitement dimmed when Riley didn't come inside for breakfast. Had he overslept? Just gotten distracted with chores?

She fixed Riley a plate and set it down on the kitchen counter near the back door, intending to deliver it as soon as she was free after breakfast.

"Will we get to sing at the revival again tonight?" Camilla asked as she placed her plate on the cart.

"Yeah, will we?" Lissa shouted, from her place at the table.

"I don't know, but you need to finish up. Almost everyone else is already done and doing their chores. Camilla, go put the clean silverware away, then you need to hurry upstairs and take the sheet off your bed so it can be washed."

Annie surveyed the serene scene. Tess was washing the last of the dishes, while Becky dried, and Camilla gathered the forks and spoons. Laura was off somewhere with the boys, and Mrs. Alton stood at the far counter, putting away the supplies she'd used to make breakfast. Annie wiped off the table, all except the spot where Lissa still dawdled. She pushed each chair in all the way so no one would trip, and stopped and leaned on the last chair. How different would her life be next month?

Laura strode into the kitchen and looked right at her. "May I speak with you privately, please?"

Nodding, Annie followed her out of the kitchen and into the quiet parlor. Laura sat on the settee and patted the space beside her. Sitting, Annie couldn't help wondering, *what now?*

Squeezing her hand, Laura smiled. "Stop worrying. I want to run to town and see how much was collected last night. The reverend told me he'd deposit the money in our account at the bank this morning so that we wouldn't have to keep it here overnight."

Annie nodded. "Sounds like a good idea."

"I'm hoping it's enough to pay off all the accounts I've charged since receiving Mr. Morrow's last payment and to purchase some additional supplies to hold us over until we close."

A sharp sting lanced Annie's heart. "So we truly are shutting down the school?"

Pain filled Laura's eyes. "I don't see an alternative. I've talked to everyone I know who might be able to help, but with the war just being over and the Confederate dollar now worthless . . ." She sighed and shook her head. "Nothing but a miracle or Mr. Ramsey's change of heart could stop us from closing now, and I don't see either of those happening."

Annie sat up straighter and smiled. "A miracle of sorts happened to me last night. I repented of my sins and received God into my heart. So . . . maybe He will yet work a miracle for us."

Some of her joy faded when Laura didn't seem the least bit delighted. "Aren't you happy for me?" she asked.

Cupping her face, Laura offered a halfhearted smile. "Yes, of course. It's just that, well . . . I've never made peace with God for taking Milly at such a young age."

"Milly? That's Mr. Morrow's daughter, right?"

Laura nodded. "She contracted a disease when she was around Tess's age and nearly died. We were all so glad when she started getting better, but I was devastated that her sight never returned. Milly was my best friend, and her blindness changed everything."

"How did she die?" Annie asked softly.

Laura turned her head and seemed to be staring out the

window. "It was a tragic accident. Mr. Morrow was having a special addition built onto his home to make life easier for her. She got bored and went exploring while her nurse had run downstairs for a moment. Milly wandered into the construction area and fell from the second story. A workman had gone down to his wagon for something and hadn't erected a barrier to block the opening in the wall. Milly broke her neck in the fall." Laura blinked her eyes. "She was only twelve."

Annie took her friend's hand. "I'm sorry. I know how hard it must have been to lose your best friend." Soon, she would know just how Laura felt.

"Now you understand why educating blind children has been so important to me."

Gathering her composure, Annie nodded.

Laura still maintained her faraway gaze. "But I have a feeling certain things are about to change."

"What do you mean?"

Laura hopped up. "I need to get to town. We can talk about that later. Can you work with the children on their arithmetic and spelling until I get back?"

She nodded and stood. "Sure. How long will you be gone?"

Walking to the door, her friend shrugged. "I'm not sure. Not too long, I hope."

Ambling back to the kitchen, Annie's thoughts swirled. Her heart ached for young Milly, and for Laura dealing with such a deep loss when she was so young. She paused at the doorframe, checking on the girls. "Are you-all about done?"

"Yes," Tess said. "Just a few more things to dry."

"Lissa, are you finished eating?" Annie asked, even though it was obvious the girl wasn't in the room. She winced at her deception. The children would still need to learn that she wasn't blind.

"She went out to the privy, Miss Annie." Becky hung the

towel she'd been using on a peg to dry. "And Mrs. Alton went out to the garden to hunt for some vegetables for lunch."

"All right. If you're finished, run upstairs and strip the sheets off your beds."

The girls shuffled from the room. Annie surveyed the near spotless kitchen. She turned toward the back door, eager to finally have a chance to run Riley's breakfast to him, but his plate was gone. She sighed and grabbed the broom. She couldn't sweep away the things that were to come, but maybe her new-found faith in God would give her the courage to face them head-on.

CHAPTER SIXTEEN

*R*iley dragged an old, hardened pair of chaps from a dark corner of the tack room and tossed them onto the pile of debris, leaving only the bed and a crate that held his pitiful few possessions. He grabbed a broom and knocked down the cobwebs in the rafters and swept the dust, horsehair, and dried manure from the corners and out the door. Miss Laura's request for him to get the barn in order for their leaving and to repair the equipment so they could sell it would keep him busy for a while. He had mentally prepared himself to leave the school when she had told him it was closing, but at her request, he had agreed to stick around and take care of the barn and the animals and make sure those raiders didn't come back and harm them.

But he agreed just so he could keep watch on Annie for a little while longer.

He kicked at a warped board poking out from the wall. A loud bang reverberated through the room, making hens on the other side of the wall squawk. What had he been thinking to ask Annie to touch his face like that? When the children had studied his face with their small fingers, it had tickled a bit, but when Annie had—why, he almost kissed her. Good night, he barely knew her. Yanking off his hat, he pushed back his sweaty hair. What had he been thinking?

He snatched the feather tick off his bed, strode outside, and whacked it against the fence rail, raising a dusty cloud. Across the yard, Annie and Tess were hanging up the freshly washed sheets, his included. Her efforts were mostly wasted, since he had yet to spend a whole night on the bed. Maybe one of these days . . .

Another loud clap reverberated across the yard as he slapped the mattress against the rail. Letting her touch him had been a stupid mistake—one he couldn't repeat. He'd be leaving here soon, and there was no point in giving Annie false hopes that something might develop between them. He had to do a better job of keeping his distance.

"Hey! Hey! Stop that. Can't you see we're hanging laundry?" Annie marched toward him, a deep scowl puckering her brow.

He hadn't seen her since last night. He waved his hand in the air, trying to disperse the dust. "Sorry. I wasn't thinking, I guess."

"Good thing for you there's not a gusty breeze—or you just might find yourself rewashing sheets." She hiked her pert nose in the air, her hands on her shapely hips, every part of her body aimed toward him except her eyes.

Riley grinned. "I said I was sorry."

"Oh, fine then." She stood there, as if she didn't want to leave, and toed the dirt with the tip of her shoe. "What are you doing, anyway?"

"Cleaning out the tack room, at Miss Laura's request. She

thought there might be some things in there worth selling."

Annie frowned. "I hate to think we're so hard up that we have to resort to selling things. It's a cryin' shame that skunk of a man can just waltz in and take our home." She crossed her arms over her chest. Suddenly her expression softened. "That didn't sound very Christian. Sorry."

Riley couldn't help it when his brows shot up. He was pretty sure this was the first time she'd ever apologized or talked about her new faith, for that matter.

"You're taking us to the service again tonight, aren't you?" She cocked her head.

Just once, he'd like to see a spark of interest ignite in her pretty, brown eyes. He kicked up a clod of dirt, sending it sailing toward the house. It slowed to a stop in the grass that needed trimming. "Yes, I will be. Miss Laura already asked me to drive all you-all." He leaned on the fence rail and stared out at the pasture, where Gypsy grazed peacefully beside Bertha, the two having become fast friends. He had a fleeting thought to buy her, but then he had little money at the moment and no idea where he'd be in a month.

"That Reverend James sure knows how to preach a good sermon. What did you think of it?"

Riley grunted. Next to thoughts of Annie, the preacher's message had been foremost on his mind. Both had kept him awake last night until the wee hours. He didn't want to admit that the man's message had flamed to life a hope he'd long ago stomped out. He'd never understand why God took his young brother, and although the pain had dulled over the years, he'd never forget Timothy. But why had God let his parents die? Why were their lives cut short? Why weren't they there when he needed their love? How would he ever forget the things he had seen men do in the name of war? And why wouldn't God protect a house full of blind children from a money-hungry villain? For a long time, he'd hardened his heart—didn't want to believe in a God who tolerated such deeds, but just as good manners had been instilled in him when he was young, so had the Christian faith. He couldn't understand why good people suffered so much, but the truth was, he was as tired of fighting God as he was the war.

"That was a rather personal question I asked. You don't have to answer me." Annie spun around and started back toward her laundry. "I should finish my chores anyway. It's not right that I make Tess hang all the laundry by herself."

"Annie, wait." He reached out and grasped hold of her arm, gently pulling her to a stop. "I didn't mean to not respond. It's just that . . ." He released her and stared up at the sky. "I've had to face a lot of hard things the past few years—my brother's sudden death, the war, and now my parents' murders—and it all made me angry at God. I'm not proud of that, but it's the truth. Reverend James's message hit the target more than I care to admit."

Her cautious expression exploded into delight. "Me too. I've been to church services the seven years that I've lived here and heard the similar words many times, but last night they finally pricked my heart. I just had to make things right with God, and if someone with a past like mine can, I know you can." She smiled up at him, and he saw her useless eyes alight with her newfound faith. "Just don't close off your heart. You're a good man, Riley Morgan."

He watched her go, and he longed to follow after her, to pull her into his arms and tell her he'd take care of her. She'd stirred up feelings he thought had died with Miranda's betrayal. But what was the point?

He was selling his ranch and had no idea where he'd end up. Even if they could have a future together, did he want to marry a woman who was blind?

And that was the crux of the matter.

There was little doubt he liked Annie and was growing to care for her far more quickly and in a deeper way than he had Miranda. He wasn't sure why. Maybe because she needed his protection more than a woman who could see and take care of herself.

He exhaled a laugh. Who was he kidding? Annie didn't need him. She was as independent as any woman he knew. She'd be fine, no matter where life took her, and that road most likely would not veer in the same direction as the one he'd soon travel down.

As he walked back into the barn, he realized he'd created a dangerous hazard for Annie and the children by tossing all those things out of the tack room as he'd done. He started sorting out the trash from the useful items. The boys could polish the bridles and halters that he'd found, and then they'd be worth a bit of coin. He'd fixed a broken holster that was more suitable for the trash heap than useful, but Miss Laura said he could keep it since he didn't have one.

He dragged a moldy, half rat-eaten horse blanket behind the barn. Later, he'd move the pile away from the building and bury or burn the unwanted items. Back in the barn, he rubbed the back of his neck, trying to decide what to do next. He hoisted the saddle block and moved it back into the tack room. Tonight, he needed to give his saddle a good polishing. He ran his hand over the fine leather. It was very generous of his uncle to give him something so valuable as a horse and saddle.

A sudden thought nearly buckled his knees. He needed to write to his relatives and let them know about his parents' deaths. He hadn't even considered that before. Maybe Annie or Miss Laura had some paper he could use.

He looked around the dim tack room to see if there was anything else that needed tending. High up on the far wall sat a small window that someone had boarded over from the outside. If he removed the boards, the room would air out and be a bit cooler, and he could build a new shutter for it in a day or two. He looked around for something to break the boards, but the room was near empty. Looking up, he spied a sturdy rafter, and jumped up, grabbing hold of it. He tucked up his legs and kicked at the boards. The first kick loosened them, and the second and third knocked them free, sending fresh air and sunlight streaming into the dim room.

Outside, a feminine screech set his feet in action. Fearing he'd hit one of the children, he raced out the barn and around the side, where he spied a phaeton with a colored man driving and a female passenger sitting beside him. The falling boards must have spooked the horse that was still prancing sideways, nostrils flared. The driver was working the reins and cooing to the frightened animal.

Riley slowly approached, his hands held out. "Whoa, there. You're all right." The black horse bobbed its head and began to settle. Riley grabbed hold of both reins in one hand, just below the horse's chin, then he placed his other hand above the horse's nostrils until the animal calmed. The driver set the brake and relaxed. Riley's gaze shifted to the woman, and he sucked in a breath.

Miranda.

◄——— ★ ———►

Annie helped Mrs. Alton finish up the last of the lunch dishes while Tess and Henry put the younger children down for their afternoon rest. Riley hadn't come in to eat—again. His plate still sat beside the one Mrs. Alton would deliver to her husband. One of the children had mentioned hearing someone arrive just before they sat down, but then Annie had gotten involved with the meal and forgotten about it until now.

Curiosity drove her to the window. A fancy buggy sat in front of the barn, and a colored man stood beside it, looking as if he were talking to the horse. From where she stood, she couldn't tell if Riley was on the other side of the animal or not.

"What you looking at, child? I hope nobody sees you peeking out that window."

Annie drew back. "There's a buggy out there with a colored man standing beside it."

"Guess he must have come to see Mr. Morgan, since nobody has knocked on the door." Mrs. Alton looked around the clean room, a satisfied smile on her face. "I'll mosey on home and give Chester his lunch. See you in a few hours."

Annie waved and checked the room again. What would happen to everything? The dishes and cooking pots would be sold with the house. Or perhaps there would be a sale to get rid of everything. She shuddered at the thought of the townsfolk haggling over their household items.

Pushing open the back door, she stepped outside into the afternoon sunlight. She probably ought to weed the garden, but she was afraid to do that chore with Riley around. She feared having to explain how she managed to do such a task if she couldn't see.

Now that she'd given her heart to God, her lying bothered her even more. But how was she going to get out of the mess she'd created without hurting people?

She plopped down on the back step. What was she going to do?

Until she came to the Wilcox School, she'd never had anyone look at her with anything but contempt. She'd been a street urchin. A guttersnipe. Most people didn't even waste the time of day to glance at her, which had made picking their pockets easier and more rewarding. The ones who had looked down had usually sneered and gone out of their way to walk around her. It wasn't until she came to Waco that folks treated her like a real person, even though many still cast her odd looks because they thought her to be blind.

If she told them that she'd tricked them all these years, they would hate her. The easiest thing would be to just leave town and go somewhere else. But that felt like the coward's way out. What would God expect of her? She knew the Ten Commandments prohibited stealing, but she hadn't read anything in the Bible about lying. Still, she knew it was wrong, but she had no idea what to do to remedy the situation.

A woman's raised voice pulled Annie to her feet. She stared at the barn. Why would a woman be in there talking to Riley?

She longed to sneak over there and listen, but that was hardly proper behavior for a woman—especially a newly professing Christian. And besides, the driver was still standing by the buggy and would see her. Wandering alongside the house, she wandered toward the servant. The horse lifted its head, ears flicked forward, and watched her. The man turned around also, and his eyes widened for a moment then he ducked his head.

"Afternoon." Annie turned her body so she could view the barn without the man noticing, but all she could see was the back of the woman's pink bell-shaped dress. A silk dress, if she wasn't mistaken. With spiraling black trim all around the bottom. A matching bonnet covered her head, but the edge of her curled dark hair peeked out below it. Lest she appear interested, Annie forced her attention back to the servant. "Would you or your horse care for some water?"

He shook his head. "Nah, miss, but thank you kindly. I just watered Jasper when we passed through town."

Annie noticed he didn't mention being thirsty himself, but she let it slide. "All right then. I should probably head back inside. Good day."

The man nodded. As she turned, her gaze was drawn back to the barn. She could hear the trill of the woman's voice but couldn't make out what she was saying. The woman backed up a few steps, and Annie hurried to get around the side of the house before being seen. She hoped Riley had been so taken up in his conversation that he hadn't noticed her. As soon as she rounded the corner, she clung to the side of the house like a tree frog, and peeked toward the barn.

The woman backed up several more steps, bringing her outside and into clear view. "Well, I certainly never—" She spun around and marched toward the buggy, her lips pulled tight as if she'd sucked on a lemon.

Annie shrank back and hurried up the porch steps and into the house. She scurried to the window and peered out. Riley stood in the yard, arms crossed, staring at the buggy.

◄——— ★ ———►

Riley stomped out of the barn. "I came home expecting to marry you."

She paused beside her buggy, looking more angry than sad. "I'm sorry, Riley. I tried waiting, but I was wasting the best years of my life. You could at least try to understand."

"I was busy trying to stay alive, Miranda. Men were shooting loaded guns at me." He yanked off his hat and smacked it against his leg. *Why couldn't she think of someone other than herself?* "I wrote you as often as I could. I can't help it if you didn't receive all of my letters."

Miranda's lips pinched tight, an expression Riley remembered well. "I can see now that coming here was a mistake. I just felt I owed you an apology for not trying harder to notify you about my marriage. It all happened rather suddenly." She waved her gloved hand in the air. "I felt bad when Mother told me that you had showed up at the door expecting to find me at home." Miranda turned her back to him, and her driver offered his hand to assist her. She hiked up her nose and her skirt, climbed in the phaeton, and turned back to him. "I just arrived at Mother's yesterday and was too exhausted to attend the revival, but Mother did, and she told me you showed up at the revival last night with a pretty blonde on your arm. You can't be too heartbroken if you've already replaced me." She swiped her hand at the driver, who hurried around to the other side of the buggy and climbed in.

Riley moved toward her, not wanting to holler the thoughts on his mind. "That was Annie, and she's blind. I was helping her."

"That's not what Mother said." She faced the front, and the driver clucked to the horse. The buggy—a brand-new one if he wasn't mistaken—rolled forward without so much as a squeak. The driver made a wide turn, and Riley heard the back door bang. It was just as well that Miranda left before he had to explain her presence. He watched her ride away, nose stuck up in the air. She was a pretty thing with her dark hair and fiery blue eyes, but she was as spoiled as three-day-old fish. He didn't need her. Was probably better off without her. But the fact that she'd chosen someone over him still rankled him.

He saw it clearly now; she would never have been happy married to him. He came from a family who had a decent home and land, but they weren't wealthy, by any means. Miranda was better off with a man who apparently could give her the things she was accustomed to.

He rubbed the back of his neck and stared down the road at the buggy as it grew smaller. Truth be told, he was glad she'd come. Now he'd not have to wonder about her. She seemed happy enough with her decision, not that there was much to be done now.

He walked back to the barn, relieved to have that chapter

of his life over. Maybe one day he'd find another woman that he'd want to marry.

He snatched up a pitchfork and began tossing down clumps of hay into a stall. He tried thinking of the ranch and how he needed to find a buyer—of how he still needed to write that letter to his uncle and other relatives—even thought of his parents, but after a moment, Annie appeared in his mind.

Somehow he had to find a way to remedy that. He couldn't fall in love with Annie. She wasn't the kind of woman he ever thought he'd be interested in.

No, she was spunky, a hard worker, sassy at times. He leaned on the handle of the pitchfork and grinned. Oh, yeah, she was sassy.

But she was also loving and kind—at least to the children.

He set the pitchfork in the corner and climbed down to the ground floor. Maybe staying here until the school closed wasn't the best of ideas.

CHAPTER SEVENTEEN

With clean sheets on all the beds, the children resting, and Laura upstairs in their room writing the first of the letters to the parents about the school closing, Annie needed something to do. She wandered the house, memorizing each and every item—the way the chairs were neatly tucked under the table, the way the blue gingham curtains were pulled back and fluttering in the warm afternoon breeze. Trying not to think of the woman who had visited Riley, she walked out onto the front porch and sat down. But questions battered her mind.

Who was that woman in the fancy clothes with that nice buggy? Why had she come to see him?

Jumping restlessly to her feet, she paced the porch. Why did that woman have to show up just when Annie realized how much she was starting to like Riley?

She leaned against a post and stared up at the blue-gray sky. She hoped the clouds would fill with rain and dump their load, cooling things down, but she wasn't going to hold her breath. "Father God, it sure would be nice to have some rain."

She cleared her throat. Talking to God, especially out loud, felt strange—awkward. But maybe with practice it would get easier. "God, I sure hope You've got a plan for me. I have no idea what to do when the school closes. If it pleases You, Lord, would You work a miracle and keep it open?"

The town drew her gaze. She ached to go talk to Reverend James to share her dilemma and seek his wise advice. Talking to him after the service was difficult. Others vied for his attention, and she and Laura needed to get the children home and to bed, and she had to have someone escort her back if she stayed.

Ambling across the porch, she glanced over at the barn. Loud hammering emanated from inside, but she couldn't see Riley. She glanced over her shoulder at the empty road. If she hurried to town, maybe she could see the reverend and get back before anyone missed her.

Before she could change her mind, she pushed her feet into motion, hurried down the steps, and out the front gate. She kept an eye out for travelers, but not a soul was on the road midafternoon. Holding her hand over her eyes to shade them from the hot sun, she bemoaned the fact that she hadn't taken time to get her straw hat. But it was upstairs in her room, and if she went to retrieve it, Laura would pelt her with questions.

As she entered the peaceful town, she drew to the far side of the road and slowed her pace, going from hitching post to hitching post, keeping one hand touching the rough wood, in case anyone was watching. It seem that everyone was taking an afternoon siesta from the hot summer sun. Several businesses had their doors open, and not a single person stood out on the boardwalk talking. There was just one horse—a black with four white stockings—tethered straight ahead in front of the bathhouse.

Turning, she hurried down a side street until she reached the town square. The empty area looked so different from when it had been filled with people. A layer of dust coated the many wooden benches sitting in haphazard rows. Hmmm. Where could the minister be? Keeping her eyes trained on the courthouse, she felt her way along the benches and she meandered to the front, sitting down in the shade of a pecan tree. The minister wasn't there, but she could still sense God's presence.

"Lord, what should I do? Should I tell everyone the truth—that I faked being blind—and have them hate me, or make things easy on myself and the children, and just go away and start over someplace new?"

The idea of leaving Waco left her shivering in spite of the heat. This place had become her haven of rescue. The only place she'd ever had true friends. And yet, she stood to lose them if they knew the truth. There was no easy answer.

"Well, howdy, miss." Reverend James strolled across the square, holding something in one hand. He touched the tip of his hat in greeting, his wide smile chasing away any apprehension Annie had about coming to see him. She guessed the man to be in his late forties, probably about the same age as her daddy, if he was still alive.

"Good afternoon, Reverend." Annie stood. "I was wondering if I could speak to you about something."

He glanced around. "I reckon so." He set down the plate that covered what Annie guessed was a slice of pie then pulled another bench over a respectable distance in front of hers. He held out his hand. "Please—Miss Sheffleld, isn't it?"

Annie nodded.

"Have a seat, miss."

Annie obliged and straightened her skirts before looking up. "Please don't let me keep you from eating."

He glanced at his plate then his puzzled gaze shot back to hers. "How did you know I had something to eat?"

She ducked her head, uncomfortable with his stare. "Well, I smell something sweet, and it thumped when you set it down."

"Ah, of course." He visibly relaxed.

He so easily believed her deception, and tricking him made her feel as low as a wagon without wheels. Tears filled Annie's eyes, and the years of lying and deception overcame her.

The reverend leaned toward her. "What's the matter, child? Are you doubting your conversion?"

She pressed her lips together and shook her head. "It isn't that, Reverend. I know I'm different, I can tell, but . . . but . . . I've—" She shook her head, unable to voice the hideous words. She couldn't bear to see the grimace of disgust that would surely form on his face when he learned the truth.

He rested his elbows on his knees and clasped his hands in front of him. "I know it can be difficult to speak of some things, and if you'd prefer to confide in a woman, I'm sure I could find one who would be happy to listen." He sat up and looked around, but not seeing a woman he thought might help, resumed his position. "Or, if you're comfortable, I'm a good listener. Baring one's soul can make a person feel better. Freer."

She had to tell him, but she hadn't expected confessing to be so hard. She steadied herself and took a deep breath. Long ago, she'd learned that if you had something unpleasant to do, it was best to do it quickly and get it over with. Glancing up, she dared to look into his eyes. "I've been living a lie for the past seven years, sir, and before that, I was a thief."

His brow crinkled, as if he were struggling with a thought. A faint, indulgent smile twittered on his lips. "Everyone lies at one time or another, even me, although I try very hard not to."

"But I bet you've never stolen anything."

He looked off to his left, staring across the square. "Not since I was a child, and my father took a switch to my hind end and made me return the items to the mercantile." He grinned. "I had to work a week to repay ol' Mr. Thatch, even though I only snitched a few lemon drops. But I learned my lesson."

Annie twisted her hands. She'd known stealing was wrong, but the only consequences she'd faced, other than having to outrun the person she'd robbed, were those she suffered when she returned empty-handed. If her father had found a place to sleep inside, he would make her stay out in the cold or the rain and go without dinner. She learned to steal to survive, but she'd never liked it. If only she could pay back all those people, but their money and their valuables were long gone—all except for the one watch she'd buried.

"When you repented of your sins last night, God forgave them, Miss Sheffield. He takes a dirty vessel—us—and when we repent, He washes us clean by the blood of His Son, Jesus, who died on the cross to set us free. Do you understand?" His kind eyes gazed upon her face, as if begging her to believe him.

She nodded. "Yes, but what if I've sinned today?"

He smiled. "We all sin every day, whether in a lustful thought, or gossiping, or hating a neighbor whose cow destroyed part of our garden. We're human, and humans sin. Just continue to ask God's forgiveness."

She took a deep breath. It sounded so simple. "But what if everyone believes a lie about you? How do I go about fixing that?" She stared into his eyes and didn't look away. It had been so long since she'd done that with anyone but Miss Laura and Mrs. Alton that she squirmed on the bench.

The minister stared at her for a long moment then his brows lifted. "You can see?"

Annie broke his gaze and stared at the grass smashed down from yesterday's crowd. She nodded.

"Praise the Lord."

Her gaze jerked up. What an odd reaction.

"I felt so bad that you couldn't see after talking with you, that I prayed half the night for a miracle for you, now we have it. You're such a young, pret—uh, never mind." He lifted his head toward heaven, as if praying. "I see your dilemma. Everyone in this town thinks you're blind?"

She nodded. "Everyone, that is, except Miss Laura and Mrs. Alton, our cook. You see, I was just thirteen years old when my father abandoned me in Waco." Even after so long, saying the words pricked her heart. A wagon pulled by two bays drove down the street with a thin man guiding them. "After three days, I was starving and filthy. I found the Wilcox School for Blind Children, and Miss Laura didn't have the heart to turn me out, even though she knew I was just pretending to be blind." Her eyes stung again. "You see, I'd never had a home before. Hadn't worn a dress, been clean, or had a full stomach in years. Everything I wanted was at that school—but I wasn't blind. And Mr. Morrow insisted that only blind children could live there."

The reverend sat back, hands in his lap. "That is quite a quandary."

"I know. For a long while I've wanted to end the charade, but I didn't want Miss Laura to get into trouble. And what will the children think?" She blinked her eyes and wiped her cheek when a tear trickled down. "I don't want them to hate me. I—I couldn't bear it."

"They won't." He shook his head. "Children are sympathetic and resilient. Once they learn why you did what you did, well, I think you'll be surprised. Most will probably be happy that you aren't blind."

His words soothed her worry. "But what about the townsfolk?"

"Well, you'll face a harder road there. Adults are far less forgiving than young'uns. Still, I think you need to come clean, for your own sake. You won't have peace in your heart as long as you continue to deceive people."

Annie watched a blue jay soar toward them then land on the stage. She'd always admired the pretty birds even though they often bullied smaller creatures.

He caught her gaze. "What about that young man who escorted you last night? Does he know the truth?"

She nibbled her lower lip and shook her head. "No, and I have no idea how to tell him. He'll hate me for deceiving him."

"I'm sorry I don't know the man, but if he cares for you as I suspect he does, once he gets over the shock, I imagine he'll be delighted."

"Why?" Annie couldn't hide her surprise at his comment.

The man smiled. "What if you learned one of those children you love so much wasn't really blind? Wouldn't you be happy for them?"

"Of course, but this is different. I've tried very hard not to lie to him, but I've still had to pretend not to see when I've been around Riley." She shook her head. "I'm sure he'll hate me for tricking him."

"Then he doesn't care about you as much as I think he does."

She stared into his eyes and saw nothing but seriousness there. Dare she hope he could be right?

"Now, how do you intend to tell the town? Would you like to come up front tonight and get it over with all at once?"

Annie gasped and shook her head. "No. No, I'm not ready yet. And I feel I need to tell the children—and Riley—first."

The reverend's moustache wiggled while he worked his mouth, thinking. He nodded. "That would be the wise thing.

I'll be here tomorrow night also. If you're ready by then, just let me know. I'm happy to stand up beside you and offer my support."

Annie smiled. "Thank you, Reverend James. I appreciate your offer, but I do hope you won't be disappointed if I need more time to prepare myself."

"Not at all. I'll keep you in my prayers. God will tell you when the time is right, as you continue to seek Him."

She stood, feeling better. If she didn't get back soon, she'd be missed. "I'm much obliged to you, sir. Your visit has changed my life."

"Thank you. I appreciate your telling me." He smiled. "See you tonight?"

Annie nodded, her burden feeling lighter than it had in a long time.

"I'll be praying for you—and your young man."

She opened her mouth to explain that Riley was just a friend, but decided she rather liked the idea of him as her young man. She smiled. "Thank you."

A few people were around—a couple strolling on the west side of the square, the man who drove the wagon had stopped in front of the feed store, and two children played tag up the street. Annie really needed to hurry before someone she knew stopped her or Riley came looking. It would be hard to explain being in town alone.

Taking a shortcut, she dodged down an alley, quickening her pace as she all but ran past the rear of a saloon. Empty bottles dried on the back porch, awaiting refilling. The place reeked like an outhouse, and she didn't stop to consider why. Two buildings down sat another saloon, an even more dilapidated one. Something flapping out an upstairs window drew her attention, and she glanced up. Her mouth dropped open. Waving like a flag was a frilly, red corset. All she could do was stare. She didn't even know they came in red—with black lace.

As she started to cross an alley, she noticed two men standing in the front of the alley, next to the saloon. She ducked back, and peeked around the corner, holding her breath and hoping they hadn't seen her. She shuddered, realizing how precarious a position she was in. If a man were to discover her alone, hiding behind a saloon—fingers of fear clawed their way down her spine. *Protect me, Father, please.*

She weighed her options. Run across the alley and hope they didn't see her? Wait until they left and hope someone didn't come out of the saloon and find her? But she needed to get back as soon as possible. Laura would worry if she went looking and couldn't find her, especially since she hadn't left a note. Peering around the corner again, her breath lodged in her throat, as if she'd sucked a piece of food down her windpipe. One of the men was the odious Otis Ramsey.

Why was Ramsey still in town? She thought he had slithered back to wherever he'd come from by now. She couldn't let him of all people find her in town alone. The way he'd looked at her back at the school made her want to run to the Brazos, jump in, and scrub herself clean. Looking back the way she'd come, she contemplated making a wide arc, doubling back, and then going the long way home, but that would take more time, and she would surely run into people who knew her.

Mr. Ramsey bellowed a laugh. "It won't be long before that property is mine, as it rightfully should be. I sure outsmarted those dimwitted females."

Annie silenced her gasp with a hand over her mouth. The hair on her arms stood on end. Was he talking about her and Laura, or some other women? Fred Barker, the man talking to Mr. Ramsey, was known around town as a troublemaker. Annie's curiosity soared. Why would Ramsey be talking to him?

Turning away from the saloon, Mr. Ramsey stepped up onto the boardwalk. He muttered something about a buyer then disappeared from her view. Mr. Barker turned her way. She gulped and shrank back, plastering herself against the wall of the saloon. Rank smells rose up around her, and through the wall, she heard a deep laugh. The man's footsteps grew closer.

Annie's gaze darted left and right, but there was no place to hide. She slid toward the back door of the saloon, a door propped open with a small barrel, holding sand and cigar stubs. Without taking time to think what she was doing, she dashed inside, and placed her hand over her pounding heart. *Please don't let him come in here.*

Just to her right was a closed door, and behind it the person who'd been laughing. She could hear the shuffle of feet from inside the room. If anyone opened that door, she'd be found. Across the entryway was a room with a lock on the door—the liquor room, she surmised. Sweat trickled down her back, and she felt as if insects were crawling up and down her arms, and she rubbed them. She never dreamed she'd ever be in a saloon. If she wasn't so nervous about what could happen and wasn't so pressed for time, she just might tiptoe to the front and see what the inside of a saloon actually looked like. But even though Mrs. Alton wasn't there, Annie could hear her scolding. "Girl, have you taken leave of your sense?"

Peering out the door, Annie released her breath. If Mr. Barker was coming in the back entrance of the saloon, he would have been there by now.

With no one in sight, she rushed out the door and quickened her pace as she passed a pair of rickety privies. Something thudded against the side of one, and she nearly jumped out of her skin. A loud keening rose up. Annie skidded to a stop. Had someone locked up a dog? Other than mistreating children, the thing she despised most was people mistreating animals.

Besides the foul stench, a privy was dreadfully hot on a day like today, even one with so many cracks in it. "Anybody there?" She waited a moment and glanced around, reached for the door, then gave it a yank. It stuck.

The whimpering inside silenced, as if the creature was holding its breath, awaiting escape.

With two hands on the handle and one foot braced again the doorframe, she wrenched the door open on a loud creak. Her fingers flew to her mouth, as she stared inside, unable to believe what she saw.

A small, filthy child let out a screech and cowered down, looking at her with wide blue eyes.

CHAPTER EIGHTEEN

*A*s you can see, the land is good and fertile, but the house needs some work," Riley said to the land agent as they walked around the house he'd grown up in. For the ninetieth time, he wondered if he was doing the right thing in selling the place. A shaft of sunlight reflected off a piece of broken glass, making him squint. He should have returned home, picked up all the shards, and fixed the place up like he'd planned, but something kept holding him back.

"It does need some work, but at least it's not a sod house or a dugout. Whoever buys the place won't have to build from scratch. That's generally a plus." Mr. Johnson pushed on the side wall. "The chinking needs patching, but the wood is sturdy, and the windows need to be replaced. 'Course, there are still plenty of people who prefer not to have glass in their windows since it's expensive and breaks easily and it blocks the flow of air. That's an important thing to consider here where it gets so hot."

Riley nodded, remembering the day his pa had surprised

his ma with the new glass. She'd been prouder than a hen that had laid her first egg. The first few days after his pa had put in the windows, she'd insisted on keeping them shut—to keep the dust out. He grinned. The temperature in the house had risen so high by evening supper, they'd all been nearly as roasted as the prairie chickens they'd eaten. His pa had grumbled about returning the windows and had taken his plate outside to finish eating where it was cooler.

"I doubt I'll have any trouble selling your property, Mr. Morgan."

Riley wasn't sure if that was good news or not. "With the war just being over and people so strapped for cash—not to mention what happened here—well . . . I figured it might take a while to sell the ranch."

Mr. Johnson nodded. "Things with the Indians are settling down and will even more with all our men coming back, and that's true about cash being tight. But there are many folks leaving the South and coming to Texas where the war was kinder. And they're not all poor folks." The land agent rubbed his index finger over his thin mustache. "I feel certain I can get the price we discussed and maybe even more."

Nodding, Riley scanned the familiar dips in the land, the trees, and the picket enclosure up on the hill. He felt like a traitor selling off the land his father had loved and the house his ma had made into a home, but he needed a fresh start. He needed a place where the memories didn't haunt him, and if he got the price he was asking, he could do just that. Start over somewhere else.

"Mind if I go inside?" Mr. Johnson asked.

"No, go ahead and have a look around, though things are still a bit of a mess. I'll just walk up the hill until you're done."

The man glanced where Riley pointed, and nodded.

Riley couldn't help wondering if this was one of the last

times he'd visit his family cemetery. A heaviness weighed down his steps, and the walk seemed far longer than the last time he'd come. He opened the gate of the thigh-high fence and stepped inside the small graveyard. A blackbird squawked at him and hopped along the fence top, then flew off. Grass and weeds battled the few wildflowers that covered the graves. If not for the slight humps in the ground and the five crosses, not a soul would know that a family rested there. A whole family, save one.

His throat tightened as he removed his hat out of respect for his family. Would his parents still be alive if he hadn't ridden off the day Timothy died? If he hadn't gone to war?

His lips trembled, and he tried to stop them, but could not. He placed his hand over his mouth and chin to still them, and then his eyes started watering. Staring up at the sky, he blinked, determined to regain control. He couldn't have the land agent see him blubbering like a baby. Sniffing, he stooped down, gathered up the dried bundle of wildflowers he'd left last time he visited, and flung them over the fence. Then he tossed aside a small limb that had fallen from the oak overhead and plucked several weeds. *Would the new owners tend the graves? Or would the fence and crosses rot until one day there was nothing but a hill here, like when they first arrived?*

Riley blew out a deep breath. He couldn't have it both ways. He could stay, tend the graves himself, and try to rebuild his life here, with all the memories of the tragic events that had occurred like an albatross around his neck. Or he could leave and get a fresh start.

Standing, he made his decision. This place would always hold a special place in his heart, but it was not his future. Some of his army buddies had been from Dallas, a relatively new town, and he had a hankering to go there and see if its land was as rich as they'd said. He allowed his gaze to rove the property again. Other than his family, his only real regret was losing all his father's horses. He'd hoped to continue the line of Morgan horses, but maybe once he was settled, he could buy some stock animals from his uncle. "Please keep watch over this land and my family, Lord. Send someone here who will tend this place and not let my family be forgotten."

He stared at each grave—those of his parents, his younger brother, and the babies he'd never known. Then he slapped his hat on and headed down the hill. At least *he* would never forget them, that was certain.

An hour later, he drove back to the school with the wagon loaded with food he'd rescued from his ma's root cellar. Crates filled with jars of canned peaches, apples, green beans, and so much more, clinked in the bed of the wagon behind him. There was no sense letting it all go to waste or leaving it for the next family when the children at the school needed the food. His mother would appreciate knowing the food she worked so hard on was going to such a good cause.

He started to turn into the schoolyard, but noticed a woman and child walking up the road. The lady's blue dress swayed like a bell, and she held the hand of a small blond child—a boy if the pants were an indication. He glanced at the woman again.

Annie.

What was she doing walking from town without someone escorting her? Foolish woman. Didn't her experience with those raiders prove how dangerous it was for a female to be walking without an escort? Especially one who couldn't see.

Shaking his head and the reins, he clucked to the horse and guided it into the yard, and parked under a tree. With his jaw clamped down so tight his teeth might crack, he set the brake and jumped down, his long legs swallowing up the ground between him and the fearless woman. He'd be surprised if steam wasn't spewing from his ears by the time he reached her. "Where in the world have you been?"

She merely blinked and smiled, as if his accosting her on the road was an everyday occurrence. "I took a walk into town."

Riley's eyes widened. "Are you daft? Are you just begging for something bad to happen?" He stomped to the edge of the road, hands on hips, and stared out at the wilderness. "What if you got off the road and wandered out there?" He swatted his hand in the air. "Don't you know there's all kinds of critters in there?"

Annie walked and stopped beside him, the child cowering against her far side. "What?"

"How can you stay on the road when you can't even see it? You're a brave, spunky woman, Annie Sheffield, but you're not invincible." There. He'd finally said what was bothering him.

"I never said I was invincible. And if I get off the road, the grasses and flowers brush against my dress."

Her sensible response cooled some of his irritation. So she knew how to not get lost. But she was still defenseless. "Annie, why didn't you ask me to take you to town? I'd have been glad to."

She poked the pert nose in the air. "You weren't here, as I recall."

"You could have waited."

"I didn't know where you were or how long you'd be gone, and I had to get back before anyone noticed me gone." She sucked in a breath and covered her mouth with her fingertips.

Riley pushed his hat up off his forehead, suspecting there was more to the story than she was telling. "Why?"

She looked down at the boy, patted his cheek, then turned back. "All your gruffness is scaring Josh."

He peered down at the filthy child who had buried his

face in Annie's skirt, as if she were his mother. Who was he, and where had he come from? Leave it to Annie to bring home a stray child as if he were a pet. Regret for frightening the waif forced him to take a deep breath before speaking again. "Annie, you can't be wandering the streets alone, not when you can't . . ." He waved his hand in the air as if she could see it. "You know."

She scowled. "Didn't you hear me? Your barking like a guard dog is frightening Josh." She turned around and bent toward the boy. "It's all right, Josh. This is Mr. Morgan. He might sound cross, but you don't have to be afraid of him. He works at our school."

The boy peeked around Annie and stared at him. Light streams cut a path through the grime on his face, as if he'd been crying. Cautious blue eyes studied him. Riley smiled and squatted down on his boot heels, hoping to make amends for scaring the boy. "That's right. I do odd jobs at the school and tend the animals. Do you like horses?"

Josh nodded and then ducked his head, as if expressing his opinion was not something he was used to doing.

Riley stood, and leaned toward Annie, lowering his voice. "Where did you find him?"

"In town."

"I gathered that since that's where you're returning from. Care to be more specific?" He started walking, just to keep up with Annie.

She hiked her chin and kept the boy on her far side. "What does it matter? He's an orphan in need. I could hardly walk off and just leave him, could I?"

"Are you aware he can see?"

She stumbled, but righted herself before he could reach out. "That doesn't matter."

"What about the rules?"

Annie frowned. "Rules aren't important when a life is at stake. And besides, why should rules matter now that the school is closing?"

One way or the other, he had to make her realize that she wasn't invincible, but she did make a good point. He peered down at the stubborn set of her chin. For someone who made such foolish choices at times, he had to admit she had thought this subject through. He lightly took hold of her arm, and she stiffened. "Here, let me guide you before you march clear past the school."

Though her scowl remained, she allowed him to help her. She may have thought she'd dodged his questioning about why she had no escort, but she was wrong. The first time they were alone, she would get a lecture.

———— ★ ————

Annie couldn't wait to get inside the school and escape Riley's questions. Why did she have to run into him, of all people? If he'd just been another few minutes returning in the wagon, she'd have been safely inside, and he'd never have seen her.

What would Riley say if he knew she'd been behind a saloon all by herself? Or that she found Josh in a privy?

In spite of it all, she bit back a grin as she imagined those beautiful eyes of his widening in shock.

He stomped up the steps and held the door open for her. The delicious odor of stew wafted her way.

"I've got to get the wagon unloaded, but don't think this is the last of our conversation. You can't put yourself in danger like that, Annie. I just about had apoplexy seeing you all alone on that road."

She lifted her chin, secretly happy that he was concerned, but too stubborn to acquiesce. "I wasn't alone. Josh was with me."

He snorted a laugh and leaned into her face. "A fat lot of help that little guy would be if someone tried to toss you over their saddle and ride off."

He was right, whether she could see or not. Neither she nor Laura should be walking into town alone, but it was impossible for them to both go every time there was a need. "I have to get Josh cleaned up and talk to Laura."

He nodded. "All right. We'll talk later."

"About *what*?" She lifted her face and tried to sound coy.

He tweaked her nose. "You know *what*." He backed out the door, spun around, and trotted down the steps. The longer he stayed and ate Mrs. Alton's food, the healthier he looked. His sunken cheeks had filled in, and the dull flicker in his eyes when he first returned to Waco had brightened to that of a prairie fire. She sighed.

"Annie's back." Tess cocked her head from the table where she and the younger girls were counting buttons. "And somebody's with her—a small child, I'm guessing."

Laura strode in from the kitchen, drying her hands with a towel. She glanced at Josh, her eyebrows lifted, and then her questioning gaze shot to Annie's. Crossing the room, she bent down in front of the boy. "I'm Miss Laura, and this is my school. What's your name?" She spoke gently.

He ducked back behind Annie, and Laura straightened. "Tess, come here please."

The girl did as told. She stopped next to Miss Laura and tilted her head up. "Yes, ma'am?"

Laura brushed her hand across the girl's shoulder. "Miss Annie has brought us a new guest. Would you please take him in the kitchen to Mrs. Alton? He needs a good scrubbing, then I'm sure he would enjoy some of our cook's delicious apple bread and a glass of milk, if there's any left."

At the mention of food, Josh crept out of hiding.

Annie patted his head. "It's all right, Josh. You're safe here."

He looked up at her, as if measuring her words. *What kind of life had he lived to be so fearful?*

"You go with Tess, and I'll be right here. I promise. I just need to talk to Miss Laura for a few minutes, and then I'll come and sit with you. All right?"

He nodded. Annie placed his little hand in Tess's, and the girl led him toward the kitchen. At the door, he glanced back over his shoulder at Annie with eyes that melted her heart, and she smiled to reassure him.

"Let's talk on the porch," Miss Laura said.

"I can't." Annie shook her head. "What if he looks for me and doesn't find me? I don't want him any more frightened than he already is."

"Then come over here."

Annie followed Laura to the far corner of the parlor. "Where did you find that boy, and why did you bring him here?"

She bit her lip, wondering just how much to tell Laura. She wouldn't be happy to learn what she'd done.

"I see the wheels of that quick mind of yours turning. You might as well tell me the truth and be done with it."

She blew out a breath. "All right. When you and the children were resting, I went into town to talk to Reverend James."

Laura's eyes widened. "Alone?"

Annie hesitated, then nodded.

Laura leaned back against the wall, and shook her head. "I might have known you weren't out working in the garden. Who does the boy belong to?"

"I can hardly bear to say the word out loud."

"Just say it. How bad can it be?"

"All right then." She leaned close to Laura and whispered. "He's the child of a—a—lady of the night."

"And what's he doing here?"

"His mother died last week, and he's been living in a saloon. The man who runs it didn't want him—said all Josh did was cry and that he was too little to do any substantial work—so he gave him to me."

Laura pinched the bridge of her nose. "You are aware he is sighted, aren't you?"

Annie rolled her eyes at the ridiculous question. "Of course I am. I'm not blind, you know." She peered over her shoulder to make sure none of the children had overheard her sarcastic remark, but the three girls were busy practicing their arithmetic by counting and sorting buttons.

Laura giggled and shook her head. "Only you would say something like that."

"Well, what was I supposed to do? The man I talked to behind the saloon didn't want him, and you can see how neglected he is. I just couldn't leave him there to be mistreated. He's so little and sad, Laura."

"All right. I understand. I don't guess it matters since we're closing anyway. I'll fix him some bathwater and get him cleaned up. I don't suppose he has any clothes, does he?"

Annie shrugged. "I don't think so. That man didn't give me any. He just said that Josh was three, and his mother's name was Lotus."

"He can stay here for now, but I don't know what we'll do with him when the school closes."

Annie smiled. "Thank you. I knew you'd understand. I just couldn't leave him behind. Kind of like how you couldn't say no when I first arrived."

Laura nodded then wandered over to the table and sat down with the girls, while Annie hurried to the kitchen. Josh glanced up from eating the apple bread and watched her. His solemn expression made her heart ache. What had he endured living in such an awful place? Had his mother treated him well? Had she loved him?

She must have for him to miss her so badly.

A knock sounded, the back door flew open, and Riley entered, carrying a crate on one shoulder. Josh leapt from his chair and dove under the table, cowering against Annie's legs. Mrs. Alton shook her head. What had the poor boy endured?

"It's all right, Josh. It's just Mr. Morgan." Annie ducked her head and patted the youngster's shoulder. "Remember?"

Josh peeked out at Riley, then climbed back up on his chair and resumed cramming the apple bread in his mouth by handfuls. Riley watched them for a moment, and Annie found it hard to avoid making eye contact with him.

"Where do you want this, Mrs. Alton? It's some food from my ma's cellar. There's lots more in the wagon, too."

The older woman clapped her hands to her cheeks, her wide smile reflected in her eyes. "Why, bless your heart, Riley Morgan. What a kind, thoughtful thing to do."

Riley smiled and set the crate on the end of the table. "It's what Ma would have wanted."

Annie wondered if sharing the food his mother had prepared was hard for him. He didn't have much to remember his folks by, and now there would be even less, because of his generosity. Riley Morgan was a kind man.

CHAPTER NINETEEN

nnie tucked Josh into a spare bed in the boys' room. Clean and with his long, blond hair cut to look like a boy, he was a cute little thing. His big blue eyes stared up at her. All day he'd followed her around, preferring to stay by her side rather than interact with the other children. His lower lip wobbled, tugging at her heart. Annie cupped his cheek. Poor little thing. "Don't you worry, sweetie, Rusty and Henry will be right here, and I'm right down the hall. If you need to go to the privy, just wake Henry, or come and get me. I'll leave the upstairs parlor lantern lit so you can see. All right?"

Josh glanced at Henry, as if the older boy frightened him.

"I'll be glad to help you get to the privy if you need to go." Henry flopped over onto his side and laid his head on his arm. He yawned, soliciting a yawn from Josh.

"Me, too," Rusty added.

"See, Henry's a nice boy and so is Rusty. Everyone here is kind, so please don't be afraid." She smiled. "We'll take care of you."

His eyelids drooped, but he popped them open again. Annie brushed her hand over his hair and hummed a hymn. Soon, both of the younger boys were asleep. She stood and tiptoed toward the door. "Goodnight, Henry. Sleep tight."

"He sure don't talk much, does he? Wonder why?"

"He's missing his mama, and he's in a strange place with a bunch of people he doesn't know. I don't think we should expect too much out of him just yet."

"I know how he feels." Henry pushed up onto his elbows, his face turned toward her. "You think it would help if I told him about when my mom died?"

"That might help, but keep it simple. Josh is even younger than Camilla."

Henry nodded and fell back on his bed. The floor creaked in several places as Annie walked down the hall to her room. In the upstairs parlor, instead of blowing out the lamp as she normally did, she turned it down. The blind children and she and Laura didn't need the light to find their way around, but Josh might.

In their bedroom, Laura sat reading a book. Annie walked to the window and peered out. She was glad that it had taken a while for Josh to settle down and go to sleep, because she so disliked going to bed when the sun hadn't set. Twilight was settling in, and the night creatures were winding up. The fingernail moon barely illuminated the silhouette of the barn. Was Riley already sleeping? She'd managed to avoid him most of the day by staying in the house and helping Josh learn his way around, but she knew that he would pester her with questions the first chance he got.

"I'm sorry that you didn't get to go to the revival tonight. I know the reverend's sermon really touched you, but with Josh coming—well, it would have confused him to go back to town so soon."

Annie turned around. Laura's book lay open across her chest, and the light from the lamp cast dancing shadows on the wall. "I know you're right, but I sure did want to go. Maybe tomorrow night."

"We'll see how the boy does tomorrow and then decide." Laura caught Annie's gaze and her eyebrows lifted. "Now that everyone is asleep, you can no longer evade me. I want to hear the whole story." Her expression said that she wouldn't take no for an answer.

Sighing, Annie headed for her bed and plopped down. "It all started when I discovered a woman visiting Riley."

Laura's mouth opened, and her no-nonsense expression sparked with interest. "What woman?"

Annie shook her head. "I don't know, but she was all dressed up in a fancy gown—silk, if I'm not mistaken, and she had a new buggy that didn't even show any wear, and a colored driver."

Setting the book aside, Laura sat up. "What did she want?"

Annie hiked her chin in the air and crossed her arms over her chest. "Did you expect me to eavesdrop?"

Leaning forward, Laura's eyes gleamed. "Of course. How else are we to know anything?"

Grinning, she relaxed her stance. "I tried, but that servant was out there and would have seen me. All I know is that the woman said her mother saw Riley with me at the service, and that it hadn't taken him long to find someone else."

"Oh dear. That must have been Miranda."

"And who is she?"

Laura stared in the direction of the window for a long moment. "She was Riley's fiancée, but she got married last year at Christmas, while he was off to war."

Annie gasped. "That's horrible."

"I don't think he found out until he returned home—at

least that's the story going around town." Laura shook her head. "Miranda was young and somewhat spoiled. I guess she must have gotten tired of waiting for Riley to return. I'm not condoning her actions, mind you, just trying to understand."

Annie didn't understand how a woman could be engaged to Riley and choose someone else. She stared down at her hands, her heart aching for him. Not only did he return home to find his parents dead and his home ransacked, but his fiancée married? No wonder he was so grumpy when he first came here. He had good reason.

"So what does Miranda have to do with Josh?" Laura carried her book to the desk then blew out the light, but not before Annie counted four letters stacked up and ready to go out to the children's parents. "I fail to see how the two are related."

"Just that I was upset over some things and needed someone to talk to. You were resting, I think, so I went into town and visited with the reverend."

"Annie, you didn't."

She stared into the darkness, but a tiny flicker on the lamp's wick drew her attention. "Yes, I did, but I was careful, and there were hardly any folks out and about. I went to the public square and sat on one of the benches, and a short while later, here came the reverend, as if we had an appointment. He's real easy to talk with."

"You never should have gone alone. What if those raiders had come back? They could have taken you, and I'd have never known what happened."

"I'm sorry, but it's almost as if I was compelled to go." She bolted upright. "Do you think God called me to town so I'd find Josh as I did?"

"I don't know about God having anything to do with it, but I guess it could make sense, considering how things turned out. Just where did you find the boy?"

Annie wrestled with what to tell her, but she wouldn't lie again. She was sick of lying. "Behind the One-Eyed Jack saloon."

"Annie! My word. What were you doing there?"

"Hiding." Suddenly she remembered seeing Otis Ramsey. She told Laura about nearly running into him. "And he said he'd outsmarted those dimwitted women and the property would soon be his. Do you think he meant us?"

The sheets rustled as Laura moved on her bed. "I don't want to believe that's the case, but it does stand to reason he was referring to us. Maybe I shouldn't be taking that man at face value." She paused, thinking. "In the morning, first chance I get, I'll pen a letter."

"To . . . ?"

"Mr. Morrow's lawyer."

Annie yawned and settled down again. "The man from the saloon said I could have Josh if I wanted him, just like he was giving away an unwanted puppy or a set of clothes that no longer fit him. Can you imagine such an awful thing? Said he was too young to pull his weight and all he did was cry."

"Some people can be cruel, but I sure don't know what we'll do with the boy. I'm already notifying our students' parents that they need to come and get them."

"But what if you find out that we don't have to leave?"

Laura sighed. "All this has made me realize that it's time for me to do something different."

"Like what?" Annie held her breath, afraid what that might mean for her.

"I'm not quite sure just yet." Laura squeaked out a yawn.

Annie's heart pounded as she felt it was time to make her own confession. "I'm sensing it's time to make a change too. I can't keep pretending to be blind."

Laura was silent for a long while, and Annie wondered if she'd fallen asleep. "I don't see how you can tell people without them getting upset over how we've tricked them all these years. I'd hoped when the time came, maybe we could just leave town and never have to tell people."

"I know it won't be easy, but I feel it's what God wants me to do."

"I sure hope you're right."

Annie did too. Confessing would be the hardest thing she'd ever had to do. In spite of her concern, the heaviness of sleep tugged at her. Tomorrow she'd worry, but tonight she hoped to dream of a handsome ex-soldier.

◄——— ★ ———►

Laura stared out the back door to the garden. Mrs. Alton was talking to Annie and the children about vegetables and how the different ones were cooked and used in recipes. She pulled an ear of corn off a stalk and passed it around. Laura couldn't hear what she was saying, but each child felt the silk, ran his or her hand down the husk, then handed it to the child sitting beside them. Josh sat on Annie's lap and took the corn next. After he briefly touched the silk, Annie took the ear then tickled Josh's cheek with the hair-like end. He rubbed his face against his shoulder and looked up at her with a tiny smile. The girl would make a wonderful mother when the time came.

Riley passed behind the group, carrying a fence rail over one shoulder. His head turned toward them, and a smile danced on his mouth. Was that warm smile for the children or Annie? When he first showed up, she'd been tempted to send him on his way, but they sorely needed a man's help. She and Annie were so busy keeping track of the children and tending the garden and caring for the animals that things like fence repairs, the roof, and the barn had been neglected for far too long.

She leaned against the doorjamb and smiled to herself.

Maybe Annie wouldn't be the only one to have a chance at romance. For a long while, she'd been discontent. Not that she didn't love the children and teaching them, but she wanted to be a mother—and to be a wife. Sean had been disappointed yesterday when he learned they wouldn't be attending the revival. She couldn't help wondering if he'd been looking forward to seeing her, as she had him.

The love she had once felt so strongly was flaming up anew, giving her hope for the life she'd dreamed about so many times. She resented Otis Ramsey prancing around her house like a proud peacock, but in truth, he gave her the reason she'd been looking for to make a change.

Was she being selfish? Unfair to the children? Hadn't she exhausted all her options in searching for a way to keep the school open?

Yes, she knew she had. There was really nothing else she could do. The girls would be fine going back home with their parents. Her only real worry was the boys and Annie and now Josh. She hoped her letter would reach the director of the Texas Blind Asylum in Austin and that they could take in Henry and Rusty, but with the shortened deadline, she may just have to take them there herself and hope for the best.

A loud pounding at the front door barged into her thoughts. She hurried through the house and opened the door, her smile fading. "Mr. Ramsey."

He lifted his chins—all three of them—in the air and looked down his nose at her. "I want to know if the rumors I've heard are correct."

"Uh . . . I'm sure I don't know what you're referring to." Her mind raced, but she couldn't think of a thing that would have him so out of sorts. The man had several spots on his shirt, two brown and two yellow—coffee and eggs—she suspected.

He glanced past her. "Where are all the children?"

She looked at him steadily. "I don't see how that's any concern of yours."

"Do you or do you not have a new child here—a child who is not blind?" He lifted his head another notch, as if he'd just won that round.

Her thoughts scrambled in a hundred different directions. How had he heard about Josh already? What would the boy's presence mean to them?

The sound of someone clearing his throat behind Mr. Ramsey made Laura realize there was someone else on the porch—someone who was completely hidden behind Otis Ramsey's bulk. She threw the scoundrel a questioning glare, and he stepped to the side, revealing a man barely over five feet tall. The stranger adjusted his spectacles and smiled.

"This is Mr. Hastert, and he's come to have a look at the house to see if it meets his expectations."

Of all the nerve! Laura stepped outside and closed the door to keep the men from entering. "Now see here, Mr. Ramsey. I've a school to run. We may have to vacate soon, but until then, you need to understand that there will be no tours. We have half a dozen blind children here, and I can't have strangers wandering through the house disrupting their routine. Is that clear?"

Mr. Ramsey's lips puckered and his nostrils flared.

"Oh, uh, I do beg your pardon, Miss Wilcox, but I was under the impression we had your approval to see the school." Mr. Hastert cast a perturbed glance at Mr. Ramsey, backed off the porch, and spun around and headed toward the buggy.

"You'd better hope you didn't cost me a sale, Miss Wilcox."

Laura had never encountered a more pretentious buffoon in all her life. How the man could be any relation to kind Mr. Morrow was unfathomable. "I do believe it's time for you to leave, sir."

Riley stepped around the corner of the house, carrying a post. "Everything all right here, Miss Laura?"

She lifted her brows at her unwanted guest, as if to ask if they had a problem.

Mr. Ramsey scowled at Riley then leaned toward her. "No woman tells me what to do. I'll be back tomorrow, and that urchin who doesn't belong here better be out of this house."

"Or what?" Laura stood rigid, wishing she was another inch or two taller, so he'd have to look up to her. Riley set the post down and stepped onto the porch, standing a few feet away, arms crossed, with a menacing glare on his face. She appreciated his presence more than she could say.

Mr. Ramsey backed up a step, but like a bullying dog that wanted to get in one more snap, he growled. "Or I'll cut a week off your deadline."

She sucked in a breath that brought a smug smile to his lips. "You wouldn't."

"Oh yes, I would. In fact, I just did. My uncle had strict rules about only blind children allowed at his school, and you've broken those rules. You have two weeks to vacate these premises."

"B—but that's preposterous. I can't possibly get the children to their parents and find a place for the orphans in such a short time." She didn't want to beg, but for the children's sake, she would.

"Two weeks, Miss Wilcox."

"You're leaving now," Riley said.

"And just who are you?" Ramsey said, one side of his lip curling up.

"He works for me, and I suggest you do as he says."

Ramsey glared at her then turned and lumbered down the stairs with Riley following. She shuddered. What a disgusting man. She dropped into a rocker, tears blurring the vision of Mr.

Ramsey struggling to climb into the buggy. How would she manage to do everything that needed to get done in just two weeks?

She would have to get the letters posted to the girls' parents right away, and she needed to make plans to take the boys to Austin as soon as she could. At least the reverend's donation would make that trip possible. But what about Annie? She feared for the young woman who'd never known a home other than this one. Laura could only hope Annie's newfound faith in God and maybe even her growing relationship with Riley would be enough to sustain her.

CHAPTER TWENTY

nnie meandered out to the barn, her heart aching. Laura had told her of Mr. Ramsey's visit and how he said they needed to remove Josh from the house and find someone to take in the orphan. But how could they send the grieving little boy away? And where to? He was so young and hadn't even gotten used to being with them yet, and she had promised him she'd take care of him. She felt lower than a skunk's belly.

She inhaled the familiar barn scents, although she didn't miss the chicken odor. In his efforts to clean up the barn, Riley had built a small covered chicken coop beside the barn with some spare wood and wire he'd found. She ambled over to his horse. "What are you doing in the barn on a perfectly nice afternoon?"

Scratching the mare under her chin, Annie admired Gypsy's pretty face. "It's ironic that you're called a Morgan horse and your owner's last name is Morgan." Riding the mare had been pure fun, and she longed to do it again. What fun it must be to take off across the countryside, galloping with the wind whipping her face. To run away from the difficult things she must face in the next few weeks.

"I don't know how to tell the children—or the towns-folk—that I've been lying to them. Do you have any idea how difficult that is? No, I don't guess you do."

The mare swished a fly with her tail and closed her eyes, as if she hadn't a care in the world. If only Annie didn't.

⟵ ★ ⟶

Riley stood on the far side of the corral, where he'd just finished mending a broken rail and watched Annie walking confidently toward the barn, as if being unable to see was no issue at all. He lifted his hat and swiped the sweat off his brow, then shook his head. That woman had more gumption than most of the soldiers he had fought beside the past few years. He slipped between the rails and strode across the enclosure and through the gate. Dare he hope Annie had come looking for him?

He ground his teeth together at the involuntary notion. Annie invaded his thoughts more and more each day, and he had no idea what to do about that. His future was so uncertain. He didn't even know where he'd be in a few weeks. The last thing he should be thinking about was another woman, and yet here he stood watching her pet his horse's nose, and he couldn't help being jealous. What kind of man did that make him? A lonely one? Desperate?

She bent, and he saw her mouth move, but he couldn't hear what she said to Gypsy. He didn't want to be attracted to Annie—much less care for her, not after the way Miranda had treated him.

A hawk screeched overhead and soared away, pulling his gaze upward. The hot breeze did little to cool the sweat running down his back from his labors. He stared at the vivid blue sky. *God, I know we haven't been on the greatest of terms lately, but that preacher said You are always ready to hear a man when he calls to You. Would You help me out here? Show me what to do where Annie's concerned.*

When Annie wrapped her arms around Gypsy's neck, Riley's mouth went dry, remembering how good it had felt to hold her close as he had the other night.

But could he ever fully trust her? If he gave her his heart, would she crush it like Miranda had? No, she'd never deliberately hurt him. Annie was not Miranda, and he was now a man and not a lonely boy in the throes of war who missed his family and the girl he'd left behind.

She stepped back from the horse and brushed her sleeve across her eyes. Was she crying? Before he thought things out, his feet pushed into motion. "Is something wrong?"

She jumped and spun around, her hand on her chest. "Oh, I didn't hear you." She swiped her hand across her eyes. "I must have gotten dust in my eyes."

"You don't have to pretend with me. I can tell when something is bothering you."

"You can?" Her eyes widened—those lovely deep-brown eyes.

"I think so. Are you upset because of Mr. Ramsey's visit?"

Annie ducked her head and nodded. "He said Josh has to leave the house."

"Yeah, I heard. I came around the side of the house when he was here and getting pushy with Miss Laura."

A sweet smile tugged at Annie's lips, and his gaze was drawn to them. "She told me you chased him off—you and your fence post."

He stood a bit straighter at the pride in her voice. "I don't like men who get rough with women. And for the record, I set the post down so I wouldn't be tempted to use it to smash that snake."

Annie giggled. "I appreciate that you stood up for Miss Laura and for all your help lately. You're a good man, Riley Morgan, and you're very good with the children." She lifted her face toward his and blinked her eyes; this time he had a sneaking suspicion it had nothing to do with dust. "And that's why I think you're the perfect person to take care of Josh."

If she'd told him she could see, he wouldn't have been as shocked. "Me? I'm in no position to care for a young child. That boy needs a mother, not a war-weary man like me."

She shook her head. "A loving father is just as effective as a mother."

He took a step closer, still unable to believe she was serious. "I'm living in a tack room with one makeshift bed. That's no place for a child."

"Miss Laura said you've cleaned it all out and that it looks better than she's ever seen it before. Besides, the tack room is only temporary, and a child needs love more than a house."

Why did he get the feeling she was speaking from experience?

"Please, Riley." She lifted her hand as if to touch his arm then dropped it to her side. "I told Josh I would take care of him. How can I do that if he isn't even here? I'll help you."

He glanced up at the ceiling. His heart ached for the poor, little guy who hadn't yet said a word, but keeping him was out of the question. "I can't. I have work to do."

"If you could just keep him with you until I leave, I'll take him with me."

Riley couldn't help the sarcastic laugh that slipped out. "Annie, be serious. It's one thing for you to tend children here, where you know every inch of the house, the barn, and the yard, but what happens when you leave? You have to be realistic. Where are you going to live? Who will take care of you?"

She hiked that pert chin in the air. "I can take care of myself. I don't need help."

He stepped forward and clutched her upper arms, giving her the tiniest of shakes. "You are not invincible, and you have to stop thinking that you are. Yes, you're an amazing woman who doesn't let your inability to see get in your way, but it's a whole different issue when you're caring for a child."

"Ha! What do you think I've been doing for the past seven years?"

"Yes, but you haven't been doing it alone. You've had Laura and Mrs. Alton to help out."

She hung her head as if finally defeated, and it nearly broke his heart. "What if Josh gets put with a family who's mean to him like that saloon man? Could you live with that?"

His grip tightened. "How do you know he was mean to him?"

"Mrs. Alton said Josh was the dirtiest child she'd ever seen, maybe except for me when I first came here. He has bruises on his arms and legs. Too many to be from a normal child's activities. That poor little boy needs someone to love him."

Riley closed his eyes. She wasn't playing fair, and he suspected she knew it. "Annie, I don't have anything to give a child."

Her head snapped up, and her hands lifted to his waist. "Don't say that, because it's a bald-faced lie. You have lots to give. You're kind to the children and gentle with them, and I know it's true, so don't bother denying it." A fire burned in her eyes that ignited a flame in his soul. "You'd make a wonderful father, even if the child wasn't your own. And you have a nice house, too. All it needs is a bit of work."

Ah, he finally had a legitimate defense. "I've decided to sell the ranch."

Annie's eyes widened and she gasped. She stiffened and

jerked back, forcing him to release her. "You can't be serious. How could you sell your home? All my life, all I've ever wanted was a home. I finally have one and it's being taken from me." Tears glimmered in her eyes. "You have one, and don't want it or appreciate it. I just don't understand that."

She pushed past him, but he couldn't let her go with her so upset at him. He gently grabbed one arm, making her stop.

"What do you want?"

"Annie, a home is not a house. It's people who make a house into a home. All of my family is gone, and I don't want to live in that house with so many memories of what I did wrong. I want to start fresh with a place of my own, where I can make my own memories. Can't you understand that?"

She shrugged. "I never had much of a family until I came here, so no, I can't understand it. I just know there's a little boy who needs you, but you're too focused on your own losses and hurt to see that. You have a good heart, Riley. Don't be afraid to love again."

She pulled away, and this time he let her go, but he couldn't turn loose of what she'd said about never having much of a family. Just what did that mean?

———— ★ ————

An hour later, as Riley was repairing the barn door, Annie walked toward him with Josh in tow. He wasn't sure what her game was, but he was prepared. There was no way this side of the Brazos River that he would adopt that boy. It wasn't fair to the child.

Annie's smile wobbled a bit as she approached. "Um . . . Miss Laura needs to talk to the children to tell them about . . . well, you know. She asked me to see if you might be willing to take Josh for a short ride on Gypsy." She turned her face toward the boy, and Riley studied her pretty profile. Short sprigs of light-brown hair curled around her forehead while her long braid lay along the back of her yellow gingham dress. Her nose was straight, not too long or too short, and her chin turned up just the slightest bit on the end. "Have you ever ridden a horse, Josh?"

As far as he knew, Josh had yet to utter a single word. What had the poor child experienced being around the rough people one encountered in a saloon? His heart hurt for the boy, not enough that he wanted to accept responsibility for him, but he *could* give Josh a ride on Gypsy.

The boy peeked up at Riley then glanced past him and into the barn. He'd brought Gypsy in from the pasture so he could give her a good rubdown, then he'd planned to ride out to the house and do a little straightening up. He could still do that with the boy along, he supposed. But he wasn't going to go all softhearted and change his mind.

He stooped down to make himself look less intimidating. "Would you like to go for a ride on my horse with me?"

Josh shrugged one shoulder and leaned against Annie's skirt. His gaze shot between Riley and the open barn door again, looking more interested than scared.

Annie stroked Josh's short, blond hair. "All the other children have already had a chance to ride. You want your chance, don't you?"

Riley smiled at her tactic. Josh shook his head.

Annie slid her hand down the boy's arm and took hold of his. "Let's go have another look at Gypsy. She's the horse that you fed a carrot to yesterday." She led him into the barn, and Riley followed. He couldn't help admiring how her soft speech and gentle touches made the shy boy more comfortable. He made a mental note to do the same so he wouldn't frighten the child.

Annie held her hand out flat, and Gypsy sniffed it looking for a treat. "See, isn't she a nice horse?"

Josh watched her with wide blue eyes and tucked his hands behind his back. From his viewpoint of standing just about three feet tall, the horse had to look gigantic. Riley stooped down next to the boy. "Would you like for me to pick you up so you can pet Gypsy?"

Josh backed up against Annie, but didn't look overly frightened.

"Maybe he could help you saddle the horse." Annie lifted her brows as if saying he should have thought of such a thing.

He stood there trying to decide just what a boy so small could do, when Annie offered another idea.

"Why don't you let him sit on your saddle before you put it on the horse, so he'll get a feel for it?"

Now that was a good idea. Riley stooped down and held out his hand to Josh. Bright blue eyes only a few shades lighter than his stared at him, as if judging his trustworthiness. Riley couldn't help wondering again if the child had faced cruelty at the hands of men. He seemed far more comfortable with the women. Riley had smiled at him at their mealtimes but hadn't approached him.

Josh glanced up at Annie, then ever so slowly, reached out and laid his hand in Riley's. The child's was dwarfed by Riley's bigger one, but his trust stirred something deep within. Smiling, Riley gently closed his hand and pulled the boy toward him. "My saddle is in the tack room on a block. I'll need to lift you up to set you on it. Is that all right?"

Josh tightened his lips. Annie patted his shoulder, and the boy nodded and held up his arms. Riley smiled at how quickly Josh overcame his obvious apprehension. "Thatta boy."

Riley swung him up into one arm and smiled at Annie when Josh didn't make a fuss.

"Oh, before I forget, Miss Laura wants to know if you'd ride into town and post these letters for her." She pulled a collection of nearly a half dozen letters from her apron pocket and held them out.

He didn't want to take them, certain they were the summons for the children's parents, but he did. If Annie was aware of their importance, she did a great job hiding her emotions. His throat thickened at the thought of saying a final good-bye to her, so he carried the letters and the small boy into the tack room, where he lay the missives on the bed and set the boy on the saddle. Josh's eyes went wide and he seized the horn, his short legs spread wide across the saddle, feet dangling more than a foot above the stirrups. He sat there for a moment looking as if he were wishing he was anywhere else, but then his lips turned up in a charming smile that revealed matching dimples.

Looking over his shoulder, Riley wanted to share the boy's happiness with Annie, but the little sneak had vanished, leaving him alone to care for Josh. Well, it was his own fault. He had agreed to watch the boy for a short while.

He shook his head. What a big mistake that was going to be. The moment he lifted Josh in his arms, it was like adding coffee grounds to water. The two together blended, fit. His heart reached out and connected with the young orphan. He was afraid his plans to give Josh back to Annie were going to be far more difficult than he hoped.

CHAPTER TWENTY-ONE

*L*aura wrung her hands as she paced the parlor, waiting for Annie to return from the barn. They both thought it would be less traumatic for Josh to not be present when she broke the news that the school was closing. The children all waited patiently, as they did when their teacher was about to begin class or read to them, but this time the story wouldn't have a happy ending.

Tess perched on the settee with Lissa, Camilla—still not fully awake from her afternoon nap—and Becky on the far end. Henry sat in a side chair, while Rusty pumped the rocking chair, forward and back, as if trying to break a wild mustang. She loved each of them so much. Tess for her mothering, Becky so quiet and shy until there was a competition, sweet Lissa with hair almost the color of Annie's, and darling Camilla with her charming accent and insatiable curiosity. And then there were the boys. Henry was always quiet and such a hard worker, while Rusty with his loud exuberance kept everyone smiling. Oh, how she would miss them.

She batted back the sting of tears and stiffened her spine. The back door opened and closed when Annie walked through the dining room. She smiled halfheartedly and stopped at the wide doorway to the parlor and leaned against it. Mrs. Alton had prepared dinner early, preferring not to be present when the sad news was broken. The fragrant aroma of chicken soup and biscuits filled the house and would soon fill their bellies.

A highly fulfilling era of her life was quickly coming to a close, and while she definitely was sad, there was an excitement building. Something new was on the horizon, she just knew it. Laura took a deep breath and began. "Children, Miss Annie is already aware of the news I have to share with you this afternoon, and I want to assure you that I've done all I know to do to prevent it. There is no easy way to say this, but in two weeks, the Wilcox School for Blind Children will be closing."

An audible gasp circled the room then Tess and Becky started sniffling and their chins trembled. Annie and Henry hung their heads.

Rusty slowed the rocker. "What d'ya mean the school's closin'? Where're we gonna live?"

Laura looked at the girls, all cheerless except Camilla, who probably was too young to grasp the ramifications of the announcement. "I've sent letters to the girls' parents, so they should all be coming soon to pick you up and take you back home." She walked over to the boys, stooped down, and took hold of their hands. "There's a wonderful school for blind children in Austin. I'm sure you both will love it, and Henry, Austin has several colleges. I know how much you love learning. Maybe it will be possible for you to attend one when you're old enough."

The dim light in the older boy's eyes sparked. "You think they'd allow someone like me to go?"

She squeezed his hand. His useless blue-gray eyes looked

to be staring straight at her. "I think it's a good possibility. We'll find out more when we get there."

"A new school?" Rusty asked, as if the news interested the smart five-year-old. "How will we get there?"

"I'm not sure just yet, but we will somehow. Do you girls have any questions?" Laura stood, relieved they were all taking things so well.

Footsteps echoed across the porch, and a knock sounded at the door. Annie pushed away from the wall she leaned against. "I'll get it."

She opened the door, and Laura caught a peek of a man dressed in a white shirt, black pants, boots, and a straw hat—a new wide-brimmed style that some of the ranchers were wearing. He yanked the hat off when Annie answered the door.

"Can I help you?" she asked.

"I'm looking for Riley Morgan. Heard in town that he was working here."

Annie nodded. "You might find him at the barn, but he may not be there. He was taking one of the children for a ride on his horse."

"I want to ride Gypsy, too!" Rusty cried.

Laura shushed him so that she could hear the stranger.

"Thanks, ma'am. I'll check to see if he's there," the man said. "In case I don't find him, could you tell him that Gerald Brown was here, and I've got something of his pa's that I need to give him."

Laura's heart jumped. A memento of his father would be such good news for Riley.

"Thank you. I'll be sure to tell him." Annie closed the door then sat in the last remaining chair.

"Miss Laura, why is the school closing?" Tess ducked her head and worried her fingers in her lap, pulling Laura's attention away from the door.

"It has nothing to do with you children, be assured of that. I try to shelter you-all from things you don't need to know, but I won't lie to you." From the corner of her eye, Laura saw Annie grimace. "The man who owns this house wants to sell it, and I've been unable to locate another suitable place nor find the funding I need to continue the school since Mr. Morrow died. I've run out of options and have no choice but to close."

"Thank you for explaining, Miss Laura. Knowing that it's not your choice to close makes it easier to accept." Tess offered a tentative smile.

"All right, now." Laura clapped her hands. "I knew you'd be sad, so I asked Mr. Murphy if he'd come for supper this evening, and right after the dishes are done, he will take us for a hay ride."

Cheers rang out, but they were not quite as enthusiastic as usual. At least the news put smiles on most of the children's faces.

◄——— ★ ———►

Laura walked Sean out to his wagon, remembering the wonderful evening. After a delicious supper, they had all loaded up into his wagon. Laura had smiled to herself as Riley lifted Annie up on the gate of the wagon then sat beside her, their legs dangling down, and Josh nestled in between them. All of the children had crowded together, smiles again lighting their expressions. They sang and called hellos to people who were just leaving after the final night of the revival as they drove through town. Many of the townsfolk smiled and called hello back. She had a feeling if finances hadn't been so tight for everyone because of the war, the town would have rallied around them.

"Why so quiet? Didn't you have a good time?"

Laura smiled. "Of course. Just thinking about tonight and a few other things."

Sean's brawny torso stood out in the light shining from the parlor window. "What other things? Maybe I can help?"

She shook her head. "I don't know how I'm going to do everything that needs doing. Mr. Ramsey wants us out in two weeks."

"I thought you had three weeks until the deadline."

"We did, until Annie brought Josh home and Mr. Ramsey found out a sighted child was living in the house. He said the boy had to leave or he'd shave a week off. I made him angry, so he did it anyway."

"Is that why I saw Annie heading to the barn with an armload of bedding?" He chuckled. "Leave it to the two of you to finagle a way to keep the boy."

She lifted her chin and gave him a mock glare, rather proud of how they remedied the situation. "All that greedy coot said was that we had to get Josh out of the house."

Sean laughed heartily. "So you put him in the barn with Riley?"

"Well, isn't that better than giving him to someone who'll make him work for a meal or two a day like that saloon owner did?"

"It is, but what happens in two weeks?"

Laura glanced over at the barn, a conspiring smile lifting her lips. "I'm hoping for a miracle."

"I didn't think you believed in those."

"This time I do. Haven't you noticed how Riley and Annie are attracted to each other?"

"Laura." Sean's deep voice scolded. "You're not meddlin', are you?"

She shrugged and grinned. "Maybe. But don't you see, they'd make the perfect set of parents for that boy."

"Do they know this?"

She swung her skirts back and forth, like a schoolgirl.

"Annie thinks we're trying to get Riley to keep the boy, but I want to see them get together. They need each other."

"And Annie needs a home. I'm just not sure that's the best thing for her." He shook his head. "How can she run a home and care for a young child alone if she can't see?"

Laura's heart pounded like the spoon Rusty often hammered on the table when his meal didn't arrive as fast as he expected. "Well, everyone is going to find out soon enough, so I might as well tell you now. Annie—she isn't . . . uh . . . blind."

Sean frowned. "You mean she can see some, like lights and shadows?"

"I mean she isn't blind at all; she can see everything."

His eyes widened, and he turned and stalked over to his horses, leaning against the back of the closest one. That was hardly the reaction she'd expected. "Aren't you happy for her?"

He was silent for a long moment, and all she could hear was the chorus of night creatures. Stars covered the sky, winking at her, as if telling her everything would be all right.

"Of course I'm happy for Annie, but you lied to me." He turned back around, his wounded expression barely visible in the faint lighting. "I never thought you'd do such a thing."

She walked over to him. "Sean, I never told you Annie was blind. In fact, I've never told a single person that."

"It's still a lie to deceive people. I would think you'd know that."

"Of course I do, but Annie was so pitiful when she first came here. She was so hungry and desperate that she pretended to be blind so I'd take her in." She crossed her arms and stared at the stars, blinking back tears at the memory. "Her father had abandoned her. What would have happened to her if I'd said no?"

He heaved a loud sigh and placed his hands on her shoulders. "I understand what you did, Laura, but I wish you would have confided in me. I'd have kept your secret."

She lifted a hand to his cheek, the day's light stubble tickling her palm. "I know you would have, but things were different between us back then. You were still upset with me for choosing the school over a life with you."

He closed his eyes and shook his head then gently pulled her against his chest and held her. "I was never angry with you, sweetheart, but rather at myself for making you choose. If I could do it all over I would do things far different."

Laura's breath caught in her throat. All these years she'd thought he was upset at her. "What would you do differently?"

He stroked her head in a loving caress. "I'd never make you choose between me and the youngsters. There was no reason when you could have had us both. I let my pride keep me from the woman I love for far too long."

The tears she'd held at bay now trickled down her cheeks. "Oh, Sean. Do you mean you *still* love me?"

He cupped her cheeks. "Sure do. And I still want to marry you."

Laura's heart pounded hard. The thing she secretly had pined for all these years was within her grasp. "Are you asking?"

He stiffened. Then he spoke. "Are you saying you'd agree if I did?"

A wide smile tugged at her lips. "What was the question?"

Sean's big hands ran down her head and cradled her cheeks again. Tears glimmered in his eyes. "Would you marry me, Laura, darling?"

She nodded. "I'd love to."

His lips crushed against hers, and her joy knew no bounds. All the worries of the past weeks fled as her future began to take shape. After a moment, Sean threw back his head and laughed. "Just think, I came here tonight expecting dinner and a hayride, and I'm leaving with a fiancée."

Annie's hand halted in midair at Sean's boisterous laugh. What in the world was there to laugh about? She shook her head and resumed patting Josh's back. The boy had had a harder time going to sleep on the tack room bed than she'd expected. Riley sat a dozen feet away in Bertha's stall. With the excitement of taking the children on a hayride, the poor cow had gotten overlooked. The gentle *swish swish* of the milk drifted in the open door, and she matched the pace of her patting, feeling a special kinship as they both worked so closely together.

Something must have happened on today's ride to change Riley's mind, because he said he was willing to give keeping the boy a try. Josh had smiled a lot more since they returned from their ride and had moved at the table so he could sit next to Riley at supper, although he grew a bit apprehensive when he learned he had to sleep in the barn. And yet, he still never uttered a peep. His breathing deepened, and she dared to halt her ministration. When he didn't move or fuss, she pushed up from her spot at the head of the bed and tiptoed out.

When she reached the stall, she blew out a deep breath. "Asleep. Finally."

Riley twisted his neck and glanced up, a solemn expression on his face. "Will getting him to sleep be that hard every night?"

She shook her head and smiled. "No, it's just that this is new to him, and I think he's a bit confused why he's here instead of with the other children. But he'll get used to it and to you."

He sat up after a few moments and rolled his shoulders. "I think Bertha's done." He stood and, wiped his hand on his pants, and held it out to her. "C'mon, I'll walk you back to the house and put the milk in the cellar."

"No, I think it's better if I stay here. I wouldn't want Josh to awaken and find himself alone."

He nodded then took the bucket and walked outside, his long-legged gait quickly taking him out of view. Was he angry at her for pretty much forcing Josh on him? He hadn't said a lot to her on the hayride, but then they couldn't talk about much with all the children there, chattering or singing.

She walked back into the tack room and stared down at the little boy. She longed to make things good for him. To see him smile again so she could enjoy his beautiful dimples. To hear him talk. "Please, Lord, let Riley be a good father to Josh," she whispered.

The second the words were out of her mouth, she knew the truth. She wanted to be Josh's mother. But even more, she wanted to be Riley's wife. Leaning back against the saddle block, she blinked her eyes, trying to comprehend when her feelings had taken such a sharp turn. When had she fallen in love?

"What's wrong? You look like you've seen a ghost." His gaze searched the room as if hunting the source of her disturbance.

"Um . . . nothing's wrong. I just thought of something rather shocking."

"Oh." He glanced at Josh, looking a bit like he wondered what he'd gotten himself into.

"How'd your ride go today?" Annie longed to meet Riley's gaze. To stare fully into his eyes and see if her love for him might be returned.

"Fine, I reckon. Josh seemed to enjoy it. When we arrived at the ranch, he had a big smile on his face, and when it was time to leave, he was eager to climb back in the saddle." He reached for the blanket and started to cover the boy but then stopped. "Do you think I should put the quilt over his legs?"

Annie shook her head. "No. Even with the window open, it's still warm in here. No wonder you often sleep outside or in the stalls." She wasn't certain because of the low lighting, but she thought maybe Riley was blushing.

He cleared his throat. "It is cooler, but that's not usually why I don't sleep in here."

"No?" Her curiosity shot off like a racehorse at a starting line.

"No." He turned then lightly took her arm. "Let's go out so we don't wake Josh."

Smiling at his concern, Annie stepped down into the barn and walked over to Gypsy's stall. But her smile dimmed as she realized that if she hoped anything could develop between her and Riley, she had to tell him the truth.

He reached out and patted the horse then forked his fingers through Gypsy's mane. "I don't sleep well, because I sometimes have nightmares about the war."

Annie laid a hand on his arm, wondering at the horrors he had seen. "I'm sorry."

He shrugged. "Josh was actually a big help today. We went back to the ranch, and he helped me clean up. The place looks much better, and good thing, because Mr. Johnson came by while I was there and said he already has someone who's interested. One of our neighbors may buy the land to expand his holdings—Mr. Brown."

Brown? Why did that name sound familiar? Suddenly, she gasped.

Riley grabbed her arm and reached for his gun. "What is it?"

Annie giggled. "Sorry. I just remembered something I was supposed to tell you."

He relaxed and holstered his gun. "For pity's sake, Annie. I just about shot Bertha."

She laughed softly, drawing the old cow's curious stare. "I'm really sorry. It's just that a Mr. Brown came looking for you. He said he had something that belonged to your father that he needed to give you."

Riley started. "Like what?"

"I don't know. He must have arrived right after you and Josh left."

Riley reached out and stroked Gypsy then glanced outside, as if considering riding over right then. "What else did he say?"

"Nothing."

"I'll ride over and see him tomorrow."

"Good idea. If you can wait until Mr. Ramsey returns to check about Josh being out of the house, I'll watch him for you."

"Watch him for *me*?" Riley's brow lifted. "You say that like he's my son or something."

Annie shrugged and stared at Gypsy's face. "I guess I was just hoping."

"Don't get the cart before the horse." It was time to come clean with him about her blindness, but she feared he would hate her when he learned the truth. Summoning every ounce of strength she had and saying a prayer for courage, she lifted her head. "There's something important I need to tell you, and I hope you'll wait to hear my explanation before getting upset with me."

"What's that? You didn't bring home any other children today, did you?"

She gave his arm a playful shove. "No, silly. It's just that—"

Heavy footsteps pounded in their direction, and Riley yanked her behind him and drew his gun. Annie peeked around his arm, hoping it wasn't another group of raiders. Surprise washed over her when Laura and Sean ran in. Their buoyant smiles disappeared in the face of Riley's gun.

"Whoa!" Sean lifted his big hands, and Annie had a hard time not giggling at the sight.

"Sorry." Shoving his pistol back in his holster, Riley blew out a breath. "I almost shot you. What are you doing running into the barn like that? It's not raining or nothin'."

The biggest smile Annie had seen on Laura's face in weeks also danced in her eyes.

Laura glanced at Sean, who looked her straight in the eye and grinned, then turned back toward her and Riley. "Sean and I are getting married," Laura squealed.

Married? That was the last word Annie ever expected to hear her friend say.

nnie waved good-bye to Riley and Josh as they went out the back door after lunch. "I sure hope Riley has an easier time getting Josh down for his nap than I did getting him to sleep last night. Maybe I should go help him."

Laura shook her head and carried her plate to the sink. "No, he needs to learn how to care for the boy himself."

Annie's heart sank. If he did that, he wouldn't need her. "I almost told him last night."

"Told him what?"

"You know." She flicked her eyes toward Tess and Becky washing and drying the dishes then pointed to her eyes. Annie wished she'd waited to tell Laura until later, but in all the excitement last night about Laura's engagement, she forgot about it. In spite of the hard days ahead with the school closing, her friend had hardly quit smiling. If only her own future were as secure.

Someone pounded on the front door, and Laura and Annie

glanced at one another. Laura sighed. "I suppose that's Mr. Ramsey."

"Probably is that curmudgeon at the door since he didn't come earlier," Mrs. Alton muttered as she wiped down the stove then placed the rag in the washbasin for Tess to rinse. She grabbed the lunch she'd saved for her husband. "Guess this is a good time to head out. Don't forget I won't be back this evening. I just put a pot of beans on to simmer for your supper, so make sure you stir them." She waved and closed the back door.

Annie wished she had some place to hide, but she still needed to wash off the table and help the girls finish cleaning up. Otis Ramsey made her skin crawl with his leering gazes. Still, her curiosity pulled her to the doorway.

"Mr. Ramsey." Laura spoke without enthusiasm.

"Afternoon, Miss Wilcox. Is that boy gone?"

He peered through the open doorway, and Annie saw that, once again, he'd brought another man with him. When he glanced her direction, she ducked back.

"Yes, the boy is no longer staying in the house, as you requested."

Demanded was more like it, Annie thought.

"Good. Now, I've brought Mr. Phelps here to have a look at the place. I'm sure you'll be accommodating, all things considered."

Annie could almost see Laura rolling her eyes. Didn't the man take a hint?

"I thought I made it clear that we operate a school here. We have a schedule to keep. I can't have you parading people through the house anytime you like."

"It's costing me considerable money to stay in this town, and it's unreasonable of you to not allow me to show it to prospective buyers."

"No, it is not. If you'd like to walk around the outside of the property when the children are inside, that is fine. If you wish to come inside the house, I insist you make an appointment."

"You insist? Don't you know I could throw you out any time I like?"

Annie dared another peek. She rarely ever heard Laura so riled.

"Maybe I'll just cut another week off."

"Try it, and we'll see what the sheriff has to say. I found my lease agreement last night, and it says I'm to have a thirty-day notice when the owner of this property decides not to lease it any longer. So that still gives me three weeks before we have to be out."

Mr. Ramsey sputtered like a pot of stew boiling over on a hot stove.

"If you wish to show the house, you may do so from ten to eleven or three to four on Saturdays. Good day." Laura shut the door and collapsed against it, looking spent.

Annie walked into the room and clapped. "You're one plucky lady."

Giving her an embarrassed grin, Laura shook her head. A knock—not so hard as the last—echoed through the room. Laura's eyes closed as if she were steeling herself for another battle. She turned and opened the door, her body stiff.

"Mr. Carpenter! What a nice surprise."

Annie's heart clenched. Becky's father? He couldn't have possibly received Laura's letter yet. What was he doing here?

Laura stepped back and let him in, also looking a bit confused. "It's good to see you again."

"I came to bring a wagonload of cotton to town. Heard a rumor about the school. I'd planned to come and visit Becky on my way out of town, but if what I heard is true . . ."

"Please, come in and have a seat, sir. Let me explain what's going on."

The short, thin man with graying black hair perched on the edge of the settee. His fingertips held his wide-brimmed hat that reminded her of the kind the Mexican residents wore. His wide moustache turned down on the ends, and his frown deepened as Laura told him what had happened.

He muttered something under his breath, then glanced up with wide brown eyes. "Please, pardon me. But it irritates me to no end when selfish men accomplish their agenda. If I were a rich man, I'd build a house for the school, but as it is, I barely manage to pay for Becky's tuition. Her coming here has been the best thing that has happened to her." He shook his head. "Her mother and I will be delighted to have her home again, but it makes my heart hurt that she won't get to finish her training here."

"Becky is a fast learner, Mr. Carpenter. Her skills have vastly improved to the point that she's able to take care of herself for the most part. She does still need help getting her hair braided and finding something that's out of place, but if your family will be consistent to put things in the same place and have plenty of patience, Becky will do fine. Read to her. Give her arithmetic problems to figure. And, please, give her plenty to do. Let her help with the meals, laundry, and other household duties."

He nodded, and his eyes lit up when Becky and Tess walked into the room.

"Miss Laura?" Tess cocked her head.

"Yes, I'm here, and so is someone else."

"Hey pun'kin."

Becky jerked her head toward Mr. Carpenter's voice and she held out her arms, hurrying toward him. "Papa?"

"Yes, I came for a visit, but . . . how would you like to go home today?"

Sadness gripped Annie, just like it always had when one of

the children left, only this time it was worse. Becky wasn't leaving because she'd reached the point where she knew all they had to teach her; instead, she was being forced out because of a greedy man.

Annie swirled and ran through the dining room and kitchen and out the back door. Why didn't God do something? Could it be His will for the school to close?

She swiped at the tears burning her eyes and hurried to the barn. How in the world could she handle saying good-bye to all six children?

———— ★ ————

Riley rode Gypsy to the barn and dismounted. When he reached for Josh, he heard a noise coming from the barn. Sniffling, if he wasn't mistaken. He dropped Gypsy's reins, and carried Josh to the house. Maybe Miss Laura would keep an eye on him—unless by chance she was the one who was upset, but he doubted it. Not after the way she'd glowed with joy last night. A wagon he didn't recognize was parked out front, with sprigs of cotton, probably the remains of a shipment someone brought to town, floating out of the back of the wagon like dandelion fluff. He hoped whomever the wagon belonged to wasn't a prospective buyer, pestering Miss Laura.

"Are you hungry?"

Josh nodded.

"Let's go see if Mrs. Alton left us some food." He went around to the back of the house instead of knocking on the front door and disturbing Miss Laura if she had legitimate company. He knocked lightly on the door, and when no one answered, he opened it and peeked in. Not a soul was in the spotless kitchen. His ride over to Mr. Brown's had taken far longer than he'd anticipated, and he could hardly wait to tell Annie his news.

He found two plates under a towel and set one on the table for Josh. "Sit down and eat. I'm going to see if Miss Laura is busy. All right?"

Josh eyed the plate of cold roast beef, cheese, and stewed apples, then licked his lips and nodded. The boy reached for his fork and started to stab an apple.

"We ask God's blessing before we eat here." Josh scowled, but then he ducked his head as he'd seen the other children do. After a second he looked up as if waiting for Riley's approval. Nodding, Riley smiled and closed his eyes, said a short prayer, then looked at the boy again. "Go ahead and eat. I'll be back in a minute."

He stopped at the dining room door and called, "Miss Laura?" She'd told him to come in at mealtime without knocking, but he still felt odd entering a part of the house other than the kitchen or dining room without being invited. When she didn't answer his call, he turned to go back, but a rash of footsteps coming down the stairs stopped him.

Miss Laura led the way, followed by a man he'd never met who carried a satchel and quilt under one arm. Becky was right behind him, followed by a stoic Henry, and Tess, who was dabbing her eyes with a hanky.

Miss Laura spotted him as she lowered herself from the final step. "Oh good, Riley. I'm glad you're back. We missed you and Josh at lunch."

He smiled. "My business took me a lot longer than I expected."

"Well, I hope it was good news."

"It was wonderful news." He glanced at the man and nodded a greeting. "What's going on?"

"Becky's father was in town to deliver a load of cotton and stopped by to see her. I told him what happened, so he's taking her on home." Laura introduced him to Mr. Carpenter.

Although he didn't know Becky as well as some of the other children, his heart still ached to see her go.

"We said our farewells upstairs because I didn't want the younger children to get up when we just got them down for their naps. Did you want to say good-bye?"

"Sure." He crossed the room and stopped in front of Becky, who leaned against her father's leg. He squatted on his boot heels and gently tugged on one of her blonde braids. "I'm sorry to see you go, sweetheart, but I know you're glad to get to be with your parents again."

Becky nodded then launched herself at him, hugging him around his neck. His gaze connected with the girl's proud father, and he smiled.

A few minutes later, the wagon rolled away, taking the first of the children. Miss Laura and Tess had tears running down their faces, and Henry didn't look that far off from crying himself. Annie had come from the barn, all red-faced, and kissed Becky good-bye, then she had turned around and fled back to the barn.

"Miss Laura, Josh is finishing up his lunch. I'd like to go talk to Annie. Would you mind keeping an eye on him?"

"I'll help," Tess volunteered.

"Thank you. If he's tired, maybe you could have him lie down on the settee, then I'll fetch him as soon as I can."

Laura nodded, and he hurried to the barn. He found Annie in the very back, sitting on an upturned crate. A sharp pain lanced his heart to see the stubborn, independent woman in tears. He crossed the space between them and lifted her to her feet, pulling her into a hug. Her arms wrapped around his waist, and her tears wet his shirt.

"Becky's gone, isn't she?"

"Yes. I'm sorry. Don't be upset."

His words of comfort only brought more tears. He held her,

leaning his cheek against her head. It pained him to see her in so much anguish. He brushed his hand along her hair, and for the first time, he had to admit how much he cared for her. What did it matter if she couldn't see? She was braver and had more spunk than any woman he knew. "Shh . . . things will work out."

She shoved at his chest, but he didn't let her go. "How can you say that? Nothing will work out. All the children are leaving. I hate that Otis Ramsey!"

"Hating the man only hurts you, not him. I've been angry for so long, and it was all a waste of time. You've got to give your doubts and fears to God, and trust Him that He is working out His will."

———— ★ ————

Annie's breath caught in her throat. Riley was talking about God? She knew what he said was true, but she'd let her pain and anger cause her to lose control of her emotions. She felt so safe, locked in the circle of his arms, that she never wanted to leave them. She glanced up, their gazes connecting for a mere moment before she looked down. Riley lifted her chin, cupped her cheeks, and wiped away her tears with his thumb. "Don't worry about the future, Annie. I'll take care of you."

Her heart jolted. Did he mean what she hoped he did? Guilt threatened to steal her joy at Riley's declaration. She had to tell him that she wasn't blind. She looked up again, determined that nothing would stop her from telling him the truth. But then his lips crashed down on hers, and she grabbed hold of his shirt with both hands. He kissed her like a starving man, spreading delight to every part of her, then suddenly, he pulled back and turned her loose.

"I'm sorry, Annie. I shouldn't have done that."

"Why did you?"

He shrugged. "I don't know. You just looked so lonely."

"Kissing me is your way of comforting me? Is that how you comforted Miranda?"

His brow wrinkled. "What? How do you know about her?"

She tugged free of his grasp, hurt beyond words at his rejection. Why had he kissed her? Was he just comforting her as he said?

"I just do, and I don't need your comfort, especially if you're going to be sorry afterwards." She hurriedly left the barn, but he followed.

"Annie, wait."

What a horrible day. Annie rushed out, just wanting to get away from the man she loved—a man who didn't care a bit for her. He was right about a home being people, because she'd never wanted a home as much as she wanted him.

CHAPTER TWENTY-THREE

hree days later, Annie ran upstairs after breakfast to change her soiled apron. She found Laura in their room counting coins at the desk. She had several stacks of eagles and double eagles as well as some smaller coins—more money than she'd ever seen at one time, and yet she knew it wasn't nearly enough to accomplish all that she needed.

Eyes filled with regret, Laura slid two double eagles toward Annie. "I wish I could give you five times that amount. I feel bad that I haven't paid you a fair wage all these years."

Annie placed her hands on Laura's shoulders and hugged her from behind. "You gave me a home, food, clothes—you gave me life. I'm sure I'd be dead by now if not for you."

Laura smiled in the mirror that was set above the desk. "I don't know how I could have made it without you all these years. You have been such a blessing. But what will you do?"

Untying her apron, Annie shook her head. "I don't know. Probably travel to a new town and start over."

"I'd hate to see you leave town." Laura turned in the chair. "Maybe Sean could add a room and you could stay with us."

"Thank you, but no. I will miss you terribly, but I have no desire to live with a newly married couple, and that wouldn't be fair to you. And besides, I think it's best for all if I leave town. There will be some folks who will never forgive me for deceiving them." She nudged her chin at the coins, hoping to change the subject. "So who are the other stacks for?"

Laura slid over two gold eagles. "These are for Riley, but it hardly seems enough for all he's done."

Annie ducked her head at the mention of Riley. She'd avoided him as much as possible in the past days, but he hadn't made any special effort to talk to her. At least she could be happy that he and Josh seem to have developed a good relationship.

"These coins are for Mrs. Alton, and this eagle is to get the boys to Austin."

"What about you? Did you save any money for yourself?"

Laura smiled. "I don't need money. Sean will take care of me."

Sitting on her bed, Annie stared at her friend. "But what about your wedding?"

"We don't need much. I'll wear my Sunday dress, gather some wildflowers, and I hope you'll stand up with me."

"It would be my honor."

Laura pocketed the coins. "Well, I'm about to make a few people either happy or disappointed, depending on their expectations."

Annie stared at the pair of double eagles in her hand—forty dollars. More money than she'd ever had, and yet she suspected it wouldn't go very far when she had to find a place to live and buy food. Maybe she could find a nice boardinghouse to stay in. That way she wouldn't be alone.

She'd have to find some kind of employment, but what was she suited for? She didn't have enough education to be a teacher. Maybe she could find someone who needed a nanny.

One way or another, she would have to earn some money. Suddenly, she sat up as a distant memory flashed across her mind like lightning in a spring sky. The watch. Of course. If it had survived burial the past seven years, she could probably sell it. But would selling a stolen watch be dishonest? She couldn't return it to its owner because she had no idea who he was, and selling it would help her find a position where she'd be helping others. Surely that would be all right.

She trotted downstairs. It wouldn't take her long to go to the tree and dig up the watch. As she reached for the door handle, Laura called. Annie closed her eyes for a moment then turned.

Several crates sat on the dining table with books and other items stacked beside them. The children huddled around the table as if awaiting orders. Laura crossed the room toward her. "I wonder if you might take Camilla and Lissa outside and occupy them while the rest of us pack. Rusty is with Riley and Josh, but the younger girls are a bit bored."

The girls would slow her down, but she could kill two birds with one stone. "Of course."

The usual ten-minute walk took thirty with the young girls in tow, and the trees had grown since Annie had last been here. But she'd know her tree when she saw it.

"I'm tired." Camilla lagged back, slowing Annie's steps.

"I know, sweetheart, but we're nearly there."

"Where are we going? Seems too far for town." Lissa stumbled, and Annie jerked up on her arm to keep her from falling. "Are you all right?"

"Yes, Miss Annie, but I'm kinda tired too."

Annie's gaze searched the tree trunks. If she didn't find the one she was looking for in the next few minutes, she'd have to give up for today. The leaves overhead rattled in the stiff breeze, and their skirts threatened to trip them up. She glanced up at the sky, and noticed the thick gray clouds overhead. A storm was blowing in, and the last place she needed to be with two little girls in a Texas thunderstorm was outside.

Suddenly, she spotted her target. "All right, girls, you can sit down and rest a few minutes, and then we'll head back home."

"I think I got dust in my eyes." Lissa rubbed her hands over her eyes.

"Don't rub them. It will only make them hurt more. Try blinking fast. Here, sit down." She helped the girls down behind a large oak to help block the wind. "Give me five minutes, and I'll be ready to go."

Annie ran her hands over the heart engraved in the tree. *RM loves AM*. She'd always wondered if the couple were married since their last initials were the same, but she supposed she'd never know. Kneeling, she dug out the rocks that covered her treasure. She could have kicked herself for not remembering to bring a shovel, but then that would have been hard to do with the children in tow and even harder to explain if someone saw her.

Using one of the rocks with a pointed end, she dug the dirt away, finally revealing the small pouch. She longed to check the watch—to see if the oiled canvas had protected it, but there wasn't time. Sprinkles tapped her head and dampened her back. They had to hurry and return to the school.

"C'mon, girls. Let's get going." She stood, and a heavy gust nearly knocked her over. She turned around and stared at the empty spot where her two wards had been. Her heart lurched. "Camilla! Lissa!"

Thunder shook the rafters of the barn, and rain poured down outside, forming a river that ran into the barn. Hoping to keep Josh occupied so he didn't become afraid, Riley tossed the boy in the air and was rewarded with his giggle. They had grown closer in the days that Josh had stayed with him. Josh still didn't talk, but he was making more sounds, and Riley felt he'd talk once he became more comfortable.

Riley threw him even higher, and when Josh dropped down, he wrapped his little arms around Riley's neck. Josh laid his head on Riley's shoulder, and the final piece of the wall shielding his heart cracked and crumbled. He took a deep breath, receiving the love the tiny orphan offered.

He was stupid to refuse when Annie had first asked him to take Josh, but he'd been afraid. Every person he loved had died. But he hoped and prayed that nothing would happen to Josh. He walked to the doors and stared out at the deluge. In Texas, weather seemed to be all or nothing. They'd go months without rain and then get a month's worth in a few hours.

Josh relaxed, and Riley realized he'd fallen asleep. He carried him to the tack room and laid him down. Love for the child already swelled in his chest, but unless Annie were there with them, they weren't complete. He crept out of the tack room and back to the main doors. He never should have apologized after kissing her. He saw the joy in her eyes fade when he did.

Odd, how her eyes could be so expressive and so ineffective. But her sightlessness no longer mattered. He loved her enough that he wanted the chance to make a life with her. But had he already ruined his chances with Annie by shoving her away one too many times?

A blur to his right caught his attention, and he narrowed

his gaze. Annie? What in the world was she doing out in this weather? He rushed to the tack room and snatched up a horse blanket and met her at the door.

"Riley! I lost Camilla and Lissa. I can't find them. You've got to help!"

He brushed the water from her face and cupped her cheeks. "Hey, slow down. Where did you lose them?"

"We went for a walk, toward the river, and the storm blew in." Tears mixed with the water still dripping from her hair. The pain in her eyes nearly tore his heart out. "I lost them."

"I'll find them." Suddenly, he realized what she said. "Why were you clear down by the river?"

She shook her head. "We can talk about that later. Just saddle Gypsy, and let's go find them."

"I'll go. You need to stay here with Josh."

"No, I can't. I've got to help find them. They've got to be scared and drenched." She grabbed hold of the front of his shirt. "Oh, Riley! What if they fall in the river?"

He set her back and opened Gypsy's gate. He hurried into the tack room and grabbed his saddle and blanket. Annie already had the horse out of the stall. He tossed on the gear then turned back to her. "I promise I'll find them."

"I told you, I'm going with you."

Riley touched her shoulder, hoping she'd have the sense to understand. "Annie, you'll only slow me down."

Anger fired in her pretty eyes, and he rushed to smother it. "You're the most confident and capable woman I know, but you need to know your limitations. A blind woman can't search for the lost."

She winced and her lips pressed so tightly together that they turned white.

He cupped one of her cheeks. "I love you, Annie Sheffield, but in this case, you'd only slow me down."

She stared at him long and hard, as if she could see clear into his soul. He could no longer deny his love for her. He only hoped she'd forgive him for what he said.

"Riley—"

"I've got to go. We can talk later, darlin'."

"Riley, let me go with you. I can see."

He shook his head then stopped it in midshake. "What?"

"I can see. I've always been able to."

Her gaze bore into his, and he knew the truth. Just like Miranda, Annie had deceived him.

———— ★ ————

Annie paced the length of the parlor then crossed to the front door again. She searched the horizon, but there was no sign of Riley or the girls. The storms had passed, but darkness would soon settle in across the land. "Please, God, help Riley find the girls," she repeated.

Laura plodded down the steps. "Tess is having a hard time going to sleep in the room all by herself."

"Yeah, Josh wasn't too excited about sleeping on the settee again." Annie glanced at the little boy, who lay on his back, relaxed in sleep. Her love for him had grown so much, but would Riley take him away, and never let her see him? She looked outside again, not wanting to think about such a horrible thing. "I should go out and help search."

Laura wrapped her arm around Annie's shoulders. "It would be dark before you reached the river. Riley and Sean will find them."

"It was good of Sean to go help look for the girls." Annie was quiet for a few moments then she turned toward Laura. "I–I told Riley I could see."

Her friend's eyebrows shot up. "You did? How did he take it?"

She shook her head. "Not good. In fact, he just scowled and didn't say a word."

"He needs some time to get used to the idea, but I'm sure he'll be happy once he does."

"I don't know. He seemed awful upset." Annie narrowed her eyes and stared at something moving their way. "Look! There he is!"

They pushed through the doorway together and rushed down the steps. Riley rode into the yard, holding Camilla, who was sound asleep. Lissa sat behind him, her little arms around his waist. Riley lowered Camilla to Laura while Annie reached for Lissa, and they carried the girls inside. Riley dismounted and followed. He stopped at the doorway. With Lissa's wet clothes seeping into Annie's dry ones, she turned, her gaze landing on his muddy boots and pant legs. She lifted her eyes, encountering his icy cold stare, and her heart dropped to her boot tips. He would never forgive her.

"If you'll just give me Josh, I'll be on my way."

Annie set Lissa in the rocker and went to the settee and picked up Josh. Her heart skipped a few beats as her hands brushed Riley's when she passed the boy to him. He took the child and turned away. "Riley, please."

He spun around, his lips puckered and eyes narrowed. "Tell Miss Laura that I'll finish up this workweek. Then Josh and I will be leaving."

He didn't wait for a reply, but stalked away, taking with him Annie's dream of their life together.

CHAPTER TWENTY-FOUR

riday afternoon, Annie sat in the porch rocker more glum than she could ever remember being. The girls' parents had picked them up this week. Laura had gone with Sean to talk to the minister about tomorrow's wedding, and they'd taken Henry and Rusty with them to get each boy a new pair of shoes. The house was oddly empty.

Annie ought to be doing a final cleaning in the girls' room, but she didn't have the heart. Too many good-byes had been said, and with Riley ignoring her and keeping Josh away, she felt as if all her strength had drained away.

She had to make a decision where she would go. She thought of going to Austin so that she could check in on the boys from time to time, but then she'd have to travel with the newlyweds, and her heart wasn't in it. She'd have to make a life for herself that didn't include Riley.

She could not imagine saying good-bye to Laura. Riley and Josh were leaving after the wedding and heading back to his place. She thought of the news Laura had shared—about how Mr. Brown had a stallion that belonged to Riley's father, as well as several of the Morgans' brood mares that he'd bred to his stallion in a swap. All three mares had foaled, and Riley would be able to raise Morgan horses as his father had. "Thank You, Lord, for that blessing."

How ironic that Riley would now live at the house he'd said he didn't want while she had to leave the house she loved. Her eyes blurred as she thought of his icy glares. Any future she might have had with him had washed away in the flood of her lies.

Annie was so tired of good-byes. The best thing for everyone would be if she took a stage while Laura was in Austin, then she could travel until she found a place she liked. Her only decision now was where to go. She'd heard the Hill Country was nice, so maybe she'd go there.

She stared up at the sky. "Lord, would You please show me what to do?" The sound of hoofbeats drew her attention to the road. A sick feeling coursed through her. Not Otis Ramsey. Not today. She stood and hoped to slink away before he saw her.

The buggy drew to a stop, and a man stepped out to help Mr. Ramsey down. "Miss Sheffield, isn't it?"

Annie paused, wishing she could ooze down under the porch like rainwater. "Yes. May I help you?"

"I'm sure you can. I saw Miss Wilcox in town, and she said that I could take a look at the house today."

Annie glanced toward the barn, hoping Riley would notice their unwanted guest, but he wasn't in sight. "I suppose you can go look around if you want. Nobody's in there right now."

He lumbered up the porch. "I wouldn't feel right looking around on my own. Please, would you show me around?"

Annie stared at him. His polite words were so uncharacteristic that she felt sure he was up to something, but she had no idea what it could be. "I suppose I could do that."

Leaving the front door wide open, she gave him the grand tour of the downstairs.

"Let's check out the upstairs." He held his hand out toward the stairs. "If you'll be so kind as to lead the way."

Annie shook her head and backed away. "No, if you want to see the upstairs, you go on up on your own."

He scowled. "Perhaps you could just explain the layout to me."

She did, then followed him through the kitchen and out the back door.

"You look to have a rather large garden. However did you manage?"

"Oh, we just did. You'd be surprised how resourceful blind people can be."

He spun around, his right fist clenching and unclenching. His eyes narrowed, his expression menacing. Annie backed, her heart thrumming.

"Especially . . ." He took a step toward her. " . . . if they are not all blind."

How did he know? Had she been too careless when he was around? For a brief moment she considered telling a falsehood, but she was done with lying. She swallowed the lump in her throat and nodded.

"You've made a mockery out of my uncle's kindness. I know his rules—oh, he told me all about this place, more times than I could count. No children who can see—or young women—for that matter, are to attend this school." He turned and paced across the narrow porch and back. His hand raked through his thin hair, making it stand up like sparse wheat in a field. Suddenly, he spun around and stood close to her. "Ten dollars per child per month—that's the stipend my uncle paid.

Since I inherited everything from him, the way I see it, you stole that money from me, you pretty, little thief. I think some payback is due." He backed into the corner where the porch and kitchen wall connected, arms on either side of her to block her escape.

She glanced out the side of her eyes at the barn. Would Riley hear her if she screamed? Was Mr. Ramsey just fuming or did he have something else on his mind? Her heart thundered so loud it was a wonder he didn't hear it. In all the years she'd been a pickpocket, she'd never once been cornered. She sucked in a breath and tried to duck under Ramsey's arm, but he caught her around the middle and tugged her up against him.

"Just settle down, you little nymph, and we can have some fun." His slobbery lips angled down her neck. Annie pulled at his hands, but when that didn't work, she doubled up her fist and rammed it backward over her shoulder, colliding with his eye. He let out an enraged howl and dropped her.

Annie dashed to her left, intending to jump over the fence rail but Ramsey grabbed her skirt and threw his arm around her again.

"C'mon, you little minx. Give me a kiss."

Annie pulled on the man's little finger, breaking his hold. She spun around and slapped his cheek. "I'd rather kiss a pig."

He shoved her back, and she stumbled on her skirt and would have fallen if he hadn't lifted her up. He narrowed his gaze and rubbed his cheek with his free hand. "My uncle thought he was smarter than me too. He also thought he'd get away, but he didn't—and neither will you." He spun her around and pressed her against the wall. The edges of the wood pressed into her back, sending pain through her. "I intend to make sure you never steal from anyone again, just like I made sure my uncle never wasted another penny in this God-forsaken town."

His hand closed around her throat, and his warm breath, which smelled of onions, made her stomach churn. Annie didn't have time to react. She grabbed at the fingers closing off her breath. "You killed your uncle?"

The gleam of pride that sparkled in his eyes was the only answer she needed.

Panic flooded Annie. He had killed his own uncle—kind Mr. Morrow. He wouldn't hesitate to hurt her. She pounded on his arm, but the city man had more strength than she'd given him credit for. How ironic that she might die for a crime she'd long ago forsaken. His fingers tightened, sending pain radiating through her neck. She gasped desperately, trying to breathe. The light of day dimmed, and a fog of darkness threatened to steal her life away. *God, help me. Please.*

———— ★ ————

Riley paced the barn, waiting for Josh to finish his nap. When the boy awakened, they'd ride over to the ranch and work on the house again. They had a lot of work ahead of them but the house was a far sight better than a tack room.

He leaned against the barn door, marveling again at how God had returned to him something that was lost. Well, not lost exactly, but borrowed. His father's horses.

After the wedding tomorrow, he and Josh would ride out for good. Mrs. Alton had already given back some of his ma's canned goods since most of the children had left. They'd make do.

But every time he thought of riding off without Annie, he got a sick churning in his gut. He was still mad at her—no, not mad. Hurt. Why hadn't she told him the truth?

And he was angry with himself for not realizing it. How many times had he wondered how she got around so well? Now he understood why she could be so independent. Laura had explained why Annie had done what she did, but it still hurt that she hadn't been honest with him once they started growing close.

He stared at the house. What was she doing in there with everyone else gone?

Where would she go?

He shook his head. The foolish woman was so independent that she didn't realize the danger she put herself in. She needed someone to watch out for her, and in spite of everything, he wanted to be that person.

Riley peeked in at Josh, who was napping. If he hurried, he could find Annie and try to make things right. He'd prayed the past few days and asked God to show him what to do. Annie never left his thoughts.

He headed to the back door of the house out of habit and rounded the corner, and what he saw caused his heart to leap. Otis Ramsey had his hand on Annie's throat, and her frantic gaze snapped to his, a second before her eyes rolled up in her head.

Riley took a flying leap over the porch railing and grabbed Ramsey by the tender spot right above the collarbone. The man yelled in pain and released Annie. She collapsed in a pile of blue gingham, and Riley howled and flung Ramsey clear off the porch. The city slicker landed hard, groaned, but didn't move for a moment. Riley turned to Annie. Her lips were blue but color was returning to her cheeks. A shuffling sounded behind him, and he turned. Ramsey staggered up and lumbered toward him. Riley jumped off the porch and met him with fists raised. "Just what's going on here?"

"Nothing." Ramsey's gaze darted past Annie to Riley, his lips turning up in a snarl. "Just head on out of here."

"Not in this lifetime. What did you do to Annie?"

His expression paled for a moment then hardened. "She

merely passed out from the heat, and I was attempting to assist her."

"Liar," Annie squeaked out, her voice raspy. "Attacked me—killed Morrow."

The second his uncle's name left Annie's mouth, Ramsey lunged at Riley. The man's weight pushed Riley backwards, and he landed against the stairs. Using them as leverage, he tucked in his knees then kicked Otis Ramsey backwards, as if he were nothing but manure on his boots. The man's feet pedaled backwards, his hands pinwheeled, and he stumbled—then he went down hard. A loud breath wheezed out, and Riley yanked his gun from his waistband. When the man didn't move, Riley rushed to Annie's side. He dropped to his knees and scooped up the woman he loved. He patted her pale cheek. "Breathe, sweetheart. Breathe."

Nothing happened. She'd spoken moments earlier but had now lapsed into unconsciousness. Tears blurred his vision of her pretty face. "No, God, please."

He tilted her head back, and her mouth fell open. His hand brushed across the redness on her delicate neck, and he leaned down, compelled to breathe for her. He blew breath after breath into her, praying, begging God to save her. He couldn't lose her now.

How could he live without her?

Suddenly, she gasped. Riley's eyes flew open and hope battled despair. "C'mon, darlin', breathe. Don't leave me."

She flailed her arms, as if to fight him off, and Riley wrapped his arms around her. "Hey, it's me. Riley."

Her panicked gaze collided with his as she continued to suck in precious breaths of air. He smiled as he realized she could actually see him. Tears ran down his face, and one dropped onto her cheek. He bent down and kissed it off. "I love you, Annie Sheffield. Don't you dare think of leaving me."

Her worried expression fled, and slowly she caught her breath. Riley cradled her in his arms, thanking God for saving her.

"S—sorry." The croaky word didn't sound at all like Annie's voice.

"It's all right, darlin'. Laura explained everything, and I understand."

She closed her eyes and leaned her cheek against his shirt, and tears—this time of joy—once again blurred his view of his beloved.

⟵ ★ ⟶

"You'll be all right while I take this—this scoundrel into town?" Riley nodded at Otis Ramsey, who'd been slung over his saddle and tied securely on.

Annie was glad the man's face was on the other side of the horse, because she never wanted to see him again. She gazed up at Riley, grateful to finally be able to look him in the eye. He captured her gaze and held it for a long, enchanting moment.

"Do you know how much I love you?"

The warmth in his gaze sent a thrill running from her heart all through her. "No, but I hope to find out."

He grinned. "I won't be gone long."

"Josh and I will wait right here until you or Laura return."

He smiled and ran his knuckle down her cheek. "I'm really sorry, Annie. Sorry for what that snake did. Sorry for getting so upset with you."

"No, it's not your fault. I wanted to tell you for so long, but I couldn't find the words. I tried that night when Laura and Sean burst in with their news."

"Well, let's put it behind us and think of the future. See you soon." He bent and kissed her forehead then held his hand against her cheek. Then his head dipped down, and she thought he might kiss her, but he looked down instead, and then he chuckled.

Annie looked to see what was so funny, and she saw Josh tugging on Riley's pants, his lips puckered, waiting for a kiss. Riley picked up the boy and tossed him in the air, receiving a joyful squeal for his efforts. He hugged Josh and placed a kiss on his cheek. "You be good for Annie, all right?"

Josh pointed to the road, but Riley shook his head. "No, you can't go this time. I'll be back soon. Don't worry." He hugged Josh again then set him down and gazed at Annie with another look of deep love. He tipped his hat to her then headed down the stairs. Suddenly, he stopped and just stood there, his back to her. She admired the width of his shoulders, his narrow waist, and long legs. He lifted his hat, a trait he often did when frustrated or contemplating something. Then he spun around and marched back to her, a determined look in his eye.

"Annie, I know this is short notice, and things between us have been up and down since we met, but would you—" He looked away, staring off in the distance then he turned back to her. "Annie Sheffield, would you marry me?"

Her mouth dropped open, and the dreams she'd thought were dead came scrambling to life again. "Marry you?"

Riley nodded, looking both nervous and hopeful.

"When?"

He lifted his hat and forked his fingers through his dark rumpled hair again. "Would tomorrow be too soon?"

"Tomorrow!"

Riley shoved his hat down and a sheepish grin tugged at his lips. "Yeah. I know it's fast, but with Laura leaving and the children gone, you'd be alone in the house. It wouldn't be right for me to stay in the barn, but I don't want to go off and leave you here by yourself. It just makes sense to marry quickly."

She blinked, stunned down to her toes, and tried to comprehend that he had asked her to marry him. Tomorrow.

When she didn't answer, his enthusiastic expression dimmed. "Is that too soon? I know women have to prepare for weddings. Or do you think it would upset Laura for us to marry the same day as her and Sean?"

Annie shook her head, and Riley's shoulders sagged.

"No, you won't marry me? Or just not tomorrow?" He glanced over at Josh, rocking the chair back and forth.

Annie touched his arm. "No, I don't think it would bother Laura."

He stared at her for a long moment then grinned as comprehension dawned. "Does that mean yes?"

Annie couldn't contain her smile. "Yes, of course. I mean, if you're certain that's what you want."

"I don't have a single doubt, darlin'." He pulled her into a tight embrace and proved his point, and when he let go, Annie was dizzy with joy.

"Let me go so I can get back soon." He dashed away without waiting for a response, grabbed the reins, and walked Gypsy toward town. He looked back over his shoulder and waved.

Annie's heart sang with delight as she watched the man she loved walk—very quickly—toward town. "Thank You, Lord, for working everything out in such an amazing way."

Oh, what a difference twenty-four hours could make.

CHAPTER TWENTY-FIVE

*A*nnie stood at the back of the church beside Laura, waiting for their double wedding to start. Laura had been so thrilled to learn of Riley's proposal that she'd insisted they get married at the same time.

"Are you nervous?" Laura asked, looking so pretty in her lavender silk dress that Sean had insisted on buying her at Mrs. Petree's mercantile. Annie smiled at how she'd teased her about not needing any perfume because the dress reeked of gardenias.

"Yes, but not for the reason you're thinking."

Laura locked eyes with hers. "I know. But you're doing the right thing. Most of the people of Waco are the forgiving type. You'll see."

"I sure hope so."

A side door opened, and Sean and Riley entered, looking handsome, all cleaned up, and spit-shined. They stopped at the front, standing on either side of First Baptist's minister,

Rufus Burleson. Riley glanced at the front row where Henry, Rusty, and Josh sat; then his gaze found hers, sending her heart into a tizzy.

The pianist starting playing—the women's cue to move forward—and Annie stepped up beside Laura and walked toward their soon-to-be husbands. Annie never had dreamed she could be so happy. Not only would she soon have a permanent home—the ranch Riley had decided not to sell—but she would have a family. She'd be a wife and mother.

And in less than fifteen minutes she was.

"It's my delight to present to you Mr. and Mrs. Sean Murphy and Mr. and Mrs. Riley Morgan."

The crowd that filled the church cheered and clapped. Several men tossed their hats in the air. Sean and Laura walked forward, and Annie saw the admiring smiles of their friends and acquaintances. Would they still be smiling when she and Riley proceeded down the aisle?

The minister stepped to Annie's side, and Riley wrapped his arm around her waist in a show of support. They'd discussed today's events, and he agreed that it was time to come public with her news. "Mrs. Morgan has requested to address you before we are dismissed."

Annie looked down the aisle into Laura's smiling eyes. Her friend nodded as if saying, "Go ahead."

Give me strength, Lord. Her gaze traveled the crowd of curious faces, many she knew but others she didn't. "Most of you-all don't know how I came to be in Waco." She told them of how her father left her, but avoided the part of her being a pickpocket. Then she explained her desperation to find food and shelter and how she discovered the Wilcox School for Blind Children. "It was everything I longed for—a home, decent clothes, food, so . . . so I pretended to be blind so I could live there."

Several loud gasps were heard around the room. An uncomfortable silence followed. Some men glanced at their wives, while others narrowed their gaze at her.

"I want you-all to know how sorry I am. It was an act of desperation that I've regretted ever since. I wanted to come clean, but the rules of the school said I couldn't stay if I wasn't blind, so I pretended just so I could have a home. I hope you-all can understand and will forgive me."

Annie glanced up at Riley, and he smiled. Then he wrapped her arm around his, as he'd done so many times, and escorted her down the aisle through the crowd of stunned townsfolk.

At the back of the church, Laura wrapped her arms around her. "You did well. And doesn't it feel better not having to keep this secret?"

Annie exhaled an audible sigh and nodded. "Yes, it does."

They proceeded outside to wait for the crowd to congratulate them, and Mr. and Mrs. Alton were the first outside to wish them all happiness. The two then said a quick good-bye and scurried to the school where the beloved cook was making a special wedding luncheon to celebrate instead of a public reception, which both couples had agreed to forgo.

The crowd slowly exited from the church. Sean and Laura received the more enthusiastic well wishes, while many folks—but not all—chose to avoid her and Riley altogether. Annie glanced up at her husband, wondering if she should have waited. Holding Josh in one arm, he smiled and patted her back. "Stop worrying. Give people some time, and they'll come around."

Soon the crowd thinned, and Laura turned to her. "Well, I'm certainly glad to have that over and done with." She glanced up at Sean with a sheepish grin. "The handshaking, I mean, not the wedding."

He grinned. "I know just what you mean. Never shook so many women's hands in my whole life."

Laura giggled like Tess did when she was tickled.

"C'mon, wife," Riley said. "Let's head back. I'm starved." He gave Josh a jiggle and set him down. "You want to hold your new mama's hand, son?"

The boy looked up at Annie, his blue eyes shining, and held up his little hand. "Mama."

All four adults caught their breath at the first word they'd heard Josh utter. Annie bent down and scooped up the sweet child. "Yes, darlin', I'm your mama now. And Riley is your papa."

Josh grinned wide, and mouthed the word *papa*, though no sound came out. Riley smiled and hugged Annie and Josh together. Her joy soared as high as a hawk in the summer sky. She took her son's hand and they swung him to the ground and walked out of town, back to the school. Soon she would leave the home she loved so much, but now she didn't regret it for a moment.

← ★ →

Laura walked through the house that was so dear to her and remembered all the children who had passed through it. They would always be on her heart and in her thoughts, but she was ready and eager to start life as Sean's wife. With Mr. Ramsey in jail, probably for the rest of his life, she couldn't help wondering what would happen to the house. It would probably take a long time for the legalities to be sorted out in any case.

Riley and Sean sat in the parlor, talking about the qualities of Morgan horses. Sean said they were too small for his liking, but Riley insisted they made up in smarts and stamina what they lacked in size. Josh sat at Riley's feet playing with some rocks he had brought in, while Henry and Rusty sat on the porch.

Her personal belongings were already stacked in Sean's wagon, and as soon as Annie finished packing, they'd all ride over to the Morgan ranch to deliver her things. The one thing that bothered her was knowing that Riley, Annie, and Josh would have to live in the house as it was until he could finish repairing it, but the happy newlyweds probably would barely notice any inconveniences.

Someone knocked on the door, and Sean rose to answer it. Laura hoped it wasn't another well-wisher. She was ready to leave here and have Sean all to herself. He invited the tall, thin man to come in, and he did.

The older man removed his gray derby hat and pushed a pair of wire-rimmed glasses up his slender nose with his index finger. "I was told in town that I could find Miss Wilcox here."

Laura stepped forward. "I'm Miss Wilcox."

Sean cleared his throat and raised his brows.

"Uh, rather, I'm Mrs. Murphy. We were just married, you see." She smiled happily at Sean.

The man looked from her to Sean and back. "Congratulations. This is a happy day indeed." He opened a valise, pulled out a stack of papers, and handed them to Laura. "These are for you."

Annie struggled down the stairs with a heavy carpetbag, and Riley jumped up to help her.

Laura glanced down at the thick packet. "What is it?"

Sean stepped up beside her. "Hold your horses. Just who did you say you were?"

The man chuckled. "Didn't I say? I'm Stephen Landers, Charles Morrow's attorney." He shook his head and sobered. "I've heard the stories in town about what Mr. Ramsey did, and I'm truly sorry. It was the act of a desperate man, I'm afraid."

Laura shook her head. "I'm sorry, but I don't follow you."

Mr. Landers fiddled with his hat. "My apologies, ma'am. Let

me back up a bit. I was on an extended vacation in Europe when Charles Morrow died, which explains why I didn't contact you sooner. When I returned from my trip, I learned the sad news and also discovered the letter you'd written me. I settled Mr. Morrow's affairs and made travel arrangements to come here as soon as I could." He took a breath, pulling some papers from the envelope and unfolding them. Then he held them out to Laura. "It's a deed, ma'am. Mr. Morrow left this house and its fifteen acres to you, not to his nephew."

"Me?" Laura placed her hand across her collarbone. "I can't believe it."

The attorney nodded. "It's quite true, ma'am. Mr. Morrow wrote his nephew out of his will after the man repeatedly hounded him for money and then squandered it on gambling and other unsavory pursuits." The man grew sober and looked away, staring toward town for a moment, then turned back to them. "I had a visit from the police right after I returned from Europe, and it turns out that Mr. Ramsey choked his uncle to death. At first it was thought Mr. Morrow died in his sleep, but a servant who witnessed the crime finally came forward and told the authorities what he'd seen."

Laura closed her eyes, her joy dimming as she thought of the sad ending of the man who'd used his wealth to do so much good. "He was such a kind, generous man."

"So true," Mr. Landers said. "Charles Morrow deserved better. From what I've heard since coming to town, that scoundrel nephew of his was merely trying to get you to vacate the house, so he could sell it and retain the money, most illegally, I must say."

Annie said, "Oh, that's terrible. But it's wonderful news about the house. You and Sean can live here."

Still stunned from the news, it took Laura a moment to grasp what had been said. "I can hardly believe it."

Sean hugged her and kissed the top of her head. "I have to admit being concerned that you wouldn't be happy in my tiny hovel after you've had such a big, roomy house to live in."

She reached up and cupped his hand. "You're wrong. I've been looking forward to that very thing. In fact, I think Annie and Riley should live here."

"Us?" Annie and Riley said in unison.

Laura nodded. "Yes, it makes perfect sense. Sean and I are leaving to take the boys to Austin, and that will take a week or two, then we'll come back and live at Sean's. You two can stay here until you get your house repaired."

Annie glanced at Riley, and he shrugged. "It would be a nice alternative," she suggested.

"Yes, it would relieve a lot of my concerns," Riley said. "I didn't want to take you from here, just to live outside."

"Good, then it's settled."

— ← ★ → —

That evening, Riley stood on the porch next to Annie. The three boys were bedded down upstairs, and Sean and Laura had left to go home. Come Monday, they'd fetch the two older boys and head to Austin. It had been an amazing day. If only some of his relatives could have had time to come, but at least now when he wrote them about his parents, he'd have some good news to end with.

He tugged his wife closer. "No regrets for marrying so quickly?"

Annie leaned her head against his chest, enjoying the closeness. "Not a one. What about you?"

"Does this answer your question?" He pulled her in a passionate embrace, kissing her until she had to beg to take a breath. He chuckled. "Any doubts now?"

"No," she gasped, as she struggled to settle her ragged breathing.

She looked charming, dressed like a rancher's wife in her day dress and the apron she'd donned before fixing supper. She was beautiful, not in the way of a sophisticated beauty, but in a simplified, spunky manner.

"Oh, I nearly forgot. I have a gift for you—if you want it after you hear the story about how I got it. I meant to sell it so I'd have money to start over somewhere else. I went to fetch it the day the girls got lost in the storm."

"Ah, now I understand why you were out in a thunderstorm."

She grinned. "I can be determined, when I set my mind to something." She tugged a small object out of her pocket and handed it to him.

The soft pouch triggered a memory, but it wasn't a pleasant one. He flipped back the flap and dropped the item into his hand. A watch? His heart pounded as he turned and held it toward the lantern light shining out the parlor window. He snapped open the gold cover, and the inscription made his mouth go dry. His grandfather's watch?

"Where did you get this?"

"Remember how I told you I had a rough childhood?" She lowered her eyes. "Well, the truth is, my daddy raised me to be a pickpocket, and I was a good one. I stole that watch off a youth the first day my daddy and I came to Waco."

Riley struggled to comprehend what she was saying. He studied her petite form and the color of her hair, and in that moment, he knew the truth. "You were that boy?"

Her gaze darted up. "What boy?"

"The one who stole the watch my father had just passed down to me for my sixteenth birthday."

"That was you? But your hair was blond!"

"It darkened as I got older." Suddenly, the irony of the situation was more than he could hold in, and he threw back his head and laughed. "Oh, darlin', just think. If you hadn't taken my watch, it would most likely have been taken when my house was ransacked or lost or destroyed in the war. Don't you see, I have it now because you stole it way back when."

Annie looked a bit less worried. "I suppose that is true."

"Where has it been all these years? Why did you keep it?"

"After I came here and learned that stealing was wrong, I couldn't stand to have it in my possession any longer. I found a tree a short way from here with some initials carved in it. *RM and AM encircled in a heart.* I buried it there. I had a hard time finding it again though because of how much the trees had grown in seven years, and if not for the initials, the watch might have been lost forever."

Riley shook his head as he realized the truth. He turned Annie to face him. "*I* carved those initials shortly after we moved here, Annie. AM stands for Adrian Massey, the girl I was infatuated with when I was younger."

She blinked several times, as if struggling to grasp the truth. "The Lord works in mysterious ways."

Grinning, Riley tugged her to him. "That He does, darlin', that He does."

MAY, 1870

The pounding of hammers echoed across the valley. Annie shaded her eyes and surveyed the new two-story clapboard house that the townsfolk of Waco had come to help Riley build. The sides were up, and men were laying shakes to the roof. She had enjoyed the past five years in their smaller house her husband's father had built when he first brought his family to the area, but Riley wanted her to have a house of her own—one that didn't bear the sad memories that the first one did.

Most of the women who'd helped earlier with lunch for the men had either gone home or were down by the creek with their children taking a much-deserved rest. Her dear friend Laura walked across the field toward the house, holding Rusty's hand. The top of the boy's head reached her shoulder, and his hair stuck up and his clothes clung to his chubby body from his recent swim. A shuffle sounded behind Annie, and she turned.

"Mama, I waked up." Three-year-old Melissa rubbed her eyes and yawned. "Brooks waked me."

Annie lifted her young daughter. "Well, we'd better go check on him. I imagine he's needing his diaper changed."

"I help." Melissa kicked her feet to get down. "I get diapy."

Setting her daughter on the floor, Annie entered the bedroom that had once belonged to Riley and his brother Timothy, but now served their children. Melissa scampered in and pulled a fresh diaper from the crate they were stored in. Annie leaned over the crib, and a pair of bright blue eyes sparked when they landed on her, and her two-month-old son wiggled as if asking to be picked up. Beside him and nearly twice his size, lay redheaded Colin Murphy, still sound asleep, his thumb hanging halfway out of his pink mouth. She picked up her son and kissed his soft head. "Let's go in the other room before we wake your friend," she whispered.

"Mama, I got a diapy." Melissa followed, dragging half the diaper across the floor.

Annie grinned and shook her head. Most times Melissa's "helping" caused her more work than not. She laid Brooks on the bed and smoothed down his straight blond hair that reminded her of duckling fuzz. "Did you have a good sleep?" She jiggled his fists, and a fleeting smile quirked his lips up.

"I have good sweep." Melissa used the crate that held Annie's extra pair of shoes for a stepstool and climbed onto the bed. She crawled over and kissed Brooks's cheek. "You good baby?"

Joy warmed Annie's chest. She had been so blessed. She'd never have imagined when her father abandoned her in Waco so many years ago that she would eventually realize all her dreams here. Friends, a home, a cherished man to love, and a family of her own. God had blessed her so much.

Footsteps sounded in the parlor. "Is my baby brother awake

yet, Miss Annie?" Rusty's loud voice echoed through the small house.

"Shh . . . you'll wake Colin," Laura whispered.

"I awake." Melissa slid off the bed and trotted out of the room. Annie picked up Brooks and followed her daughter into the parlor.

"I'm hungry, Ma." Rusty pulled out a chair at the table. "Swimming is hard work."

Annie smiled at Laura, who rolled her eyes. Both of them knew there wasn't more than six inches of water in the creek, but that was Rusty—making a big deal out of everything, but they loved him for it. Five years ago, Laura and Sean had returned from their trip to Austin with Rusty, who refused to be left behind. The three had become an instant family, and now Colin made four.

"Did I tell you about the new system I've read about that can help blind people learn to read?" Laura asked.

"No, I don't think so. I can't imagine how that could work, but wouldn't it be wonderful?"

"Yes. It would open so many doors for the blind. The Missouri School for the Blind has been using the Braille system for ten years now and has met with good success."

"Ma! Didn't you hear me say I was hungry?" Rusty swatted his hand in the air. "Where's that Melissa? I'm so hungry I could eat her."

Melissa squealed and dodged his grasp then ran over and hid behind Annie's skirt.

"I suppose I'd better feed this boy. He eats nearly as much as his father and—trust me—that's a lot."

"There's some pie left." Annie nudged her chin toward the counter.

"Did someone mention pie?" Riley strode in the front door.

"Papa!" Melissa ran to her father and wrapped her little arm around one knee. "Up!"

Riley winked at Annie, making her heart flip-flop. "I'm sure I heard something about pie."

"Oh, you men. All you think about is your stomachs."

"Not true. C'mere, wife." He bent over and kissed Brooks on the forehead then gently took hold of Annie's elbow. "There's something I want to show you."

Outside, he guided her toward their new house, which sat on the hillside, giving them a good view of their pastures filled with Morgan horses and their small head of cattle and goats.

"There are no men on the roof." Annie shifted Brooks to her other arm. The little tyke was growing faster than prairie grass and already getting heavy.

Riley stopped and grinned, his eyes flashing. "That's because we're done with the roof."

Annie gasped. "Truly? Can we start moving in then?"

"I want pie." Melissa lips turned down in a pout. The tiny girl completely missed the importance of the moment.

Riley set her down. "Go tell Miss Laura that I said you could have a small slice."

The girl giggled and trotted toward the old house. "Big piece."

Annie chuckled and leaned against her husband's arm. "It's a beautiful house, Riley. Thank you for insisting on building it."

He looped his arm around her shoulder and pressed his chin against her head. "I know how important it is to you to have a home."

She turned so she could look into his beautiful eyes. "That is a house. You and the kids are my home."

His eyes twinkled and he bent down, giving her a slow kiss that made her tingle all over and warmed her clear down to her toes. She was home. Truly home.

PROLOGUE

HOUSTON DAILY TELEGRAPH
March 3, 1875

We are able, thanks to a gentleman who was present, to define
the deliberations that took place under the spreading branches
of a live oak a little more definitely. Some unknown parties
(many citizens probably) seized upon the five men who were suspected of being horse thieves, and succeeded in elevating three
of the five, when the sheriff put in an appearance . . . So instead
of five men being hung, only two were hung, and one was shot.
For the sake of the reputation of Mason as a law-abiding community, we hope this correction will be made.

F ound not guilty of any wrongdoing. Praise the Lord." Derrick Denning lifted his cup of coffee in a mock salute to his wife, Leta. "As the Good Book says, 'Thou hast maintained my right and my cause.' Though I feel bad about the fines the other fellows have to pay."

The Denning family sat around the table enjoying a celebratory dinner in their cabin on the D-Bar-D Ranch. Young Ricky clapped his hands on the table, although he didn't know what they were celebrating. Leta looked into her husband's eyes over their son's head and smiled. The baby inside her stirred, as if contentedly joining in on the joy.

"I'll read up on that new law about transporting cattle over county lines before I go on any more cattle drives. Right and legal aren't always the same thing, and we want to be sure we stick on the side of the law."

"It's not right, the other men are getting fined." Leta's brother Andy stopped shoveling beans into his mouth long enough to grumble. "They didn't do nothing wrong. The cattle belonged to Mr. Roberts and Mr. Thomas."

When her husband was arrested for helping M. B. Thomas and Allen Roberts take their cattle to Llano County from Mason County, the ordeal filled her with anguish. The German cattlemen had accused both Thomas and Roberts of stealing cattle. In the court case, six of the cowhands were charged guilty and fined $25 a head. Yet the court dismissed Derrick's case due to insufficient evidence.

The German cattlemen had grumbled at the verdict. Mason County was full of cattle ranchers who were angry that justice for cattle stealing—real and supposed—was not being fulfilled through the law. German settlers and people native to Mason County alike were troubled.

Leta suppressed the niggling worry that threatened to destroy this night of celebration. God answered her prayers. Derrick was home. She and her family—Derrick, their son, and her brother Andy—could stay put in Mason County, Texas. They wouldn't have to move every year or two the way Pa had dragged them all over the map when she was a child.

Derrick set both his elbows on the table and crossed his arms, signaling he had an important announcement to make. He winked at Leta. "Since we're celebrating good news, it's time we told you the news. Ricky, what do you think about being a big brother sometime this winter?"

Ricky stopped pushing beans around his plate. "I'm going to have a baby brother?"

"Or a sister." Leta touched the palm of her hand against her womb. "We won't know until the baby comes."

"I don't want to wait until later." Ricky clapped his hands together. "I want it now."

"I'm afraid you'll have to wait."

"Can I at least have him for a Christmas present?"

Andy snickered.

Leta hid a smile behind her napkin. "The baby might come around your birthday. How would you like that?"

Ricky shrugged his shoulders. "I guess it's all right. Say, Davey's dog had puppies. Can I have one?" Leta admired how much his smile looked like his father's. "Since I have to wait so long to have my brother?"

"Your father and I will talk about it."

"Maybe I can have a horse of my own, since I have to wait for my niece or nephew." Andy lifted his eyebrows and put on his most innocent expression.

"That topic is already under discussion." Derrick grinned

at his brother-in-law. "Today I'd like to give all of you the world, but I'd better wait and see what happens next."

Good, sensible, steady Derrick. The best husband in the world for Leta. *God is so good.*

When they retired to bed later, thunder rumbled. Leta snuggled close to Derrick. The raging storms that swept across the land from time to time frightened her, and she preferred the safety of her husband's arms.

Instead of subsiding, the rumble continued—constant, moving closer and closer. More like a . . . stampede. Derrick swung his legs over the side of the bed. He grabbed his gun and headed for the main room. Leta threw on her dressing gown and followed.

Ricky sat up on his elbows in his bed in the main room, rubbing his eyes and looking scared.

Derrick ran his hand over Ricky's soft curls. "Nothing to worry about, son; you lay back down."

The boy ducked his head under the sheets as instructed, but Leta didn't for a minute think he had gone to sleep.

The rumble grew louder, the distinct sound of hooves pounding the hard earth at full speed.

Andy climbed down from the loft, rifle in his hand. "Is something after the cattle?"

That was a definite possibility. The Texas Rangers tried to keep Indians and Comancheros away from American holdings. Sometimes they were successful, sometimes they weren't.

Leta didn't like her brother heading out to fight off rustlers. She didn't like her husband going into danger, for that matter— but she knew they must. Derrick handed her a loaded rifle. She grasped it with both hands and started praying. Horses neared, almost too loud to speak. She dropped to a kneeling position beneath the window.

As Derrick reached for the front door, the hooves stopped

moving, snorting and neighing punctuating the abrupt silence. Leta lifted her head a few inches to see out the windowpane. Dark, shadowy figures on horseback formed a semicircle around the front door. Of the cattle in the pen, she saw and heard no sign.

"Derrick Denning. Come out and face justice."

Leta tensed and waited for Derrick's response. He half turned the doorknob, then dropped his hand.

The speaker held up both hands. "Derrick Denning. I will not ask again. You have two choices. Either you hang . . . " He held up a rope tied into a noose. "Or we burn down your home." A light flared in the hand of one of the other riders, and the object in the leader's right hand burst into flame—a torch. "It's your choice."

Leta gasped and the rifle trembled in her hand. Shoot the man. The thought flew in and out of her mind. They were too many, she couldn't drive them all away before someone threw the firebrand onto the dry wood of their house. She wanted to grab Ricky and run for the door. But the only exit lay through the front door—in the direction of the men threatening to burn them down.

She chanced a glance to the side. Andy stood with his rifle on his shoulder, ready to shoot. Derrick motioned for him to put the gun down.

A pale face appeared over the edge of his blanket. No! Ricky must not see this! Leta motioned for her son to sneak back under the covers.

A deep sigh drew Leta's attention to her husband. Putting down the gun, he tied a white dishtowel around his arm. He turned to Leta. "Take care of Ricky." Before she could protest, he opened the door and slammed it shut behind him.

The first quarter moon provided little light, and clouds drifted across it like wisps of smoke. Light from the torch flickered, revealing Derrick's face in sharp contrast.

"Gentlemen, whatever is troubling you, surely we can settle this like reasonable men. I come out here in peace." Derrick pointed to the white band on his arm. "Unarmed."

Rough custom said no one would shoot an unarmed man any more than they would shoot a man in the back.

The men on horseback were shadows hovering just beyond the circle of light. Leta couldn't see the faces of the men threatening her husband. "Derrick Denning, the district court of Mason County found insufficient evidence against you to convict you of the theft of cattle." *Listen to the voice.* Leta strained her ears. It had to be someone they knew, someone from their small community. "However, the people of Mason County witnessed your crime firsthand, and we find it necessary to pronounce a true judgment."

Derrick took a step back, then straightened his shoulders and moved forward. "Get off your horse and face me like a man."

The leader handed the torch to the man on his right and the noose to the man on his right and jumped from the horse. He stood in the shadows.

"We the people of Mason County have examined the testimony against you. We have determined that you were indeed with A.G. Roberts on the date in question. That you did aid in the illegal transportation of cattle over the Mason County line without proper inspection. That you knew that the cattle in question in fact belonged to a local rancher."

"How can you say what happened? The only people there were the folks on trial today."

"You admit to the facts then?"

Leta heard the smiling threat in his voice, although she couldn't see it. The end of the noose dangled where she could see it in the flare of the torch.

"Having examined the evidence, we have determined that you are, both legally and morally, guilty of the crime of cattle rustling. And that your punishment will be death by hanging."

The man with the noose nudged his horse forward.

A long, long five minutes later, Leta slumped to the floor. Only then did she become aware of Ricky crouching beside her, staring in horror out the window.

———— ★ ————

NEAR VICTORIA, TEXAS
SEPTEMBER 1874

Buck Morgan reined in Blaze when he approached the familiar sign suspended over the entrance to the family ranch: "Running M Ranch, est. 1834." As far as he roamed, across Texas and farther west, into New Mexico and Arizona territories, he always pictured this place as home. His father had worked hard to build the Running M Ranch into the best horse ranch in all of Texas. Buck loved the quality Morgan horses the family raised, but he loved the freedom of the open range. When he reached his eighteenth birthday, he kicked the dust of the ranch off his heels, coming home for only short stretches of time since.

But Ma and Pa would want to hear his current news firsthand. He owed them that much.

He spurred Blaze, and the gelding trotted forward, easing into a gallop, as if he sensed he was headed home too. His gait ate up the distance to the big house, while Buck took note of changes to the ranch. In the distance, he spotted a group of riders bringing the horses in from the pasture for the night. He turned Blaze in that direction and the horse increased his speed, giving in to the desire to reach the head of the pack.

A lanky-bodied youth on the back of a roan-colored mare

turned in Buck's direction. "Pa! Bert! Buck has come home." Buck's youngest brother, Jack, edged his mare out of the band and raced across the open space.

Buck reined Blaze in to a moderate pace and met his brother. "What did you do with my brother? He wasn't any taller than a cow's tail the last time I saw him."

Jack grinned. "It's good to see you too, Buck. Come on, let's head to the house. Ma will be so happy you're home. She'll be sending messages all across town."

Oma and Opa. Granny. Aunt Marion and Uncle Peter. Tante Alvie and her husband. His married sisters. Buck could be glad his other aunts and uncles and cousins lived scattered across Texas, or else they would've rented out all the guest rooms in Victoria.

Ma was working in the garden beside the house, probably getting it ready for the winter crop, when they approached. Her back was to him. Buck put a finger to his lips and slid off the horse as quiet as a cat.

"You're home early." The faintest trace of an accent pointed to Ma's German roots. She pulled up another weed before turning around. She dropped the weeds and the spade, her hand covering her mouth.

"Hi, Ma." Buck hugged her, surprised at how small and light the woman who had always been a tower of strength felt now that he was a grown man.

"Why didn't you write to say you were coming? How long are you staying?" Her eyes searched his, and he knew she was wishing he would stay put long enough to celebrate.

"I can stay about a week." A part of him wished he could deliver his news and ride out again in the morning, but Ma would never forgive him. He sniffed the air. "Is that rabbit stew I smell cooking? I haven't had a good bowl since the last time I was home."

"And a good *Gewurzgurke* to go with it." Ma's laughter was as light as the clouds floating overhead.

Pa, his middle brother Drew, and the ranch hands arrived, and Buck found himself the center of attention.

He didn't get any time alone with his parents until the following morning.

"Your ma tells me you're not here to stay." Pa's lips thinned. Buck's father wanted his eldest to follow in the family tradition of managing the Running M. Buck knew his reluctance still baffled his father.

"No, sir. I'm doing something I think you'll agree is important. You could say it's in my blood, since my grandpa died fighting for Texas."

"You're joining the army." Fear enlarged Ma's eyes.

"No, Ma, not since the War Between the States ended." Buck was disappointed when the war ended months before his eighteenth birthday. He had a thirst for freedom and adventure that life on the ranch couldn't satisfy. "I don't know if you heard tell that they've started up the Texas Rangers again."

Pa slowly nodded his head. "To protect the frontier and to keep law and order, the papers say."

"They need people used to Indian ways, who can ride horses as good as any Indian. All my years here on the ranch taught me that. And I even speak some Comanche." Years ago, his aunt Billie was held captive by Indians and learned the language. Buck begged Aunt Billie to speak the language to him every time he saw her, finding the strange sounds a challenge. He spoke well enough to get by.

"You're going to be a Texas Ranger." Ma looked nearly as scared as she had at the thought of him joining the army.

"Which company are you joining? One of the frontier battalions or the special force?"

Buck shrugged. "Major Jones isn't sure where to put me.

My experience with the Comanche would come in real handy with the frontier companies. Then again, he can see someone who speaks Spanish and German being valuable in the Special Force."

"German." Ma's voice dropped. "Will they send you to Mason County? Your uncle Georg has written of their troubles."

"I don't know." Buck wished Ma wouldn't worry so. "They might."

A MORGAN FAMILY SERIES

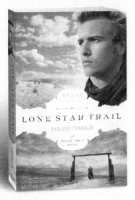

paperback 978-0-8024-0583-8

ebook 978-0-8024-7873-3

LONE STAR TRAIL

After Wande Fleischer's fiancé marries someone else, the young fraulein determines to make a new life for herself in Texas. With the help of Jud's sister Marion, Wande learns English and becomes a trusted friend to the entire Morgan family.

As much as Jud dislikes the German invasion, he can't help admiring Wande. She is sweet and cheerful as she serves the Lord and all those around her. Can the rancher put aside his prejudice to forge a new future? Through Jud and Wande, we learn the powerful lessons of forgiveness and reconciliation among a diverse community of believers.

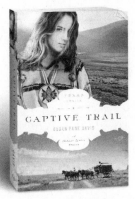

paperback 978-0-8024-0584-5

ebook 978-0-8024-7852-8

CAPTIVE TRAIL

Taabe Waipu has run away from her Comanche village and is fleeing south in Texas on a horse she stole from a dowry left outside her family's teepee. The horse has an accident and she is left on foot, injured and exhausted. She staggers onto a road near Fort Chadbourne and collapses.

On one of the first runs through Texas, Butterfield Overland Mail Company driver Ned Bright carries two Ursuline nuns returning to their mission station. They come across a woman who is nearly dead from exposure and dehydration and take her to the mission. With some detective work, Ned discovers Taabe Waipu's identity.

river north
FICTION FROM MOODY PUBLISHERS

www.RiverNorthFiction.com

www.MoodyPublishers.com